18 Fantastic Futanari Stories

Gia Maria Marquez

Published by Between the Two, 2023.

First Edition 2017

Table of Contents

18 Fantastic Futanari Stories

Gia Maria Marquez

Fanny's First Futa

Fanny dug her heels into the floor, clasping her mother's purse strap. "Please don't leave me alone with her."

"Fanny! Keep your voice down." Her mother glanced quickly at the other girl in the dorm room, but Serena had put on headphones to study. "Oh good, she's listening to music. At least she didn't hear the dreadful comment my daughter just made."

"It's not music," Fanny told her mother. "The school gives her textbooks on tape because she *says* she's partially blind and I guess she got a doctor to go along with it. If she's so blind, why doesn't she have a guide dog or a white cane?"

Fanny's mother slapped her, just on the hand, but still. "This is not the Fanny I raised, not by half! I taught you to be kind and courteous and compassionate to everyone. Anyway, people can have different degrees of blindness. It's not all or nothing."

"Oh, sure. Take my roommate's side." Fanny crossed her arms beneath her breasts. "You always take everybody else's side, never mine. You hate me. That's why you're making me share a stupid dorm room instead of staying at home with you and daddy. You want me out of the house, as far away as possible!"

"Right now I do, because right now you're acting like a spoiled little brat!" Mother's eyes blazed like she was about to give Fanny another smack. Instead, she sighed and said, "You know why we want this for you, honey. Your father and I both lived at home when we were in college. We want you to have the full college experience: the roommate, the parties, the co-ed shower..."

"Eww, mom, don't be gross." Fanny rolled her eyes. "I just wish they didn't stick me with the most boring roommate in the history of everything. All she talks about is science stuff and whenever I put my music on she asks me to turn it down because she can't hear her book. It's so annoying."

"Maybe your music is too loud."

"It's not!" Fanny growled. "And she makes me leave the room every time she wants to change. Why doesn't she just turn her back like I do?"

"The girl's probably shy. Compassion, Fanny! Where is your compassion?"

"Guess I left it at home," she said with a smirk. "Mind if I come back to the house to look for it?"

Placing a soft hand on Fanny's shoulder, her mother said, "Give dormitory life a chance, sweetie. Who knows? Maybe after a couple more weeks you'll learn to love residence."

"Three weeks is enough for me to know I hate it." Clasping her hands together, Fanny begged, "Please, mom? Please let me come home?"

"Fanny..." Her mother gave her that look that said, "Enough."

"Fine," she grumbled. "But call me later to wish me goodnight, okay?"

Glowering, her mother said, "Fanny, you're a grown woman. You don't need me phoning you every night. Try getting to sleep on your own."

Fanny couldn't believe her ears. "But... but... but..."

Her mother kissed her on the forehead and then turned down the corridor. Waving, she called out, "I'll see you next weekend, love."

This was not happening. Was her mother breaking up with her? No way. Fanny cried, "Not next weekend—I'll see you *tonight*. I'm packing all my stuff and coming home right now."

Turning briefly, her mother blew her a kiss before walking through the double doors that led to the parking lot.

Fanny ran after her, shouting, "I mean it, mom. I'll drop out if I have to!"

By the time she got to the double doors, her mother was already driving away.

"I hate you!" she screamed. "Grown woman, my ass! I'm still your little girl. I'll always be your..."

When she realized her mother wasn't turning around, she stared at the tree-lined street, and then up at the sky. How could the sun shine so brightly and the clouds dance like big fluffy cotton balls when her world was darkness and despair?

Slinking back into the cinderblock residence building, Fanny marched by a bunch of staring students. One random guy asked, "Are you okay, Fanny? Want to talk about it?"

"Shut your face," she snapped. "You just want to get me in the sack."

His buddy laughed and punched him in the shoulder while she continued toward her room. Serena was sitting cross-legged on her own bed. She had on a short cotton dress, but Fanny couldn't see anything because she had a computer in her lap. That's how she took notes from the audio textbook she "needed." Yeah right. If Fanny could work from audiobooks, she'd be in the top ten percent of all her classes.

Anger at Serena and her mom and the whole wide world surged through Fanny's arms and she took it out on their door, slamming it as hard as she could.

Serena let out a blood-curdling scream and tore off her headphones. "Fanny! What's wrong?"

Fanny knew she shouldn't, but she was so mad she asked, "If you're so blind, how come you can see it's me?"

"I'm not completely blind," Serena said, in a way that sounded calm but also puzzled. "I can see you. You're a little fuzzy, true enough, but it's mostly print that I have problems with. I've told you that before."

"Yeah, well..." She didn't know what else to say, so she just pulled her suitcase out of their shared closet and opened it on her bed.

"Are you going somewhere?" Serena asked.

Fanny tore her clothes from their hangers and jammed them into her case. "What do you think?"

"I think you're going somewhere," Serena replied, obviously trying to be funny.

"I'm going home, if you insist on knowing my every move."

"Oh." Closing her computer, Serena inched toward the edge of her bed. "Did something happen with your mom?"

"What do you care? It's got nothing to do with you."

"Oh." Serena crossed her feet at the ankles. She had on bright yellow canvas shoes and bright green ankle socks, neither of which really matched her dress, which had a pattern of little red rosebuds on a bright orange field. "Sorry. I was just interested. If you need someone to talk to, I'm always here."

"That's for sure," Fanny said. "Always here, always around, always studying or doing something equally nerdy. If I had a fun roommate, maybe I wouldn't be so anxious to get out of here."

Serena's face fell. "I can be fun."

"Oh yeah, like what? Stripping down to your bra and panties while you study? Whoop-dee-do!"

"No, I wouldn't do that." Serena's cheeks broke out in a deep blush.

Fanny hesitated for a moment before saying, "I'm not asking you to."

"I'm just a little self-conscious, that's all."

"So I noticed." Folding the top of her suitcase down, she crushed her clothes inside. "Damn it, I can't get this thing closed."

"Want me to help?" Serena asked.

"No." Fanny jumped on her soft-sided suitcase as her roommate looked on. It wasn't like her to feel bad after snapping at someone, but she did feel bad this time. She said, "I don't know what you've got to be self-conscious about. You've got a nice body, from what I've seen."

"Well, that's just it," Serena said shyly. "You haven't seen it all."

Fanny paused, looking across the room and wondering what the girl meant.

"Let me help you." Serena crossed the small expanse between their beds. "Let me zip this up."

She gave in and let Serena help. "Thanks." When it was zipped, Fanny jumped down and straightened her skirt. "You know, I used to be self-conscious, too, but then I found out things I didn't like about my body were things other people did like. Then I started feeling good about them."

"Like what?" Serena asked.

Fanny felt a blush break across her own cheeks this time. "You probably don't want to know."

"It can't be worse than mine." Sitting back down on her bed, Serena picked up her computer and showed Fanny what she'd been typing. The font was huge enough to see from across the room, so maybe Serena's eyesight really was as bad as she claimed. Anyway, that didn't matter right now. What mattered was that the notes on her computer were all about variant sexual anatomies—different genital formations, intersex configurations...

"You?" Fanny fell back on her bed, forgetting that her luggage was sitting there. She bounced back up and then took a daring step forward. "You too?"

Serena's eyes widened. "What do you mean, me too?"

"I mean..." Fanny hoped she could count on her roommate not to judge. She pulled down her panties and gathered up her skirt to show Serena. "I've been like this all my life."

A smile broke across Serena's lips as she closed her computer and shoved it under the bed. She leaned in closer, the same way she did when she was reading, and then asked, "Can I touch it?"

It didn't take much to turn Fanny on. Just the idea of someone else's fingers brushing gently down her shaft made her stiff as a board. "Touch it," Fanny said. "Stroke it, taste it, fuck it—whatever you want."

"I thought you hated me," Serena replied.

Like that mattered at this point. But, in truth, Fanny didn't hate her roommate anymore. "Do you still feel self-conscious?"

"A little."

"Don't." When Serena didn't follow through on her offer to touch Fanny's full, firm erection, Fanny touched it herself. Stroking her cock, she said, "I showed you mine. Now you show me yours."

Serena bit her lip. "I'm nervous."

"Don't be." Fanny stroked her cock a little harder, drawing Serena's gaze to the motion. "Start with your boobs, if you want."

"Show you my boobs?" Serena cupped them through her dress, whether for emphasis or to mask how big and swollen they'd grown. "I don't know. This is weird."

"Is it your first time?"

"My first time...?" Serena didn't seem to know what Fanny was asking any more than Fanny did. How far would they take this? "Okay, I just have to... sorry..."

Serena turned around. Her hands disappeared beneath her dress and she gently persuaded her stretchy panties down her thighs. Once she'd stepped out of them, she removed her dress, giving Fanny a good look at her firm, fleshy ass. She reached around and unhooked her bra, then slid the straps down her arms and discarded the garment.

Wearing only socks and canvas shoes, Serena said, "I'm so nervous."

"Why? Don't be. I want to see what it looks like."

"Okay." Serena turned slowly, shielding her breasts with one arm and her crotch with the other. "Are you sure you want to see?"

Fanny took a quick step forward and whacked her roommate's thigh with her engorged cock. "Yes! Show me!"

Serena giggled as Fanny's preliminary juices slicked her thigh. "Oh, I'm so nervous!"

"Don't be nervous. It's nothing I haven't seen before."

"Oh... okay." Slipping her arms down at her sides, Serena revealed her pretty pink nipples and then her sweet, soft cock. "Here I am."

"You're not hard," Fanny said. "Aren't you happy to see me?"

"Sure I am." Serena crossed her feet at the ankles.

"What if I do this?" Fanny asked as she unbuttoned her blouse and pulled down the cups of her bra. "Do my big titties do it for you?"

Serena's eyes lit up. She could obviously see them well enough to be moderately aroused, because her limp dick jumped before settling back down on her tiny balls.

"You asked to touch my dick," Fanny said. "And you still haven't done it."

"I know," Serena replied. "I'm nervous now."

"Have you ever touched one?"

"Only my own."

Fanny chuckled. "Well there's a first time for everything."

Serena nervously reached for Fanny's cock and took over stroking it. "Wow. You get really hard."

"You don't?"

"Sometimes, but it takes a lot of effort. Usually I just give up."

"That's no good." Fanny took her roommate's cock in hand, cupping it gently, squeezing rather than stroking. It was still too soft to stroke, but Serena seemed to enjoy the squeezing.

Serena's knees buckled and she tumbled back on her bed. "Oh, that feels wonderful, Fanny."

She'd let go of Fanny's erection, but no worries. Fanny got down on her knees without hesitation and took her roommate's soft cock in her mouth. The whole thing fit no problem, and she casually toyed with her own dick while she sucked Serena's.

"Oh, Fanny!"

Her name sounded good on Serena's lips, just like Serena's hands felt good tousling her hair. She started off gently. Her mouth's suction caused her roommate's cock to swell and enlarge. After about thirty seconds of sucking, the whole thing didn't fit in her mouth anymore. It filled her throat, daring her to gag, and she backed off. "Wow!"

"I've never been this hard in all my life!" Serena gazed down at her cock in disbelief. She wrapped her fingers around the base as if to measure her girth. "It's so hard it hurts!"

"Guess you've never been sucked off by someone like me," Fanny said, boastfully.

"I've never been with anyone—well, not like this. I did have sex before, with my old boyfriend, but it wasn't very... good."

"That's too bad," Fanny said before diving at her roommate's cock, sucking that thick spear like it was coated in honey. "God, you taste good."

"Thank you." She ran her fingers through Fanny's hair, and the gentle motion pressed her breasts sweetly together. "Oh, you're too good at that."

Fanny appreciated the compliment, and she worked even harder to make her roommate feel good. She licked Serena's swollen cockhead and then wrapped her lips around the cherry red tip. Pressing her face down into her roommate's lap, she swallowed Serena whole, until her bottom lip met those weird shaved testicles down there. Relaxing her throat, she let the girl move inside her, fuck her gently, build up speed.

Serena's breath grew shallow. "Oh God, if you keep at it I'm gonna... oh... oh no!"

"Not yet!"

"I can't... can't help it..." Serena's thighs trembled. Her whole body shook as she grasped her brightly-coloured bedding. "No!"

"No!" Fanny cried back.

Her roommate's cock exploded, splattering hot cum all across her chest. Sure she was disappointed that Serena had come so quickly, but those blasts of thick cream felt good against her tits. She aimed Serena's dick so it would shoot at one nipple, then the other, as it continued to erupt in youthful spurts.

"Wow, that feels amazing." Fanny spread Serena's load around her pink pointed nipples. "It's so warm and soft, like liquid silk. It feels amazing."

Serena looked like she was trying to answer, but she couldn't catch her breath. That, and she started giggling like she couldn't believe she'd just come all over her roommate's chest.

When she tumbled back in bed, keeping her legs spread nicely, her cock rested meekly on her bare belly. That's when Fanny noticed something very unusual. Spreading Serena's thighs a little wide, she said, "Wait... do you have a pussy?"

"Yes," Serena replied breathlessly. "Don't you?"

"No!" Fanny cried. "Does it... can I... can I stick my dick in it?"

Serena popped up, setting both palms on the mattress. "You want to?"

"Of course I want to!" Fanny stared at the pink slit between Serena's small shaved testicles. Maybe they weren't balls at all. Maybe they were pussy lips. Maybe they were both. "I've never seen anything like this. You've got a cock and you've got a pussy."

"I thought you did too," Serena said, bashfully.

"No, I've just got this." Clinging to her erection, Fanny got up on her feet. "Are you sure I can fuck you? You said you didn't like it, I thought."

"I didn't with my old boyfriend," Serena said. "But he wasn't nice to me like you are."

Ice-cold guilt drizzled down Fanny's throat and into her belly. She'd been so bitchy to Serena, and Serena thought that was nice? Obviously the girl hadn't known any truly kind people in her life. But she would. Because from now on Fanny would be compassionate and caring and kind—everything her mother wanted her to be.

"You've got a beautiful body," Fanny said.

Blushing, Serena said, "Thanks. I bet you do too, if you'd only show it to me."

Fanny didn't need to be asked twice. She pushed off her skirt and pulled off her blouse, unhooked her bra. Her towel was still wet from her shower that morning, and she used it to wipe the cum from her tits. "Here I am! One cock, two tits, no waiting!"

Giggling, Serena brought her feet up on the mattress and tucked her spent cock in the crease between her side and her thigh. Her pink slit glistened with pussy juice. Fanny's cock throbbed. If she hadn't relieved some tension in the bathroom before her mom arrived for a visit, she'd definitely have burst by now. Serena was so beautiful.

So was Fanny. She knew she had a nice body. No point being humble about it. Her tits were young and perky, just this side of large without being disproportionate to the rest of her slim body. Her skin had been terrible a few years ago, but it cleared up nicely in time for college. She wasn't sure if she liked her legs better than her ass or her ass better than her legs, but her favourite body part was definitely her cock. She loved everything about it: its shape, its thickness, the way the tip glowed like Rudolph's nose when she was turned on and just generally the way it made her feel when she stroked it.

"I've never been this turned on in my whole life," Serena said. "Fuck me, Fanny. Oh God, I need it. My pussy's so wet."

Fanny tested the waters with her finger. "Damn! Sure is."

"Put your cock in me," Serena begged. "It wasn't enough to come just once. Make me come again. Please!"

"You think I can make you cum?" Fanny knelt on the mattress and placed her thick, throbbing cockhead against her roommate's slit. "You think if I fuck you, you'll come?"

"Yes?" Serena said, insecurely.

"Well, I guess we're about to find out!"

Thrusting her hips, Fanny plunged her erection between her roommate's legs. Serena screamed and tensed up, locking like a vice on Fanny's dick.

"Damn!" Fanny cursed. "Ease up a little. Damn, you're one tight fit."

"Sorry." Serena winced as Fanny moved in her.

"Am I hurting you?"

"No, no. Sorry. I just need to relax."

"Do you ever." Fanny grabbed Serena's hips and fucked her slowly. "How's that? You're still damn tight."

"I know. I'm sorry!"

"Play with your titties," Fanny instructed.

Serena looked up at her, blushing.

"Oh, don't tell me you're too self-conscious."

"It's embarrassing..."

"No it's not. Here, let me." Fanny released her hold on Serena's hips and shifted her hands to the girl's lovely tits. "Oh God, these perfect, perky boobs.

Here, lie the other way on the bed. Put your head on the pillow. I want to fuck you good and proper."

"Good and proper?" Serena asked, realigning herself on the bed. "What's that like?"

"Like this." Placing both palms on Serena's tits, Fanny pinned her to the bed, opened her legs, and fucked her. "My cock, your cunt. Me going at you balls-deep, baby. This is fucking, good and proper."

"Oh!" Serena's hips started moving, just slowly at first. Her pussy loosened its grip enough that Fanny could plough her like a machine. Her tits formed a nice handful while Fanny's bigger breasts swung and bounced.

"God, your pussy's tight," Fanny panted. "And wet! Oh, so wet, baby. You're so damn wet I could just... I could just..."

Fanny couldn't hold out any longer. Dropping down on Serena's body, she pressed her tits against Serena's, took the girl in a full-bodied hug, and kissed her hard.

Serena moaned in Fanny's mouth. Their tongues whipped and twisted while Fanny fucked her with force. They were bucking in unison now, moving as one. Fanny's cock filled Serena's cunt again and again as their breasts smashed together. Their teeth clacked. Serena caught Fanny's bottom lip in a love bite, and that's what did it for both of them. Serena raised her hips high off the mattress while Fanny bore down, burying her cock balls-deep in her roommate's pussy.

"God," Fanny growled.

Wrapping her legs around Fanny's back, Serena cried, "Yes!"

"Yes," Fanny repeated back to her.

"Yes..."

"Oh, for fuck's sake." Fanny wanted to keep pounding the girl's cunt, but her muscles locked. She couldn't move. Her cock throbbed inside Serena's tight grip until her balls released their load. She could feel herself filling her roommate with jizz, knowing she should feel weird about it because whatever happened they'd have to go on sharing this tiny room, but too lost in ecstasy to truly care about any moment that wasn't this one.

"That feels... oh my..." With a gasp, Serena tightened her loving grip around Fanny's body. "Oh wow. That was amazing."

They gazed at each other for an orgasmic moment, and then lost themselves in another sweet kiss. When Fanny rolled off her roommate, they held each other close, both panting and covered in a slick layer of sweat. A good and proper fuck was hard work!

"I can't believe we really did that," Serena said with a sigh.

"I can't believe we really—"

Fanny was interrupted when her phone rang. She didn't plan on answering it, but she reached across the night table in curiosity.

Laughing, she said, "It's my mom."

"Take it," Serena said, tucking her feet under the covers.

Fanny pressed the talk button. "Hi mom."

"I'm sorry for taking off on you. You are just maddening sometimes, Fanny."

"I know, mom. Don't worry about it. My fault."

Her mother didn't say anything.

"Mother? You there?"

"I... I... did you just *apologize* for something?"

Serena could obviously hear the whole conversation, because she flipped the covers over her head and laughed.

"Fanny, sweetie, if you want to come home that's your choice. I've talked it over with your father, and we just want you to be happy."

"Thanks," Fanny said as Serena reached around to tweak her nipple. "But you know what? I think I'll stay here."

"Oh... okay. Whatever you want."

Fanny didn't even say goodbye before hanging up. Her mouth was too busy kissing the roommate she'd thought was boring until now.

Boring! As if...

Fanny's Futa Makeup Mirror

Fanny started talking before she'd fully opened the door. "Hey, there's an open-air showing of Blade Runner tonight on the..."

She stopped dead in her tracks when she saw what her roommate was doing.

"Serena, is that... are you...?"

Serena turned swiftly, then smiled and smacked her lips. "Am I putting on makeup? You betcha!"

"But why?" Entering their dorm room, Fanny closed the door behind her. "You never wear makeup."

Serena winked. "I do when I have a date."

"You have a *date*?" Fanny's intestines boiled with jealousy. "Since when do you date?"

"Since someone asked me out."

"Who?"

"Just a guy from one of my classes. You don't know him." Serena was obviously trying to act low-key about it when she was clearly over the moon. "Since when do you care who I go out with?"

Fanny was taken aback by the comment. "Ever since we... you know... I care what you do. Of course I care."

"Well, you can care all you want, but you don't own me." Serena finished putting on some copper-toned eye shadow and then flashed her lashes. "What do you think? Do I look gorgeous or what?"

"Or what," Fanny said, flatly. "Can you even see what you look like?"

Serena glanced at her reflection in the wall of mirrors that made up their sliding closet door. For a second, Fanny felt a little guilty for calling attention to her roommate's partial blindness. Serena wasn't ashamed of it, though, so she didn't react. She only said, "I have a good mirror, but the light burnt out."

Sighing, Fanny said, "Bring that makeup kit over here. I'll do it for you."

"Really?" Serena beamed as she brought her toolbox over to Fanny's bed. "This is so nice of you. I'm terrible at getting dolled up. I do it so rarely."

Wiping off her roommate's lipstick with a tissue, Fanny said, "Tell me about this guy."

Then she had listen to Serena prattle on about the dumb fuck for ten minutes straight. The more Serena raved about him, the more pissed-off Fanny became. She was jealous. No use denying it. She didn't want her roommate dating anybody. She wanted Serena's sweet young body all to herself.

Apparently Fanny hadn't made herself clear. She'd just assumed she and her roommate were on the same page.

It was sour grapes, pure and simple, that led Fanny to use her own makeup on her roommate's clean, soft skin. When she dragged her thick red gloss across Serena's full lips, it was almost like they were kissing. The tickly brush touched Fanny's lips every day when she put on makeup. Now it danced across her roommate's luscious lips, drawing them gently apart, so kissably smooth and glistening wet, just like her lovely pink pussy had been the day they'd made love.

And now, instead of going to the open-air Blade Runner thing with Fanny, Serena had plans with some guy? Fine, then. If Serena wanted to act like a little skank, Fanny would dress her up that way. She piled on way too much blush, making the girl's cheeks seem positively sallow.

You want to act like a crack whore? Then you're going to look like one, roomie!

Fanny had never used her liquid liner to produce thick black cat-eyes on herself, but it worked like a charm on Serena. After way too much purple eye shadow and blue mascara, the girl looked like a total slut.

"There," Fanny said, trying to conceal her jealousy. "You're all ready to go."

"How does it look?" Serena asked, making her way to the closet door. "Oh wow, are you sure it's not too much?"

"Looks great," Fanny said, lying through her teeth.

Serena stood so close to the mirror her nose nearly touched it. "Your vision's better than mine, so if you say it looks good..."

"It does." Fanny got up from the bed and opened the door. "Now get out of here. Go."

"Okay, well..." Serena picked up her purse and adjusted her short floral dress. "Thanks for your help. I don't know what I'd do without you."

"Same here," Fanny sighed as Serena left for her date.

SERENA WHIPPED THE door open at eleven on the dot.

"Good girl," Fanny muttered. "You made your curfew."

When she flicked on the light, she saw that this was no time for jokes.

Serena's bottom lip trembled as she slammed the door and back fell against it. Mascara streaked her cheeks as she slipped to the floor. Her mouth opened as though she were about to release a desperate howl, and yet she made no sound at all.

"Oh my God, Serena, what happened?" Fanny scrambled off the bed and fell to her knees at Serena's side. "Are you okay? Did your date try something?"

Serena's eyes widened as she turned her gaze to Fanny. "How did you know?"

"Ugh. Guys! They're all the same."

Wiping her eyes, Serena said, "Not to me. I mean, nobody's ever tried..."

"Tried what?" Fanny asked.

Serena stared at the back of her hand, seemingly perplexed by the colourful streak of makeup painted across it. "How much makeup did you put on me?"

"A lot," Fanny said, matter-of-factly. "What did he do to you?"

"Nothing," she said, still staring at her hand. "But he wanted to. He tried. I said no. I said I wasn't like other girls, but he just thought I meant I wasn't *easy* like them."

"I know what you mean." Fanny took her hands and held them.

"I know you know." Serena met her gaze with a glare that was at once perplexed and doleful. "Did you make me look like a hooker so he'd think he could have his way with me?"

"No," Fanny replied. "I made you look like a hooker so he'd laugh at you and kick you to the curb."

Serena's eyes turned instantly furious. "That's not funny, Fanny."

"It wasn't supposed to be funny."

With a huff, Serena pushed herself up off the ground and stomped over to her bed. "The worst thing about having a roommate is there's nowhere to go when you're mad at your roommate!"

"Sorry it didn't work."

"He thought I was *easy* because of you!" Serena howled. "I'm surprised he didn't throw money at me."

"Well, maybe if you got him off he would have."

Serena laughed, but said, "That's not funny!"

"It's kind of funny."

"No it's not." Serena playfully launched her purse across the room. "You're the worst, Fanny. Why are you trying to make my life hell?"

"I'm not," Fanny said, crossing the room slowly. "I just got jealous. Hasn't anyone ever gotten jealous over you before?"

"Pfft!" Serena rolled her eyes. "Over me? I'm a geek, I'm a freak, and I'm blind as a bat. Who'd want me?"

"I would." Fanny plucked a makeup wipe off their shared beside table and gently wiped Serena's face with it. "Ever since the last time, I've wanted you day and night."

"Really?" Serena asked.

"Don't sound so surprised. Now close your eyes for me."

"Why?"

Fanny slipped the wipe gently down one eyelid, then folded it over and cleaned the other. "Damn. It's going to take half this box to get you clean."

"You have only yourself to blame," she said, not sounding quite so angry anymore.

"I'm sorry," Fanny said. "What a stupid, passive-aggressive thing to do. And it almost got you molested."

"It *did* get me molested," Serena replied. "Well, pawed at. He kept trying to touch me down there and I kept telling him he couldn't, he shouldn't, he might not like what he found. But he wouldn't stop touching me and I tried to get away, but he was strong."

"Damn." Fanny felt genuinely awful, almost sick. "I'm really sorry, Serena."

She sighed. "It's not your fault. It's nobody's fault but his."

"Yeah, but maybe if I hadn't put all this makeup on you..."

"It's not your fault," she said, grabbing Fanny firmly by the wrist. Her eyelids fluttered, clean and clear of shadow. Her face looked bright and fresh when she said, "He felt what was down there, Fanny."

"And...?"

She shook her head. "He didn't like it."

"His loss." Fanny crawled up on Serena's bed and sat there cross-legged. "I think your body's amazing."

Serena rolled her eyes. "You're just saying that."

"Just *saying*?" Fanny asked, leaning toward Serena's naked lips. "Would it convince you if I were just *doing*?"

"Maybe," Serena replied, and by then their mouths were so close Fanny felt her roommate's breath like a warm summer breeze. "Let's find out."

Fanny took that as a green light and let her lips lightly meet Serena's. Obviously Serena wanted more than just a light touch because her tongue slipped past Fanny's teeth in a mad, mixed-up frenzy of motion. She pulled Fanny down on the bed, down on her lithe body, and they rolled together, this way and that, pawing desperately at each other's clothes.

It didn't take long to get Serena's flowery dress over her head. It didn't take much longer for Fanny to unzip her own jeans and squirm out of them. There they were on the bed: a pretty blonde in a plain white bra and sweet little panties, and a dark-haired vixen in a skin-tight t-shirt and a black thong, both girls hard as wood.

"You turn me on like crazy," Serena panted as she peeled off Fanny's top. "Oh my God, you're not wearing a bra!"

"With these little tits? Why bother?"

"Little? Yeah right." Serena dove at one and then the other, like she couldn't decide which to suck first. "I love your tits. They're the yummiest tits in the world!"

"How would you know?" Fanny said with a laugh.

"Oh, I know." Serena sucked one nipple so hard Fanny had to move her to the next. "There couldn't be nicer tits than yours. It's impossible."

Serena traced her glossy lips side to side across one nipple and then the other, back and forth between the two. The teasing little licks ramped up Fanny's desire to an almost unbearable degree. She traced one hand through

Serena's hair, but reached down with the other. Whose swollen cock should she play with: her roommate's or her own?

"Please touch me," Serena whispered before taking Fanny's nipple fully in her mouth.

Fanny moaned. "Only if you touch me too."

Nibbling gently on Fanny's nipple, Serena reached down to pet Fanny through her underwear. Fanny found her roommate's dick beneath those sweet white panties and pulled it free.

"Take me out," Fanny begged.

"Oh..."

"Please?" She squirmed under her roommate's limber young body. "You're not scared of my dick, are you?"

"No..."

"Liar!" Fanny said, stifling some laughter. Then she sang, "Who's afraid of a big bad cock, a big bad cock, a big bad cock?"

"Shut up! Am not!" Reaching beneath Fanny's black panties, Serena set her dick free.

The way they were smushed together, their cocks pressed against one another's soft bellies. They gasped in unison as each girl wrapped her fist around the other's erection.

"You've got the prettiest cock I've ever seen," Fanny said.

Serena didn't stop sucking her nipple, just moaned as they both played with each other's dicks.

"I'm so sorry your date was such a jerk," she went on. "But I'm glad you came back to tell me about it."

"Oh God," Serena said while holding Fanny's stiff nipple between her teeth. "God, you're so hard. What made you so hard?"

"You did, obviously." Fanny thrust in Serena's fist while pulling on the girl's perfect dick. "You're so sweet and sexy. I love your long hair and your tiny body. And I love knowing what's in your panties. I love thinking about how hard it'll get when we kiss."

Serena pulled quickly away from Fanny's breast. "You think about that?"

"All the time," Fanny said, sitting up on her roommate's bed.

Letting go of Fanny's erection, Serena covered her chest even though she still had her bra on. "I don't like the idea of you thinking about me that way."

"What, so I'm allowed to do nasty stuff with you, but I'm not allowed to think about it?"

Serena looked like she wasn't sure how to answer. With a sigh, she dropped her arms away from her chest. "It sounds silly when you put it like that."

"It *is* silly," Fanny said, slipping one bra strap down Serena's arm. Leaning forward, she kissed her roommate's pale shoulder. "You are so damn pretty. Do you know that? And you look better without makeup than with it. You're the perfect girl-next-door."

"Or girl-in-the-next-bed, for you," Serena said with a giggle. She didn't argue when Fanny traced the other bra strap down the other arm, and she said nothing when Fanny reached around and undid the clasp. She did gasp, though, when her bra slid down her front, tumbling into her lap.

"You've got the sweetest breasts," Fanny said, admiring the soft fullness of her roommate's flesh. "God, I've never seen anything like them."

A blush filled Serena's sweet cheeks. "Thanks."

Fanny rolled her over, until she was face-up on her own bed. "Let's see how wet we got you."

Serena burbled. "Sooo wet. You wouldn't believe it."

Pulling down her roommate's panties, Fanny held her breath until she'd exposed the full sweet pinkness of that precious pussy. Fanny had never been with anyone else like Serena: a girl with a full, swollen cock and also a mind-blowingly luscious pussy. It blew her mind that her roommate would let her inside. She felt like a commoner being allowed inside the royal court.

When Fanny approached Serena's pussy, her cock swelled with the sheer heat emanating from between the girl's thighs. "You've got one hot honeypot, baby."

"I'm not your baby," Serena replied, with a giggle to show she was teasing. She bit her finger bashfully while she held her cock out of Fanny's way. "But am I really hot? You really think so?"

"You bet I do," Fanny said as she eased the swollen tip of her cock into her roommate's slippery slit. "Oh, wow, you're hot as the sun."

"Yeah?"

"Yeah."

As Fanny pushed herself deeper into her roommate's warm and welcoming pussy, she also wrapped her fist around the root of Serena's cock. Serena whimpered. Her eyes rolled back as she teased her pretty pink cockhead with just the tips of her fingers. Fanny felt like she was watching what Serena would do to her own body alone in a locked room with no prying eyes. With someone as private as Serena, that was a huge compliment.

Fanny's dick swelled in her roommate's sweet cunt. She inched deeper down into that dark chasm and, when she'd bottomed out, she said, "My God, you're gorgeous."

Serena's eyes flew open like she'd forgotten Fanny was in the room. "Don't," she whimpered. "Don't look at me."

"Why? You're beautiful."

"No I'm not." Serena's arm flew to one side and she snapped off the light, plunging their room into instant darkness. "You're just saying that."

"I'm saying it because it's true." Grasping her roommate's tits with both hands, Fanny leaned her weight on Serena's willing body. "You're a real catch. Anyone would be lucky to have you."

"You don't know what you're talking about," Serena whispered as Fanny fucked her a little harder. "Oh God, that feels good!"

Burying her face in Serena's neck, Fanny kissed her roommate in sharp, desirous pecks. She let her hands slide around to Serena's back so their bare tits could play together. It felt indescribably amazing when their erect nipples brushed each other's naked flesh or poked together.

"Your cock feels so good inside me," Serena panted, arching her hips and driving Fanny up from the bed. "Oh, wow, fuck me harder. Fuck me harder?"

Fanny couldn't speak. She was already driving her dick into her roommate's pussy so forcefully her breath came in desperate pants. Groaning with effort, she launched her massive erection inside Serena, but she couldn't get a good enough foothold on the bed to do the kind of damage Serena was asking for.

Planting her hands roughly on her roommate's shoulders, Fanny pushed herself up. Every muscle in her ass tightened as she slammed Serena's sweet cunt. That warm pussy devoured her dick like a caged animal. All it wanted was more, more, more, and Serena's lovely whimpers encouraged her to give it. Give it hard!

"Yes," Serena said.

Either Fanny's eyes had grown accustomed to the darkness, or the moonlight suddenly found its way through their window, because when she gazed down at the girl, Selena's eyes sparkled like stars. Fanny resisted the temptation to tell her how beautiful she looked, though she did look beautiful. Instead, she asked, "How do you like this?" and slammed the girl as hard as she could.

"Oh!" Serena screamed. Her eyes bugged out and her pussy clamped down on Fanny's cock. Her erection came loose from her grip and whacked Fanny's hip, spilling pre-cum everywhere. "Oh, wow, I'm going to come if you keep that up!"

"Good," Fanny said, and slammed her again.

Serena's breasts jiggled sweetly every time Fanny rammed her, and she made this cute little yipping noise that told the walls she was close to orgasm. Then, suddenly, she started kicking the covers like she was trying to escape Fanny's clutches.

"What's wrong?" Fanny teased. "You don't want to come?"

"No," Serena moaned. "I want you to fuck me forever!"

"Forever?" Fanny asked, pushing her body hard to bring Serena closer.

"Forever and ever and ever!" Serena squealed, writhing under Fanny's fortitude.

"I'll keep you coming forever and ever and ever," Fanny assured her.

"Never stop fucking me," Serena begged as she wrapped her feet around Fanny's calves. "Promise me. Never."

Fanny's cock felt like a steel girder in Serena's little pussy. "I can't make a promise like that," she said, gasping at how amazing this girl's body felt as it hugged hers tight.

She slammed harder into her roommate, crushing Serena's rock-hard dick between their soft bellies. They were so wet Fanny struggled not to fall off Serena's tight little slip-and-slide body. Their tits were slick with sweat. They stuck together somewhat as Fanny moved in her and on her.

When their mouths met, they both moaned. Serena had one of the strongest tongues Fanny had ever encountered, and when she thought about it wrapping snake-like around her hard-on, that put her over the edge. Her thighs trembled as she gave her weight over to the girl beneath her body.

Serena's tongue whipped around hers and they held each other hard... harder...

"Oh God," Fanny moaned as she released her tension into Serena's sweet body.

Serena turned her head to the side and, panting, cried out, "Yes!"

"Yes?"

"Yes!"

Fanny felt Serena's cum explode onto her belly. The heat of that blast made her tremble, but it didn't stop at just one. Hot ropes of cum strung onto her skin. As they writhed against one another, they shared it between the two of them. Serena's jizz stained Fanny's flesh while they touched and kissed and giggled and hugged.

"Oh God," Fanny moaned as she rolled off her roommate. "That was nuts."

"*You're* nuts," Serena chuckled.

"You are."

A thought then came to mind and Fanny forced herself to sit up. She still had her black thong on with her spent cock sticking out the top, but she squirmed out of it because it was soaked with sweat.

"Where are you going?" Serena asked. "Don't leave me."

"I'm not leaving." Fanny picked up her roommate's makeup mirror and flicked it on.

The lights shone so brightly Serena shielded her eyes. "You fixed it? You bought new bulbs?"

"No, it wasn't the bulbs, it was the batteries."

Stealing her hand away from her eyes, Serena cocked her head and gazed at Fanny... then laughed. "The batteries!"

"Aren't you a science major?" Fanny teased. "Shouldn't you know that if something doesn't work you check the power source first?"

Serena laughed so hard she grasped her belly, like her sides were aching. "Oh, that's bad. That's really bad."

Tapping the mirror, Fanny said, "Take a look at yourself and tell me you're not gorgeous."

"I'm not," Serena said without looking at the mirror.

"Look!" Fanny held it closer to her roommate's face. "You are. Just look."

Serena surrendered and gazed at herself in her special mirror. Fanny often wondered what it was like to live with diminished eyesight. Did Serena wonder what it was like to have twenty-twenty vision?

"Okay, you win." Serena snapped the lights off and gazed up at Fanny. "I'm a moderately attractive person."

"*Very* attractive," Fanny said, setting the mirror on the night table. "*Extremely* attractive." She swept her legs under the covers and kissed Serena's shoulder. "*Undeniably* attractive."

Serena joined her between the sheets, tracing one hand all the way from Fanny's bare breasts to her ticklish dick. "How long do you think it'll take this undeniably attractive science major to get hard again?"

"And what will happen when she does?"

Chuckling sweetly, Serena whispered, "I guess we'll just have to wait and see..."

Full of Futa

Fanny couldn't take it any longer. A two-hour history lecture from eight until ten? *At night?* That was just wrong. Wrong on *so* many levels.

Every Monday, she dreaded that class. Fanny dreaded all her Monday classes, but that one in particular. She had to bribe herself with a fancy espresso drink from the coffee kiosk.

Tonight she'd treated herself to a large mochaccino with whipped cream, chocolate shavings, and tiny crushed-up coffee beans sprinkled on top. The little bean bits were the best part, because they were just large enough to be chewy, but small enough that they'd go down easy.

"Five bucks well spent," she told the nerd beside her.

He didn't seem to understand. Good students and bad students always experienced gaps in communication. The bad students were always looking for the easy way out. The good students couldn't imagine why—why would you *not* want to learn? That's how it went when Fanny first met Serena.

Serena was unmatched in her geekiness.

By breaktime, the caffeine and sugar had worn off and Fanny was left with an empty cup and restless legs. No way could she listen to any more academic droning. She packed her notebook into her bag and strutted from the lecture hall.

She'd tried. She really had. She'd tried, and she'd failed.

Sex was a big part of the problem. Fanny couldn't go ten seconds without imagining what dirty deeds she might get up to back in her dorm room. Her panties felt that much tighter as she fantasized.

Fanny wasn't a slut. People thought she was because she dressed like one, but lately she'd only been sleeping with one person: Serena the Nerd Queen, also known as her roommate.

What were the chances two girls with such anomalous bodies would end up housed together in the same tiny dorm? Sometime life was magic.

Fanny left the lecture hall, strutted past a cloud of smokers, and squeezed her thighs together as she waited to cross the street.

"Why's there only traffic when you're horny as hell?" she asked the elderly professor standing beside her.

His eyes bugged. "Perhaps you should launch a study on the subject."

"Yeah, right."

Inside her tight pink undies, Fanny's cock throbbed violently.

She wriggled around, begging it to wait three minutes.

When the traffic cleared, she shot across the street. Her book bag thudded heavily against her side while her short skirt flipped up with every step. She didn't even care. She was too horny to be bothered if other students spotted Fanny's French underpants.

It was almost too cold to keep wearing skirts, but she couldn't help herself. Short skirts were like an addiction. Today she'd paired hers with knee-high socks to keep out the blustery autumnal blow.

What she *should* have worn was a jacket. In only a sheer top and bra, her nipples grew sharp enough to cut glass. When she arrived at her dorm room, Serena would take one look at her and topple over with lust. Fact.

But when she arrived at the dorm, breathless and rosy-cheeked, Fanny was surprised to find the door closed. Everybody on their floor left their doors open all the time, unless they were fucking or sleeping. Even when they went to the bathroom at the end of the hall, they still left their doors open to pilfering. It was actually kind of stupid, when she thought about it, but there were lots of stupid people in college. She thought she'd be the only slacker, but nope. There were tons.

"Serena?" Fanny asked quietly. She turned the handle, but their room was locked up tight.

So what? Serena probably went somewhere. To grab a late dinner, maybe? Or maybe she went to the library to study. The possibilities were endless.

As Fanny dug her keychain from the bottom of her bag, she heard a sound she recognized. It was coming from the other side of the door: a light gasp, and then another. "Oh yes!"

"Oh no!" Fanny growled, shoving her key in the lock.

Steeling herself for what she was about to find, Fanny threw open the door and stepped into the dark dorm room.

Serena screamed.

"Busted!" Fanny stupidly shut the door, and now couldn't see a thing.

"I'm sorry," Serena squealed.

"Who's the guy?" Fanny asked, reaching blindly for Serena's bed.

"There is no guy!" Serena had the upper hand in the dark, because she really *was* blind—partially blind, at least.

Fanny heard the bedcovers shuffling, and she asked, "Who's the girl, then?"

"There's no girl. It's just me, Fanny." Serena reached for the bedside lamp and flicked it on. "See? Just me."

Maybe Fanny had been burned too many times, and she didn't trust anyone, not even Serena. She grabbed her roommate's covers and pulled them down.

Then she understood.

"Oh God," Serena cried. "I'm sorry, Fanny. I'm so embarrassed."

Serena was totally naked. Not a stitch on. Her porcelain breasts were swollen with arousal, making them even larger than their usual handful of flesh. Her pretty pink nipples could compete with Fanny's for glass-cutting prowess while her cock lay half-hard across her belly. Serena's knees were bent. Between her legs, she held what was surely the root end of a vibrator, the majority of which was inserted between her smooth white thighs.

Fanny laughed as Serena's cheeks glowed crimson.

"Fanny, I'm sorry! You must think I'm a total pervert. I bought it online..."

"Shh, baby, shh!" Fanny sat on the edge of the bed, running her icy fingers down her roommate's beautiful belly. "So you bought a sex toy. So what?"

"It's like I'm cheating on you," Serena sobbed. "I'm so sorry. You must hate me."

"Look at me, babe." Fanny gazed into her roommate's lovely face. "Do I look like I hate you?"

Serena released her hold on the vibrator and let her knees fall from position. "I can't see you that well. Come closer."

Fanny lowered her face to accommodate Serena's vision impairment, but it was a ruse. Serena stole a quick kiss, then giggled like a little girl.

Slapping her bare belly, Fanny said, "Brat."

"You're the brat," Serena teased, pulling up the covers so they veiled her naked body. "Why are you back so early? Don't you have class until late?"

Fanny groaned. "I was sick of squirming. I couldn't stop thinking about you back here, all alone." Tossing her book bag on her own bed, Fanny said, "Although I guess you *weren't* alone. You had your new best friend to keep you company."

"I'm sorry!" Tears welled in Serena's eyes as she apologized again. "You don't know how awful I feel. I betrayed your trust, Fanny. I know you're not sleeping with anyone else, and here's me buying..."

"Stop it!" Grabbing Serena's shoulders, Fanny shook her gently. "A sex toy is not a *person*. Masturbation isn't *cheating*!"

Serena's expression turned angelic. "You really think?"

"Yes!" Fanny said with a laugh. "You're so cute, the way you worry about stuff like that." Kicking off her shoes, Fanny asked, "Why didn't you just tell me you bought a vibrator? That way we could play with it together."

"We could?" Serena asked, like she'd never have imagined such a thing could happen.

"Of course!" Slipping her top over her head, Fanny said, "You think vibrators can only be used alone in the dark when your preferred partner is at a super-boring history lecture?"

Serena blushed, which was answer enough.

Sliding down her skirt, Fanny stood beside her roommate's bed wearing mismatched lingerie—baby pink panties and a foxy black bra. She watched Serena's gaze drizzle down her body, settling at the massive erection trapped inside her little-girl undies.

Fanny often wondered what she looked like, to Serena. A blur? A ball of fuzz? Patches of dark and light? If they could trade eyes for a couple hours, just for the experience, she'd do it in a heartbeat.

"Can I touch you?"

Fanny laughed. "You really have to ask?"

Serena let her arm hang over the side of the bed, reaching lazily, but falling just short of Fanny's thigh. "Come closer."

Fanny took a step forward, letting her roommate's fingers brush her cool flesh. "Ooh, your hands are warm."

"Your thighs are cold."

Pulling down the covers just slightly, Fanny cupped one of Serena's beautiful breasts. "Your boobs are warm."

"What else is warm?" Serena asked as she pushed the covers down.

Leaning across the bed, Fanny gripped the end of the sex toy. It wasn't vibrating, but Fanny knew that even before touching it. If it had been on, Serena wouldn't have been able to contain herself. Vibrators were powerful machines.

When Fanny retracted the toy from her roommate's cunt, Serena panicked. "What are you doing?"

The toy was quite large, but not painfully so. It was made of a soft material, skin-like, but hot pink. Fanny licked it slowly, running her tongue from the base to the ridge at the top.

"Mmm." The musky aroma of Serena's pussy filled Fanny's mouth. "You taste good."

"Oh." A blush spread across Serena's cheeks. "Thanks."

Fanny swirled her tongue around the tip of the fake cock, licking it like an ice cream cone. "This is why I can't concentrate in class."

"Why?" Serena asked.

"Because I remember the way you taste, or I picture you touching yourself..."

Serena casually brushed her fingers from the base of her half-hard cock to the tip. "Like this?"

Fanny grabbed her roommate's hand and wrapped it around the girl's shaft. "Like this!"

Holding Serena's hand in hers, Fanny shuttled that sweet little fist up and down her roommate's cock. She smiled as she watched Serena's tip turn a deeper shade of red.

"Keep going," Fanny instructed. She let go of her roommate's fist. "Play with yourself on your own. I want to watch."

"Okay." Serena bit her lip as she toyed with her cock. "Does this look good?"

"It looks amazing, babe."

Fanny tugged at the elastic on her panties, letting her swollen cock pop out the top. She didn't bother taking her underwear off. She wasn't like Serena—she didn't have a pussy—so there was really no need. Her panties stayed on and so did her bra, but that didn't prevent Serena from finding her erection and pumping both cocks at the same time.

"Damn, you've got talent." Fanny's legs wobbled and she fell onto the mattress, kneeling at Serena's side. "I wasn't joking when I said I daydream about you in class. You're all I think about."

"I know what you mean," Serena replied as she worked her own cock and Fanny's.

"Is that why you bought this?" Fanny asked, whacking Serena's breast with the vibrator. "So you could get yourself off even when I'm in class?"

"Yes," Serena admitted, arching her hips up and her butt off the bed. "But now that you're here, I want *you* to do it."

She opened her legs a little wider, revealing the slick pinkness of her pussy. Serena's cock was no longer at half-mast. It now stood proudly erect in her fist, like an oak tree shooting out of her pelvis.

Fanny had never been drawn to any other body the way she was drawn to Serena's.

That girl's cock was alabaster: smooth and firm and ready.

It gave way to the prettiest pussy on the planet.

A little lower, the purple pucker of Serena's ass winked in Fanny's direction.

Her ass cheeks were flawless—not a pimple, not a freckle, just milky white warmth. She had a few wispy curls of blondish hair around the base of her cock, which made it look like a monument rising out of a golden cloud.

There couldn't possibly be another girl with a body as gorgeous as Serena's.

As for Fanny, she knew she was hot, but Serena had that girl-next-door thing going for her. Fanny came off as hard, not soft. Slutty, not virginal. Rock and punk and you got a problem with that? Hope not, 'cause she's just as happy to kick you in the balls and steal your wallet.

Okay, Fanny wouldn't actually do that (unless you really deserved it) but she liked too see fear in strangers' eyes when she said something really inappropriate.

"To turn it on," Serena whimpered.

Fanny had been lost in thoughts of kicking ass while her roommate jerked her junk, but she came quickly back to reality when she felt the weight of the vibrator in her hand. She didn't need to ask how it turned on. That was simple enough. There were buttons on the base. It was in the off position now, but it went up to low, medium, and high.

"What setting did you have it on before I came in?" Fanny asked.

"I didn't," Serena said. "I just wanted to see how big it would feel in my pussy. I haven't started playing with the vibrations yet."

Fanny pressed the button for the lowest setting, but nothing happened. She shook the toy, then shook her head. "Did you put batteries in it?"

Serena's eyes widened. "Not yet..."

"You forgot?" Fanny said, laughing.

"No..."

"You always forget about batteries!"

Serena wrinkled her nose and admitted, "Yeah..."

Reluctantly pulling her cock from her roommate's grip, Fanny went to fetch batteries from the desk drawer. Her cock was so hard it bounced in front of her as she walked across the room.

"Wow," Serena said, and Fanny knew just what she meant.

"I know. This is how turned on you get me. Sucks when it happens in public."

"*Does* it happen in public?"

"Of course." Fanny unscrewed the bottom of the vibrator and slipped two batteries inside. "It must happen to you, too."

When Serena shook her head, the tips of her blonde hair flipped innocently against her pale shoulders.

"What, never?"

"Maybe when I was younger," Serena mumbled. "Like, puberty... that age... that *awkward* age."

Fanny screwed the cap back on. "But not anymore?"

"No."

"Never?"

Serena shook her head, this time with her eyes training directly on the vibrator.

Fanny pushed the button. The immediate buzz nearly turned her hand numb, so she lowered the power setting.

Serena smirked while Fanny touched the vibrating dick to the side of her own shaft. "Damn, we got ourselves a stud!"

"Is that good?" Serena asked.

"You tell me." Jumping on Serena's bed, Fanny straddled her roommate and touched the vibrator to the girl's hard dick. "Is that a stud, or is that a stud?"

"Cheeze-whiz!" Serena squealed, bucking off the mattress. "That's incredible!"

Fanny let her thighs splay on either side of Serena's. She lowered herself down until her cock pressed right down on her roommate's. Just as Serena started to sigh in that lovely girlish way she had, Fanny pressed the vibrator right up against their two cocks.

Serena screamed.

"Damn!" Fanny laughed as she lifted her body away from Serena's. "That almost made me come."

"Me too," Serena said, panting.

"And it's only on the lowest setting."

"Wow..."

"If I touch it to your tip you'll probably jizz all up your belly," Fanny said, waving the dildo like a magic wand.

"Don't!" Serena wrapped her hand around the base. "I'm not ready."

"You're not, huh?" Fanny's cock whacked her roommate's as she straddled the pretty blonde geek. "Then I guess I'll just have to fuck you until you are."

When Fanny stuck her dick in Serena's warm, wet pussy, Serena glumly said, "Oh."

"What's wrong?" Fanny asked as she thrust in the world's tightest snatch.

"I just thought..."

"You thought what?"

Serena bit her lip. "I thought you were going to fuck me with the dildo."

Fanny pulled out. "Just wanted to wet my whistle first."

Her cock emerged from her roommate's pussy slick with juice. Serena must have noticed how it glistened, because she wasted no time wrapping her fist around it.

"Good God," Fanny said as she settled next to Serena. "Your hands, babe... you've got the softest, sweetest little hands."

"They're not always sweet," Serena said, shuttling her fist up and down Fanny's dick.

"Do yours too." Fanny traced the buzzing dildo up and down Serena's dick. "You're hard as a brick!"

"So are you," Serena moaned. "You're harder!"

Fanny tickled her slit while Serena wrapped her free hand around Fanny's dick. She stroked them off in time with one another, picking up pace when Fanny plunged the vibrating cock between her legs.

"Oh!" Serena cried, raising her hips off the bed. "Wow, that's amazing!"

Every time Fanny forced the dildo deeper inside Serena's pussy, she hopped on the mattress. The girl's boobs quivered so sweetly Fanny couldn't resist plunging her face between them, taking in the wonderful scent of her roommate's skin, and then suckling those pointed nipples.

"That feels so good," Serena moaned. "Suck the other one. And fuck me harder!"

Fanny's brain was so fried on arousal she had trouble accommodating her roommate's request. She moved to the other breast, taking that wonderful pebbled nipple into her mouth. Then she gripped the dildo harder and fucked her roomie faster.

Serena's pussy clamped down the dildo, making it more difficult for Fanny to move. At the same time, Serena's fingers tightened around Fanny's dick, making it more difficult to fuck that tight first.

"You've got to loosen up," Fanny begged.

"I'm coming!"

"No." Fanny pulled the vibrator from Serena's snatch and knocked her hand away from her dick. "Not yet, baby."

"Yes yet."

Serena reached for her cock, but Fanny flipped her over and grabbed the lube.

"What are you doing?" Serena asked.

Spreading the girl's thighs with her knees, Fanny slipped the vibrator into Serena's pussy. "Be good."

"Good how?"

"Don't come," Fanny replied as she smeared lube down Serena's ass crack.

"You're not..."

"I am." Fanny pressed the tip of her cock against her roommate's puckered asshole. "Open up. You've always wanted to try double penetration."

"Have I?" Serena gasped.

"Hope so, because I sure have."

Fanny took a deep breath and then eased forward, pressing her dickhead into her roommate's reluctant hole. Serena squealed, but she didn't move. She lay flat with the vibrator sticking out of her pussy. Fanny could feel the buzz emanating from inside the girl's body.

She wanted in.

"Arch your ass," Fanny instructed. "Tuck in your knees. That's more like it."

While Serena changed positions, her ass ring relaxed enough to let Fanny pop inside. Just the tip, but the pressure that on Fanny's dick was nearly enough to bring her to orgasm. It wasn't just the tightness of Serena's asshole hugging her tip that made her want to come—it was also the low vibration emanating from her pussy.

"It's too big," Serena whined.

"What is?"

"You are!" She squirmed like she wanted to escape, but that motion worked against her. Every time she wiggled, Fanny managed to plant another half inch of cock in her ass. "Oh Fanny, what are you doing to me?"

"I dream about fucking you everywhere I go."

"I dream about you too," Serena replied, letting Fanny deeper inside her anal canal. "But not this, Fanny. I don't dream about this."

"Never?"

Serena hesitated while Fanny forced her dick down that tight chute. "Well, sometimes this."

Fanny laughed breathlessly. "I knew it. Everyone with an ass wants to try anal."

"At least once," Serena conceded. "But I never imagined I'd try it for the first time with a dildo between my legs."

"Don't you like it?" Fanny said as she fucked the girl's ass.

"Yeah. Do you?"

"God, yes!"

Fanny wasn't sure how long she'd last. The tightness of Serena's ass coupled with the vibrations from the dildo. Wow... that sensation almost made her head explode. In fact, it felt like the vibrator was sitting right up against her dick. Every time her cock retreated from Serena's ass, it started to knock the dildo out. Fanny had to grab it with her hand and cram it back in.

"Holy hell!" Serena screamed.

"Did I hurt you?"

She didn't answer.

Fanny pressed her front against Serena's back and grabbed one of those delicious swaying boobs. "God, you've got great ones. I wish mine were as big as yours."

"I know what you mean," Serena panted. "You've got a bigger cock."

"No I don't," Fanny said, even though she knew it was true. "Go on, baby. Play with yourself."

"Play with my cock?" Serena asked.

"Yeah, stroke it." Fanny fucked her roommate's ass with her huge swollen prick and turned up the power on the heavy-duty vibrator. "I'm gonna come, and I want you coming with me."

Serena screamed as the vibrator slipped past medium setting and went all the way to high. "Okay," she said.

Fanny could feel it in her body when Serena had wrapped her fist around her erection.

Planting sweet kisses against her neck, Fanny said, "I love your dick, baby. I love your dick and your tits and your hair and your neck and your shoulders and your shoes."

With a breathless laugh, Serena said, "My shoes aren't part of my body."

"I know." Fanny struggled to keep her head screwed on. "I meant your feet."

"Aww..."

"And I super-love your ass!" Fanny grunted as she pummelled her roommate from behind. "Your pussy, too. You've got the tightest little asshole and the hottest little cunt!"

"Stop," Serena pleaded. "You'll make me come!"

"Good," Fanny cried as she rammed her roommate's bum. "Come! I'm gonna come too!"

"Are you?"

"Oh yeah, baby."

They were hot and sweaty and panting and breathless when Fanny issued her final thrust into Serena's tight hole.

"Holy Moly," Serena cried. The room filled with sounds of her fist shuttling up and down her shaft. "I'm... so... close..."

"Me too!"

Keeping her cock lodged deep inside Serena's ass, Fanny fucked the girl roughly with the vibrator. The buzzing toy rubbed Fanny's dick with a heat and friction she'd never experienced. Her thighs locked and her balls quaked. She squeezed her roommate's breast, and that put them both over the brink.

"Yes!" Serena shrieked.

"Oh yeah," Fanny growled into her roommate's hair. "You are so fucking hot, baby. I want to fuck you all day and all night."

"Yes!"

"All *fucking* day and *all... fucking... night*!"

Fanny filled her roommate's ass with blast after unapologetic blast. She felt like it was never going to end when Serena toppled down on the bed and moaned into her pillow. "I guess I'll be sleeping in the wet spot tonight."

Serena's body quivered and shook even after Fanny had pulled out of her ass and withdrawn the buzzing demon from her pussy.

"Why don't you sleep in my bed tonight?" Fanny asked.

"Your bed?" Sitting up, Serena grabbed her glasses and started wiping a spectacular amount of cum from her soft white belly. "But your bed is so small."

"So is yours," Fanny said. She used a baby wipe to clean off her dick, and handed the box to Serena. "Our beds are both the same size."

"I know. Just enough room for one."

Why wasn't her roommate jumping at the opportunity to sleep all cuddled up like kittens?

Throwing down her panties and unclasping her sweaty bra, Fanny jumped into bed naked. "Fine then. Sleep in a pool of your own cum. See if I care."

Serena didn't say anything as she gathered up her makeup kit and headed out to brush her teeth. Fanny should have done that, too, but she didn't want to risk the rest of the dorm witnessing their animosity. Chances are everyone on their floor had already heard their earth-shattering sex.

When Serena came back, She took off her long, fuzzy housecoat and hung it on the back of the door. She smelled like mint and apricot scrub as she made her way up the aisle between their beds.

Without a word, she took off her glasses, turned off the light, and slipped into bed with Fanny.

Without a word, Fanny wrapped her arms around her roommate and kissed her soft white shoulder.

After a while, Serena said, "Night-night, Fanny."

Fanny kissed her again and said, "Sleep tight, Serena."

Fanny's Futa Threesome

Fanny screamed when she walked through the door. "Who's that stranger sitting on my bed?"

It shouldn't have scared her. People wandered in and out of each other's dorm rooms all the time. She felt embarrassed for shivering and shrieking the way she did.

Trying to compose herself, Fanny said to the girl, "Sorry for screaming, but who *are* you?"

"This is Angelica," Serena said.

It hadn't registered that Fanny's roommate was even around. This girl on her bed was probably just some friend Serena hadn't mentioned.

"Hello," Angelica said, with a hint of a European accent.

"Angelica," Serena said, "this is Fanny."

"Is nice to meet you." Angelica reached out to shake Fanny's hand. When they touched skin to skin, a rush of electricity coursed through Fanny's veins. "Serena has told me so much about the beautiful dark-haired roommate with the huge, hard dick."

"Shhh!" Serena said as Fanny slammed the door in a panic. "Someone might hear you."

Angelica covered her mouth. "Oh, I am sorry. I did not realize this was secret."

"It *was*," Serena hissed.

"It *is*," Fanny joined in.

Serena grabbed Angelica's shoulder. "I told you in that confidence."

Fanny looked to her roommate, feeling greatly hurt. "You've been telling people about me?"

"Is my fault." Making herself more comfortable on Fanny's bed, Angelica brushed her hand through her short hair—dyed, no doubt, because that fiery shade of red didn't exist in the natural world, or at least in the world of natural redheads. "Serena is in many of the same classes as me. I noticed her from the first day of school. In fact, I have been hitting on her for weeks."

"You never told me this," Fanny said to Serena.

Serena shrugged. "I didn't know."

With a laugh, Angelica said, "Your roommate is so innocent, Fanny."

"I thought she was just being friendly," Serena said, gazing down at the little white socks on her feet.

"You think I am just being friendly even when I brush my hand down your bum?" Angelica asked, raising an eyebrow.

Serena bit her lip. "Okay, I thought you were being *very* friendly. I didn't realize you were coming on to me."

"Until today," Angelica said, turning to Fanny. "When I ask her back to my place for sex."

Fanny didn't know how to react to someone as gutsy and straightforward as Angelica. Looking to Serena, she asked, "And instead you brought her back here... for sex?"

"For you," Serena replied.

"For sex *with me*?"

"To meet with you," Angelica clarified. "Your roommate tell me you are very important person in her life."

"If I'm so important, why are you telling strangers about my penis?" Fanny asked Serena.

Serena waved Fanny over so they'd be sitting side by side on her bed. "Don't worry—I told her about mine first."

"I am intrigued by this," Angelica added.

"Intrigued by penises?" Fanny asked.

With a nod, she said, "Penises on beautiful girls? Very intriguing indeed."

"Well, Serena doesn't *only* have a penis," Fanny said. "She's got a vagina, too."

"She knows," Serena said. "I told her."

"But why? You don't tell anyone this stuff."

Serena shrugged, then bit her lip as she looked at Angelica. "I don't know why. I just..."

Fanny's feet reacted first. She jumped up so she was standing between the two beds. "Oh my God, you want to have sex with her!"

"I just..."

"You want to have sex with her because she has a vagina and I don't." Turning to Angelica, Fanny asked, "You *do* have a vagina, right?"

Angelica nodded.

"You've never had sex with a vagina," Fanny said to Serena. "You want to try it."

"Well, can you blame me?" Serena asked. "This is college, after all. If not now, when?"

Fanny couldn't argue with that logic, except that she found herself more possessive of Serena than she ought to be. They weren't technically a couple, after all. Just because they had a lot of great sex didn't make them anything more than roommates who had a lot of great sex.

Did it?

"I still don't get why you came here," Fanny said.

"Because of you," Angelica answered. "Silly girl. She love you. You don't see?"

Serena's cheeks blazed.

"It make perfect sense that she attracted to me." Angelica stood between the beds so she was facing Fanny—looming over her, more like. Angelica was practically Amazonian in height. "Look at us. We dress the same, both in black, both punk. I have more tattoos than you, I bet. You have piercings?"

"No," Fanny said, feeling somewhat ashamed of herself. "But I'm considering getting a..."

"I have this," Angelica said, touching the ring in her lip, then the one in her eyebrow. "This, the stud in my nose, seven in this ear, five in this ear, and bars through my nipples."

"Bars through your nipples?" Fanny asked, trying desperately not to look at Serena. "Wow. Can I see?"

Angelica had no trouble sharing the moment with Serena. "I think she on the board, yes?"

Serena looked desperately to Fanny. "Are you?"

"I want to see this chick's nipple piercings, if that's what you're asking."

That wasn't what they were asking, but Fanny knew she'd go along with just about anything. Angelica's long, strong body made her insides quake. And Serena—oh, Fanny would do just about anything for Serena.

If Serena wanted to fuck a pussy, who was Fanny to stop her?

Angelica was hot as hell, a bigger, more hardcore punk than Fanny would ever be. Some girls might feel jealous—and usually Fanny would be one of them—but her cock was starting to throb with anticipation. How could she stop what had already begun?

Sex with a stranger. A student, but a stranger nonetheless. This was a big deal for Fanny. She dressed like a slut, and sometimes acted like one, but she didn't think of herself that way.

But Angelica... oh man, Angelica was smoking. She had on a black bra beneath a men's pinstriped vest. No top, but tons of jewellery—mostly silver chains around her neck and her wrists. She also had on a leather cuff which had spikes jutting out in all directions. You wouldn't mess with Angelica unless you had a death wish.

Or you craved domination.

Angelica looked like she'd be pretty good at that sort of thing.

When she unbuttoned her vest and exposed her mesh bra, Fanny could see two silver bars shimmering through. Her peachy nipples were crushed by the cups. "You want bra off?"

"I want bra off," Fanny said without thinking.

It wasn't the kind of bra with hooks. Angelica had to lift it over her head, trying not to let the mesh fabric catch on any of her facial piercings.

"Wow," Serena said. They were both staring at the girl's beautiful breasts. Would those gorgeous tits look better or worse without silver bars through the nipples? Hard to say. They'd look a little more innocent, that's for sure. Those piercings gave Angelica's look a harder edge than Fanny's.

"Now your turn," Angelica said to Fanny. "You take off top."

"Me? Oh." Fanny looked to Serena, but Serena didn't say anything. "Okay, sure."

Fanny unbuttoned her top, then tossed it on the bed. She wished she'd worn a better bra. This one was simple and white—nothing punk about it. She hadn't expected to come home to a horny Russian, or she'd have worn a black one instead.

Serena jumped down from her bed, tearing off her own top as she did so. "Here, let me."

Before Fanny had quite figured out what her roommate was saying, Serena wrapped both arms around her back. They were both down to their bras, so their nearly-naked breasts touched as Serena undid the hooks on Fanny's bra. Fanny returned the favour, and they both moved their fingertips up each other's shoulders. Slowly, and half for show, they slid their bra straps down until the meagre garments fell between them.

Serena's nipples were hard, but not as hard as Fanny's. When they brushed lightly against one another, streaks of sizzling desire bolted between Fanny's legs. Her cock throbbed inside her panties. She kissed her sweet little roommate until her cock grew so big it poked out from under the waistband.

"Oh, Serena!" She pressed her swollen dick against her roommate's belly. "Are you as hard as I am?"

"Why don't you check?" Serena said.

Angelica cleared her throat. "Perhaps I could check."

Fanny jumped. She'd pretty much forgotten Angelica was in the room, and suddenly she felt a tad self-conscious.

But Serena said, "Sure you can check." She backed away from Fanny and leaned back on her bed, wearing nothing but a summery skirt.

And panties.

Fanny got a good look at those cute floral underpants when Angelica flipped up Serena's skirt. There was a huge cock-shaped bulge under the panties, and a dark, fragrant wet patch in the gusset.

"You are hard and you are wet," Angelica said, bowing between Serena's legs for a sniff. "Ahh, you smell good too."

A deep blush took over Serena's cheeks.

"Will you let me taste?" Angelica asked.

"You want to taste *me*?" Serena asked, like she was scandalized by the question.

"I want to taste your pussy," Angelica said. She shrugged. "And taste your cock too. I would like to taste both."

Serena looked to Fanny, who cupped her own breasts because they were getting cold. Fanny shrugged and said, "Do whatever you want. It's your body."

"But I only want to if you want me to," Serena said.

Fanny's heart melted. It was so sweet of Serena to basically ask permission. Fanny said, "Go for it. I'll watch."

Angelica didn't wait for Fanny to finish before tearing off Serena's cute little panties. While she was at it, she tore off Serena's summer skirt as well. Good thing both had elastic waistbands, because Angelica's actions were a little on the violent side. It was pretty exciting to watch.

When Serena's panties came down, her cock sprang up like a jack-in-the-box. She must have been super-attracted to Angelica, because Fanny had never seen her dick so thick and hard before it had even been touched. Usually it took a bit of effort to give Serena an erection. Her dick wasn't as responsive as Fanny's.

Fanny was hard as hell, but that was nothing new.

Angelica stared unapologetically between Serena's legs. Serena's pussy only had a bit of light blond hair around it, but Angelica touched that hair gently, spreading Serena wide with her thumbs. The punk girl exposed Serena's little pink lips. They were absolutely dripping with juice.

Fanny couldn't resist. While Angelica stared at Serena's pussy, Fanny grabbed Serena's cock. It jumped in her hand, but Fanny held on tighter.

"Oh God," Serena moaned. "Fanny, what are you doing?"

"Touching you." Rubbing, actually. Fanny traced her fist slowly up and down her roommate's erection, watching a small pool of pre-cum build up in the slit. "You've got such a hot little body, babe."

Serena looked lovingly at Fanny. "Thanks. So do you."

Their moment was interrupted when Angelica shoved her face between Serena's legs and started licking.

"Oh my God!" Serena shrieked. "Oh God! That's amazing!"

Fanny wouldn't be outdone. She bowed to Serena's bare breasts and licked the girl's nipples.

"Oh God!" Without hesitation, Serena's hand landed heavily on the back of Fanny's head. "Yes, don't stop!"

Those nipples were like candy. Fanny flicked them with her tongue, then sucked Serena's small breasts into her mouth. Serena's nipples were so soft and pink. Her breasts were so white and lovely. Fanny could devour them all day long.

Then Fanny felt something strange against her hand. Was that...? Yes, it was Angelica's lips! Angelica had abandoned Serena's sweet pussy and was in the process of devouring Serena's cock. Didn't seem to matter that Fanny's hand was still wrapped around it, because Angelica's fingers were busying themselves inside Serena's tight cunt.

Serena writhed on the bed, mumbling nonsense. All this focus on her fine body was obviously doing the trick. She squirmed and moaned and made all the sweet noises she always made, and a few Fanny had never heard before.

Just when Serena's frenzy built close to its peak, Angelica popped the girl's cock out of her mouth. "Don't come yet! I want to fuck you!"

"Okay," Serena cooed, seeming exhausted beyond measure.

Angelica tore out of her tight leather pants, then straddled Serena on the bed. Fanny watched in wonderment as the punk lowered herself on Serena's pounding erection. The punk had all sorts of spider web tattoos down her back, but they stopped at her butt. The only one below her waist seemed to be the small flower on her ankle.

Fanny took a step back and watched from behind as her roommate's cock disappeared inside the stranger. From this angle, Angelica's ass looked huge—but in a good way. Angelica leaned forward, pinning little Serena to the bed. Both her palms pressed flat on the girl's white shoulders. Serena seemed to like being taken roughly, judging by the sweet sounds she made as Angelica worked her over.

"You like that?" Angelica kept asking.

Every time, Serena answered, "Yes!"

Fanny didn't know whether to feel jealous or just get in on the action. But her body knew what it wanted: it wanted Serena's tight, wet pussy.

Or did it want the full, round pucker of Angelica's ass?

Decisions, decisions. Serena's body was familiar. Fanny knew what to expect. But Angelica's ass would be new to her. Not only that, but she couldn't be sure how Angelica would react. She got a giddy thrill from the idea that Angelica might scream and kick her away and call her a pervert.

Fanny's hands took over. She grabbed Serena by the backs of the knees and heaved her closer to the edge of the bed. Angelica tumbled forward, landing with one silver barred nipple in Serena's mouth. Before she could right herself, Fanny pushed down her panties and pulled up her plaid skirt and forced her cock inside her roommate's slick cunt.

"Oh God!" Serena screamed, tightening her pussy around Fanny's erection. "Fuck me, Fanny!"

"You better believe I will," Fanny said, running her cock into the soft and infinitely warm canal of her roommate's vagina. "Oh Serena, you feel so good, so tight."

"You want tight?" Angelica asked, turning sharply. "You try my asshole."

And here Fanny thought Angelica would call her a pervert for defiling that soft, round butt.

Now that Fanny had put her dick inside Serena's pussy, she didn't want to take it out. Serena was the perfect home for her cock. She loved that warm, wet hug. She loved the velvety texture of her roommate's interior. She could live inside it.

But Angelica leaned so far down her big breasts pressed on Serena's little tiny ones. The punk stranger reached back with both hands and spread her ass cheeks wide open. Sinking her body down on Serena's, Angelica let her pussy swallow the girl's cock all the way down. "You want a tight spot? You fuck my goddamn asshole!"

Angelica didn't move. Serena didn't move. Fanny didn't move.

"You got lube?" Angelica asked.

Fanny grabbed it from the nightstand, like she was under the stranger's control.

"Good. Now put that on my crack and fuck my damn ass. You hear me?"

"Yes," Fanny said, dousing Angelina's asshole with lube. "Whatever you want."

She had to crawl up on the bed to get herself in position. As Angelica held her own cheeks open, Fanny aimed her thick red cockhead at the bull's-eye. She poked at it so gently nothing happened.

"Harder!" Angelica instructed.

"Okay, okay." Fanny heaved her hips forward, slamming into Angelica's ass. Still, it was only the tip that entered.

"Harder!" Angelica shouted.

Poor Serena panted beneath her big body.

"I don't want to hurt you," Fanny said.

"Harder!"

Fanny took a deep breath and grabbed Angelica's hips. She jerked forward, again, again, and her cock worked its way into that lube-slicked hole. Wow, was Angelica ever right! That was about the tightest thing she'd ever felt squeezing down on her cock! At first she could barely move, but she kept at it because she knew Serena wouldn't get fucked until she guided the motion hard enough.

"Oh Fanny," Serena sighed. "Her piercings are pressing into my nipples."

"How does it feel?" Fanny asked.

Serena's eyelids fluttered. "Soooo good!"

That look of luxurious pleasure turned Fanny on so viciously she rammed her cock even harder into Angelica. Both girls' bodies both recoiled against hers. Every action led to a reaction. The harder she pounded the stranger's ass, the more both girls shrieked. Angelica's pussy was obviously massaging Serena's cock nicely. Fanny couldn't help wondering which was tighter—pussy or ass. Had to be ass.

Fanny worked Angelica over, wishing she could be in every one of these girls' orifices at once. She wanted to grow three more dicks so she could fuck Angelica's pussy and Serena's pussy and Serena's sweet little ass. But maybe one dick was enough for a girl—it was certainly more than most girls had!

"Keep going," Serena said. "Oh, I'm about to come!"

Angelica started thrusting her wide hips, bucking back at Fanny while her pussy worked on Serena's dick. What a day! Sex with a stranger! And anal, for that matter. Fanny could barely hold herself together when she thought how jealous some people would be, knowing she'd fucked her roommate and a hot Russian student at the same time.

Fanny fucked the girl so hard she lost her balance right on the verge of orgasm. She stumbled back and her cock popped neatly out of Angelica's ass. Angelica groaned, but fucked Serena faster. In fact, Angelica righted herself and worked up and down on Serena's perfect cock, bouncing hard, throwing her weight around.

From this angle, Fanny could see Angelica's amazing breasts bouncing with each thrust. Serena's boobs were much smaller, but they quivered in time with the stranger's. It was such a sight Fanny wrapped her hand around her dick and brought herself to climax with a few quick strokes.

Fanny's knees trembled as thick ropes of cum shot across the expanse, landing like modern art across Angelica's backside. Orgasm art. Never to be replicated.

As Angelica bounced on Serena's dick, Fanny shoved two fingers in her roommate's pussy. There it was—the elusive G-spot, which had grown spongy but firm with arousal. Fanny petted it and Serena squealed, "Yes, yes, yes!"

"Are you coming, baby?" Angelica asked.

"Yes, yes, yes!"

Fanny reached around the stranger's body and zeroed in on her clit. Angelica howled when Fanny stroked it. "I want you both to come," Fanny said.

They were putty in her hands. They both screeched and squealed and hollered and moaned while she played with their pretty bodies. The sweetheart and the punk. What a pair. But they looked great together, Fanny had to admit. Angelica was much bigger than Serena, much tougher, but they had a bit of a "Danny and Sandy" thing going for them.

When they were done screaming, Angelica rolled off Serena, leaving the girl's dick spent and sticky on her stomach. Fanny was the only one of them who wasn't completely naked. She'd never taken off her skirt, and her cock was now tucked away inside her panties.

They were all topless, but it was impossible to say who had the best breasts. Serena's were sweet and small, Fanny's were a good handful with tight, pointed nipples, and Angelica's were full and pendulous and decorated by silver bars. It struck Fanny that the variety of female bodies was just about endless.

"I knew that would be amazing," Angelica panted.

Fanny sat beside Serena, gently stroking her roommate's thigh. "Did you enjoy yourself, Serena?"

Serena moaned for four minutes straight.

"I think she liked it," Fanny said.

"And you?" Angelica asked. "You are not upset that I seduced your girl?"

Fanny wasn't so sure Angelica had seduced anybody, but she certainly wasn't upset about it. "No, I had fun."

"So you would do it again?"

"Maybe," Fanny said. "If Serena wanted to."

Serena moaned for another four minutes, and Angelica said, "I think she wants more."

Fanny's Futa Shower Orgy

Serena was barely nineteen. She didn't get up in the middle of the night to pee. She wasn't old enough for that—not yet.

Fanny rolled over in bed when she heard her dorm mate moving around the room. "Serena? What are you doing?"

"Nothing," Serena said. "Just going to the bathroom."

"Serena, stop being stupid." Fanny flicked on the bedside lamp even though she knew its brightness would burn her eyes. "You're almost blind. Don't go stumbling around in the dark. You'll hurt yourself."

"Don't worry about me," Serena replied. "Just go back to sleep."

When Fanny's eyes stopped burning, she realized Serena wasn't wearing any clothes. Just a short robe and probably panties underneath, but hard to say.

For any other girl on their floor, a robe would have been perfectly suitable attire. But Serena and Fanny weren't like other girls, and that made them self-conscious. Serena never walked the halls of their college dorm scantily clad. For their first three weeks living in the same cramped little room, she wouldn't even change her clothes in front of Fanny.

Now things were different.

Now they undressed in front of each other almost every night. Undressed, and kissed and touched and sucked and fucked. In fact, Fanny's cock throbbed as she thought about her roomie's wet pussy, all hidden alongside her pretty penis underneath that short robe.

"What's really going on?" Fanny asked. "After everything we've been through together, don't you think you can tell me?"

Serena's bottom lip trembled.

Fanny sat up in bed, letting the covers tumble to her lap. She'd worn a stretchy camisole to bed. As the cool night air worked its way through the cotton fabric, her nipples hardened to buds. To her, they were amply visible, but could Serena see them? Fanny sure hoped so, because she loved turning her roommate on.

But Serena's vision seemed to be getting worse. Over the past couple months, Serena has started mistaking one thing for another, and then she got angry and irritable about it. Sometimes they had fights, if they were both in a bad mood, but usually Fanny put herself in Serena's shoes. Imagine how hard it would be, going to college with vision loss.

"Serena?" Fanny asked gently. "Tell me what's up, babe. Tell me what's going on."

Serena's eyes filled with tears and she took a step closer to Fanny's bed. "I was going without you."

For a second, Fanny wondered if she was dreaming all this. "Going where? To the bathroom?"

"Yeah, but no." Serena shifted, seeming nervous. "A different bathroom. In a different building."

Fanny didn't understand anything that was going on right now. "What are you talking about? What bathroom?"

"Angelica told me about it."

Now there was a name Fanny hadn't heard in a while. Angelica was a girl from one of Serena's classes. They'd had a threesome together, and it was good times. Fanny thought for sure the act would be repeated. But then Angelica fell off the map. Serena never mentioned the girl again.

Until now.

"Angelica told you about what?" Fanny asked.

"The shower," Serena confessed. "It's a shower for girls... like us."

"A shower for girls like us," Fanny repeated. "For girls... like us?"

Serena's thick glasses made her eyes huge, but she wasn't looking at Fanny. "They do stuff. You know... together. In the shower. Together."

Fanny's brain felt thick with sleep, but she thought she got the gist. "You mean it's like an orgy thing? In a shower?"

"For girls like us," Serena said, nodding.

"And you're gonna go?" Fanny asked. She wasn't sure whether she was more shocked or amazed. "And you weren't gonna tell me about it?"

Falling to her knees at Fanny's bedside, Serena folded her hands like she was saying a prayer. "I thought you'd be mad. Please don't be mad!"

"Mad about what?" Fanny asked, trying to make her voice sound calm. Because, in truth, she was pretty mad.

"I just don't want to share you with anyone else," Serena said. "I want you to be mine."

Serena's face fell in Fanny's lap, but turned to the side so her glasses wouldn't break. Fanny petted her roommate's hair, saying, "Oh, Serena! I'm totally yours. You know that. I haven't wanted anyone but you in ages."

"But you will if you come to the shower," Serena said. "The girls there will be so pretty and sexy and I bet they'll have huge cocks that actually work. Mine barely gets hard at all."

"I don't care about that," Fanny said. "Mine gets hard enough for the both of us."

Serena looked up at her. Sniffling, she said, "Really?"

"Yes, really."

"Then you don't want to come to the shower with me?"

Fanny's stomach clenched. "I didn't say that..."

Now that the idea had been planted in her head, she couldn't stop thinking about being in a hot, soapy shower with a bunch of other girls. What kind of shower would it be? A stall, like the one in their dorm? Or an open one like the kind at the gym?

"Where is this place?" Fanny asked.

Serena looked instantly deflated. "You do want to come."

"Well..."

Serena sniffled. "Oh."

"I mean, if you're going, I might as well come with you," Fanny said.

Serena nodded and got up from the floor, feeling her way around the room.

"Better get dressed," Fanny said.

Unhooking Fanny's robe from the back of the door, Serena said, "No point getting dressed. We're just going to take our clothes off when we get there."

"But it's cold outside."

"We're not going outside." Serena unhooked their towels from the back of the door and tossed that in Fanny's direction, too. "We're going to the basement."

Fanny slipped out of bed and jammed her feet into her flip-flops. She decided not to ask questions. This was feeling more and more like a dream, so why not just go with it?

After she'd put on her robe, she hugged her towel to her chest and led Serena into the hallway, which was never darkened. Serena whispered directions, and Fanny followed from in front. She hadn't looked at the time, but it must be three or four in the morning. Any time before two and students would still be up studying or talking or listening to music.

When they inched their way past the common room, the TV was still on but the guy watching it had fallen asleep on the vinyl couch. They tiptoed past, careful not to wake him, or anyone else.

"Down the East staircase," Serena whispered. "All the way down, as far as it goes."

They took the stairs slowly, their rubbery flip-flops squeaking with every step.

"Are you sure about this?" Fanny asked as they made their descent.

"Sure about what?"

"Are you sure it's a real thing? I mean, listen. Do you hear anybody else?"

They stopped moving for a second and just listened. Then Serena asked, "You think Angelica was setting me up?"

That thought hadn't even occurred to Fanny. "I don't know."

They continued on to the basement level, which smelled like damp and looked like a bomb shelter.

"Where now?" Fanny asked.

"Down the long hall." She pointed. "That way."

They walked it quickly. With every step, their flip-flops squeaked louder. Or maybe all the concrete just made it echo-ey. Either way, there was a chill in the air and it was more than just physical. There was something seriously creepy about this place.

"Seriously, Serena, where are we going?"

"The buildings are connected underground," Serena said. "We just keep going until..."

Fanny opened a heavy door, and that's when they heard it: the hiss of the shower, the wet slap of hands smacking sweet young bottoms, giggles bouncing off every surface.

Without saying a word, Fanny and Serena crept into the next unassuming concrete hallway. When they turned a corner, there it was: the mythical shower inhabited solely by girls like Fanny and Serena.

They stood together, holding hands, staring into the open room.

It was like showers at the gym. No stalls. No tiles, even. Just a steamy concrete room with shower nozzles sticking out every few inches.

The heat coming out of that room steamed up Serena's glasses, and she took them off to wrap them in her towel. "I'm gonna need your help," she told Fanny. "I really can't see now."

"I can barely see either," Fanny said, partly to make her feel better. "So much steam."

"Should we get undressed?" Serena asked.

"I don't know. You're the expert. Is someone in charge here? Do we pay admission or just walk right in?"

"Just walk in," Serena said. "Open invitation."

Fanny's cock hadn't stopped throbbing the whole way here. It was actually tenting her robe, since she wasn't wearing panties under her pyjama shorts. She could feel her nipples grazing the cotton of her camisole, and every slight sensation made her crazy with lust.

"So we just get started?" Fanny asked.

Serena threw off her robe. Wow, no panties. Nothing at all. Just pale breasts with pink nipples, a cloud of blonde pubic hair, and the soft swell of a penis hiding a dewy slit. Fanny didn't have a pussy, and she wouldn't have known Serena's was there if she hadn't had access to it so often in the past.

She suddenly wondered if the girls in the shower had cocks and pussies like Serena, or just cocks like Fanny, or a combination. Maybe she'd just have to strip off her clothes and find out.

"I'm nervous," Serena said.

Fanny tossed off her shorts. "I know. Me too."

"Maybe we should just go."

"It was your idea to come," Fanny told her.

"I know, but..."

"Don't be scared." Fanny took her roommate's hand, and derived strength from Serena's grasp. "We're in this together. Nothing bad can happen."

When they stepped into the shower, Fanny's lungs filled with heavy steam. She struggled to breathe, and found herself coughing, which attracted the attention of nearby girls. They were all strangers, to Fanny, but fabulous beauties.

Some girls were buxom with big bellies while others had slim physiques. One looked like Wonder Woman. One was more like Mighty Mouse. The only thing they all had in common were boobs, butts and boners.

Fanny felt her cock surge, and for a moment she was embarrassed. Sure she'd had a threesome once, but that wasn't the same as walking into a wet and steamy room full of other naked girls. Her dick led the way while Serena said, "Fanny? What's going on?"

"Here, come on." Fanny took her roommate's hand. "Follow me."

She'd been so overwhelmed by the nudity of strangers that she almost forgot to notice how great Serena looked. God, those little tits were like candy. She could practically taste them. And, though Serena's cock hung limp for now, Fanny was pretty sure someone in this shower could work it into a frenzy soon enough. If she spent much longer staring at her roomie, it was bound to be her!

As they entered the swath of swollen steam, some of the other girls turned. The one who looked like Wonder Woman took a step forward to ask, "Well, well, well! What have we here?"

"I'm Fanny. This is my roommate Serena."

Wonder Woman held a hand up. "We don't need names."

Too late now.

"How do we get started?" Fanny asked. "Just dive right in?"

A bunch of other girls turned to see what was going on. Tall girls, short girls, all different skin colours and hair colours. Dicks and tits of all sizes. There didn't seem to be any correlation. Girls with tiny tits had huge hard-ons. Girls with big bazongas had itty-bitty boners. But then some had massive breasts with dicks to match. It was a total toss-up.

"What are you here for?" Wonder Woman asked.

Fanny looked back at Serena, who was standing slightly behind her. Serena said, "We're here for the shower. We just want to play, like everyone else."

"What's wrong with her eyes?" somebody said.

Wonder Woman hissed at that girl, because it was such a rude question, but Serena answered by saying, "I don't see too well."

"That's an understatement," Fanny said. "She's practically blind."

Serena chewed her bottom lip, which made Fanny wonder if she'd embarrassed her roommate. But a bunch of the girl grouped around her protectively and said, "Oh, don't you worry about a thing. We'll take care of you. We'll all take care of you!"

"Thanks," Serena said, but she sounded unsure of herself. She looked to Fanny as they led her into a far corner of the shower room. In the meantime Fanny felt a number of hands caressing her body.

"What have we here?" someone whispered. "New meat!"

"MEAT!" someone else shouted as a hand wrapped itself forcefully around Fanny's dick.

They laughed as they shoved her under the shower stream. Water struck Fanny's eyes, but she couldn't wipe them because somebody behind her was holding her wrists.

"Where did they take Serena?" Fanny asked, finding it odd that she was more concerned about her roommate than herself.

"She's fine," Wonder Woman said. "Don't you worry about a thing."

Fanny could hear Serena's voice somewhere in the room, saying, "Oh! Is that someone's mouth?"

Other girls giggled, and Fanny felt a combination of jealousy and pleasure.

"Look at these tits!" Wonder Woman said, and slapped Fanny's breasts so they swung together and hit against each other. "Somebody grab them and give them a squeeze."

Somebody did, and the sensation was incredible. It wasn't just the feeling of hands (more than two!) taking hold of her breasts, pinching her nipples, twisting and squeezing them. It was also the knowledge that she couldn't pick whoever was doing this to her out of a lineup.

The only woman in this room that she could identify was Wonder Woman, who stood so close their cocks smacked like swords.

"Oh god," Fanny moaned.

"You like that, do you?" Grabbing her own erection, Wonder Woman slapped the side against Fanny's. "How about this? You like this move?"

Wonder Woman then wrapped both hands around their two cocks, pressing them together, side by side.

Fanny couldn't help herself. She started bucking in the stranger's hands, fucking those fingers, feeling wet flesh heating her already sizzling dick.

Somebody grabbed her balls from behind and asked, "Do you like getting fucked?"

Fanny gasped. "I... I... yes?"

She couldn't remember the last time she'd felt so powerless. These women could do whatever they wanted to her. She was totally in their power. If they wanted to shove a dick in her ass, how could she possibly stop them?

And then she heard Serena squealing. "Oh! What are you doing to me?"

"Serena?" Fanny called out. "Are you okay?"

Her roommate didn't respond, but five seconds later the squeals turned to moans and Serena was saying, "Oh... yes, more of that."

Fanny struggled to make out Serena through the steam and spray, but the shower insisted on filling her eyes with water no matter which way she turned. Irritation coursed through her veins, but she wasn't sure if it was because Serena sounded like she was having a better time, or because Serena was having such a great time without Fanny.

"Go for it," Fanny heard herself say. "Fuck my ass. Do whatever you want to me."

The girls all giggled and cooed as their hands rode the length of Fanny's belly. Fingers found her sopping pubic hair and wove through it like sea grasses. Hands all over. God, she'd never dreamed of such a thing.

Someone behind her said, "Pass the lube."

Someone else said, "Me first."

"No, me!"

"No, me!"

Imagine that! They were fighting over who got to fuck Fanny first.

This was too much to take in.

She was so proud of her hot, sexy body. It felt like her chest was swelling, and her breasts along with it.

While the women behind her fought over who would go first, Fanny felt a slick drizzle of lube between her butt cheeks. It wasn't too cold, probably because it had been warmed in this steamy shower room, but it felt particularly sordid when some stranger's finger escorted the slick stuff inside Fanny's asshole.

"Oh!" Fanny cried.

"Did I hurt you?" the unseen owner of the finger asked.

"No," Fanny said. "It's fine. Feels good."

"Keep going?"

"Keep going."

Fanny still couldn't move her hands around because strangers were holding her wrists, but soon those strangers guided her hands to their rock-hard dicks. They wrapped Fanny's fingers around their erections and forced her to feel them up. Up and down, actually. Their bodies closed in around her, and soon she felt multiple soft, soapy breasts pressing up against her sides and her back.

She touched as many dicks as she could find. They were all around. With water in her eyes, she still couldn't see, but she could certainly picture Wonder Woman in front of her, gripping her dick, pressing both their cocks together.

She couldn't fixate on the stranger's image. Her mind kept morphing Wonder Woman's face into Serena's, Wonder Woman's tits into her roommate's sweet ones, Wonder Woman's dick into the limp little thing Serena wore like an tennis bracelet—pretty to look at, but ultimately not much use.

"Serena," she whimpered as the stranger behind her inserted another finger into her ass.

"How's that?"

"It's fine," she said. "It's good. Keep going."

Fanny wondered what it would feel like if Serena took her from behind, though she knew that would never happen. Even if her roommate managed to get it up hard enough to insert, she could never keep it going for more than a few thrusts.

So Fanny would just have to pretend this stranger at her back was the girl she really wanted—her sweet, loving roommate.

"Fuck me," Fanny begged. "Put it in. Do it now."

"Now?" the stranger asked. "Are you sure you're ready?"

"I don't know," Fanny admitted. "But I want it."

The stranger hesitated, but another girl said, "If you don't fuck her, I will. My dick's so hard it's going to burst."

"Mine too!" another girl whined. "Hurry up so I can have a go!"

"I need it," other girls whined. "I need to shove my dick in something tight and hot."

"Oh, this hole's tight and hot," the stranger with her fingers in Fanny told the others. "Everybody have a feel."

Suddenly there were so many fingers in Fanny's ass she felt like she was being double-fisted. "Hey! What the hell?"

"Sorry," the girls said, but they kept pumping their fingers in and out of Fanny's ass. "Oh, it feels so good. I want to stick my dick in there!"

"Well, you're just going to have to wait your turn," Wonder Woman said, taking charge from in front. "One at a time, but blow your load fast and give the other girls a go."

"Oh god," Fanny moaned. How many dicks was she about to take from behind? Five? Ten? Her knees would give out before they all finished.

And what about her? Couldn't she stick her dick in someone?

Suddenly, her mind went blank. All the fingers disappeared and a mushroomy cockhead met the spongy exterior of her ass. There was lube all over, but she still tensed up as the stranger pushed forward.

Luckily, someone in front of her (probably Wonder Woman) took the opportunity to kiss her passionately on the lips. That kiss was even more of a surprise than the cock poking and prodding at her asshole.

When Wonder Woman's tongue entered her mouth, everything suddenly felt familiar and good. Fruit-scented steam travelled to her lungs and filled her chest. She could taste Wonder Woman's lipstick, which had a dense and waxy flavour. The texture coated her tongue as they kissed ravenously.

All the while, other women's hands worked her tits. She worked their cocks, almost unconsciously, while some unknown girl opened Fanny's hole with a lubed-up cock

Just the tip entered, at first. But, god, at first that was enough! A tip sounds like nothing, no big deal, but this tip felt huge, like an unforgiving helmet that wouldn't rest until it had plowed halfway to Fanny's colon.

Somebody grabbed Fanny's arm and asked, "You doing okay?"

"Yeah," Fanny said without breaking her liplock with Wonder Woman.

She could feel cocks rubbing against her thighs, against the sides of her ass, and she struggled to rub as many as she could. Meanwhile, the stranger behind her pushed deeper inside. She could feel a stretch, but it wasn't painful. Heat and elasticity. That's what it felt like. Friction. Sizzling. Hot.

Someone's hands found her cheeks, and the kiss turned into a caress. What had been rough grew soft and sweet, and when she felt a familiar pair of breasts against hers, she said, "Serena?"

"Fanny?!"

"Where did you come from?"

"I don't know!"

Her heart rejoiced as she kissed her roommate, who had miraculously carved a path into her arms. "Let me fuck you," Fanny begged.

Serena gasped, then said, "Someone else already is!"

"Who?" Fanny asked.

Serena said, "I don't know!"

"I'll move to her ass," somebody said. "You can have her pussy."

"Oh god!" Serena squealed. "A cock in my pussy, a cock in my ass?"

"You can do it," Fanny assured her.

"Oh god..."

Fanny felt around until she found a huge hard cock, then said, "Oh. Sorry."

"No," Serena said. "That's mine."

"What?" Fanny asked, in disbelief. "That's yours? You're hard?"

Serena giggled. "Guess it's the steam."

Fanny squeezed her roommate's dick, lifting it between their bodies so it stood straight up. That way, she could throttle it while her own cock found its way between Serena's soft thighs. "Oh god, it's hot down there!"

"I want to feel!" somebody said, and soon Serena's pussy was full of fingers, just like Fanny's ass had been.

"You're so lucky," one of the strangers told her. "I wish I had a nice soft pussy."

"I have one!" another stranger replied. "Want to feel it?"

"Feel it?"

"Want to fuck it!"

"You bet!"

Those two voices retreated to another part of the shower room, and a few wet footfalls slapped against the floor, following them. Fanny wondered who she and Serena were left with. All these girls were total strangers to them. Were they all students at this school? So many girls like them, and they'd never have known.

Somebody seemed to be lifting Serena from behind, and that was a good thing, because Fanny couldn't have done it. Certainly not one-handed.

While one stranger fucked Fanny's ass from behind, another placed Serena gently down on Fanny's dick. Oh, that pussy was heaven. Fucking Serena's ass was okay, but her pussy was bliss. So silky smooth, so soft, so wet. So warm!

"Oh god," Fanny said, choking out the words while her butt muscles clamped around a stranger's cock. "I don't know how long I'll last!"

"Same here," said the stranger in her ass, grasping her hips and picking up the pace. "Holy shit, I'm gonna come so hard!"

"So come," someone cried. "Give the rest of us a chance!"

"You can fuck anyone," grunted the girl in Fanny's ass.

"But I want the new meat!"

"Me too!"

"Me three!"

Everybody seemed to want Fanny's ass, and Serena's as well, but Fanny just kept playing with her roommate's dick while they kissed each other and fucked.

The room was so steamy it was like standing up in the clouds. Heaven. Nothing could harm them.

One stranger blasted a load in Fanny's ass, and the stranger in Serena's ass responded pretty much right away. They pressed their bodies together, their breasts naked and wet, their mouths smashing one into the other, not a care in the world as two strangers pulled out their spent dicks.

Didn't last long.

As soon as one cock had slipped from Fanny's hole, another one entered it. This dick didn't seem quite as fat as the last one, but it had a definite curve to it, so it struck Fanny's insides in a different way than the first.

Fanny pressed her tits against Serena's so their nipples met and mashed. She could see everything so clearly inside her own mind that she actually forgot her eyes were closed. When she opened them, shower water needled her face. She couldn't handle the heat. So she closed her eyes again and disappeared into her own mind, and into the deep kiss she shared with Serena.

Serena yelped when Fanny gripped her smooth, sweet dickhead between both palms. "Don't do that!"

"Why not?" Fanny asked.

"It'll make me come."

"So what? Then come."

"But I don't want to," Serena said. "Not yet. I'm not ready."

"I am," said the cock in Fanny's ass.

"Already?" Fanny asked. "Didn't you just get in there?"

"Yeah, but it's so tight," the stranger said. She fucked Fanny fast, scratching fingernails down Fanny's back, catching fingertips in wet hair. Fanny could feel her long locks sticking to her skin just about everywhere, but that wasn't the most significant sensation at the moment. Those sharp nails sliced through her skin, making her lean forward—which was a huge mistake, because that meant the hot shower water could strike her back, stinging the fresh wounds.

"Oh god!" Fanny cried. "That kills!"

Serena's pussy tightened around her cock while her ass clamped on the stranger's dick. Serena squealed while the stranger said, "I'm coming! I'm coming!"

"You're coming?"

"I'm coming!"

Somehow Fanny managed to nudge forward enough to knock the stranger's cock out of her ass.

The stranger cried out, "Noooo!"

Too late. Cum streaked Fanny's back and butt, sticking to her skin only momentarily before being washed away by the shower water.

Fanny and Serena tumbled toward the wall, slamming the stranger in Serena's ass up against the concrete wall. The stranger let out a pained moan and they both apologized, but they couldn't move. They were just as soon blocked in by another stranger with a hankering for Fanny's fine butt.

More lube, less prep, and suddenly another cockhead popped inside Fanny's poor worn-out hole. She held Serena's erection tighter and pumped harder in her roommate's pussy. She'd been in there countless times, but this felt different. Public. So exciting. She just kept pushing and pulling—pushing her dick in that tight, wet snatch and pulling the penis she held in her hot hands.

Serena whimpered and panted. The emotion in her voice made Fanny dizzy with lust. She pressed her mouth to her roomie's and their bouncy tits mingles while they kissed.

Everything went fuzzy while some stranger fucked her from behind. And then another. And another. There seemed to be an endless string of girls willing to fuck their asses while they pressed their chests together. They were the new meat. Everybody wanted to stick a dick in their butts, then come on their backsides. Good thing all this water could wash it away so they could start clean with the next one.

"Oh Fanny," Serena whispered. "Oh Fanny, I'm so close!"

They each had a stranger up the ass, but Fanny didn't care about that. She only cared about bringing her beautiful roommate to climax.

"Yes, Fanny," Serena panted. "Keep going. Don't stop."

Fanny tugged hard on her roommate's dick, feeling it pulse and swell between her hands. She'd never seen another cock like it. Serena's penis reminded her of marble, like something you'd see in a sculpture or a work of art. It always stayed small, always stayed limp. But not today. Today, it grew three times its normal size. It throbbed in Fanny's grip. And when Fanny looked down lovingly and blinked the water from her eyelashes, she caught sight of Serena's pretty penis spewing white ropes of cum so high they streaked the girls' tits. A dab of cum on Fanny's nipple, a dollop of cream on Serena's bouncing breasts. More cum streaked their bellies as strangers pummelled their butts from behind. The motion combined with that glorious sight to build Fanny's arousal to sky-high levels.

Serena streaked Fanny's tits with jizz, saying, "I want you to come, too."

"I will," Fanny assured her. "I'm close. Almost there."

"In me or on me?" Serena asked.

Fanny's body made that decision for her. She couldn't move fast enough to get her dick out of Serena's pussy, so she filled that warm chasm with cream. Spurt after spurt. More and more and more. It would be dripping down the girl's thighs as they walked back to their dorm room.

"Get out of my ass," Fanny said to the stranger dicking her butt. "I'm exhausted."

"Just thirty more seconds," the stranger begged.

Fanny and Serena both pulled to the side, and the strangers' cocks popped out of their asses. They both whined about it, but other girls quickly filled the gaps. Soon those two strangers were fucking two other strangers, and soapy tits were smashing together as girls with something extra traced their cocks the length of each other's thighs.

Girls fell to their knees to suck swollen cocks. Girls got on all fours to take it up the ass, or doggy-style in the puss. Veiny dicks filled mouths, filled pussies, filled any hole that would have them. Cum streaked the shower room as Fanny retreated, holding hands with her roommate.

"Ooh, it's cold out here," Serena said as they searched for their towels out in the hallway. "Are you sure you want to leave? Sounds like the others are still going."

"You can stay if you want to," Fanny told her. "But I'm ready."

They towelled off quickly and headed back to their room. Morning would come soon enough. No way Fanny would make it to her 9 A.M. class after a night like that.

But when her head hit the pillow, she was suddenly wide awake.

"I can't stop thinking about it," Serena admitted.

"Thinking about what?"

"About the shower. About those girls. Everything we did tonight."

Fanny moved from her bed to her roommate's, and they cuddled close, their skin still sticky with damp heat from the shower. She could feel her hair soaking Serena's pillow as she hooked one leg around her roomie's. "You can go back if you want. They're probably still at it, down there."

"I don't want to go back," Serena said, her voice breaking suddenly with emotion. "But even if I did, how would I get there?"

Fanny felt confused. "The same way: down the staircase, through the hallways..."

"That's not what I mean," Serena said, sharply.

Fanny had never heard her voice so tinged with anger.

"I'm losing my vision. It just keeps getting worse. Soon my whole world will be shades of light and dark. I won't be able to do anything on my own."

"Sure you will," Fanny said, but, to be honest, she really didn't know what Serena wanted to hear. "I mean, no matter what happens you'll adjust."

"Easy for you to say," Serena pouted.

"Yeah," Fanny said with a nod. "It is easy for me to say, because I'm not going through it. I'm just watching what's happening to you."

Fanny knew when to concede defeat. And now was the time.

"But you know what?" Fanny went on. "Medical technology moves so fast. There are advancements all the time. So maybe in a year or two they'll be able to do something so you can see better. I don't know."

"I don't know either," Serena said in a little mouse voice. "I hope so."

They held each other tight in the bright moonlight. Fanny could easily trace the crack across the ceiling with her gaze, but she still wasn't used to the idea that she could see things Serena couldn't. Seemed so weird that the world looked different depending on whose eyes you saw it with.

"Thanks for coming with me tonight," Serena said. "I wanted to prove to myself I could get there on my own, but if I'd gone on my own I would have felt so guilty. It wouldn't have been the same without you."

Fanny kissed her roommate's wet blonde locks. "Anytime."

"Not anytime," Serena said, turning her head to look into Fanny's eyes. Fanny wondered what Serena was seeing, until Serena went on to say, "I had fun at the shower, but I learned something, too. I learned that I don't want to do that sort of thing again."

"Why not?" Fanny asked, feeling flustered. "Did somebody hurt you? When they separated us, did someone—"

"Nobody did anything bad," Serena said, gently. "It's just... the whole time we were there, I only wanted you. It was a good experience. It was a novelty. How many girls like us get to go to shower orgies?"

"True."

"But it's not what I want for my life."

Fanny's heart beat a little faster when she asked, "What do you want for your life, Serena?"

She giggled quietly, almost in silence. "You have to ask?"

Fanny didn't know what to say.

"I want you, silly. All I want is you."

Apprehension rose through Fanny's guts like a serpent, but when it got as far as her heart it met a much greater force. Fanny kissed Serena's hair again and said, "You're like my little treat, my little reward. Other people think, 'I'll read this chapter, then I can have a chocolate bar.' For me, it's, 'I'll read this chapter, and then I can look at Serena.' Just look at you. And my heart starts to race and I just feel so good. You make me feel so good."

Serena nodded. "Exactly."

"So you want to be my girlfriend?" Fanny asked.

Serena nodded again.

"Exclusive girlfriend? Like, no threesomes, no orgies?"

"No orgies," Serena said. "Maaaybe a threesome. Once in a while. If we're both into it."

Fanny laughed. "Sounds good to me."

Serena raised her lips to Fanny's lips. "Sealed with a kiss?"

"Sealed with a kiss."

And, if they hadn't spent so long in a shower orgy with strangers who could fuck for king and country, they'd have sealed their promise with so much more. But there was always tomorrow, and the day after that. There were always midnights and mornings, lunchtimes and Sunday afternoons.

That was the pleasant part of living in a dorm room with your sweetie: she was always there and feeling frisky. Always willing to love.

Futa Farm Girl

Figures! My brand new car breaks down in the middle of nowhere, and I don't know how to fix it. I've got the best phone on the market, and I can't get a signal. Could this day possibly get any worse?

I'm hesitant to leave my Lex in the road, but what choice do I have? It's not like this rural route sees much traffic. Anyway, my balls are numb from sitting so long. I feel like I've been driving around in circles for hours, except nothing looks familiar. Before I broke down, I was getting to the point where I was actually considering stopping for directions.

Now I need to take a walk and ask to use someone's phone. Maybe get directions too, while I'm at it.

Pretty sure I saw a farmhouse back a ways, as they'd say out here in the boonies. Looked pretty run down, but I'm hoping they'll have a phone.

So off I go, trudging along this dirt road under the hot summer sun, feeling delirious and dazed. There are fields of corn as far as the eye can see, but nobody's out. No one is working. Why would they, on a day like this? Anyone with half a brain would park his ass under a shady tree.

I like to look put together, but the time comes when I have to shrug off my suit jacket. I should have left it in the car. My shirt is soaked through with sweat. I hold my jacket over my head to block out the sun, but it creates an oven effect, baking my brain. I can't think straight.

By the time I spot that tumble-down shack, my body's had it. I pull myself up two stairs and onto the rickety porch, and I slap the door with an open palm. Paint comes off on my hand, so either I'm extremely sticky with sweat or this place is falling to bits right before my eyes.

The door opens, and in the shadows I see an old man's craggy face. He's got creases in his skin like a jagged rock. The sight inspires terror in my blood. I can only hope he doesn't have a gun.

But of course he does! I see it leaning up against the wall.

This is how I'm going to die: buckshot in the brain on some tumbledown farm in the middle of nowhere. RIP Arthur Brown.

The old man says, "If it's religion yer sellin, we already got one."

"No, no," I say as he starts closing the door in my face. I hold it open out of desperation and tell him, "My car broke down. I can't get a cell signal. Can I use your phone?"

"We hain't got none of those," the old man tells me as another figure creeps up behind him.

I'd mentally prepared myself for a farmer and wife combination, but if this girl is that guy's wife, he must be hung like a stallion—because he certainly isn't loaded.

She's wearing daisy dukes like they'd never gone out of style. Long tanned legs, muscular limbs, obviously brought up doing farm work. Tight little jean cut-offs and that plaid shirt knotted below her breasts.

And what spectacular breasts! So full and round, like tanned globes. Luscious, bursting with life. If not for the flat belly, I'd wonder if she was eight months pregnant. You don't see tits like that every day.

"Papa," she says to the old man. "You're good with mechanical fix-its. Why don't you work on the handsome gentleman's car?"

Handsome! She thinks I'm handsome!

Christ, and I haven't even looked up at her face yet. Her curly blonde pigtails lead my eyes up her bosom, and straight to the face of an angel. Who'd have imagined you'd find a girl like that in a place like this?

"Yes," I say to the old man, trying desperately to ignore the boner his daughter (Or granddaughter? Or both?) has inspired in my pants. "I can pay you. It's down the road. I don't know what's wrong. It just stopped working."

He doesn't seem particularly interested in my ordeal, but he says, "Gimme the keys and I'll see what I can do."

I wrench them from the pocket of trousers that feel spectacularly tight. He isn't looking at my crotch, but his daughter (or granddaughter or whatever) definitely is, because she's cooing like a morning dove in heat.

"I'll take care of your motor vehicle." The old man fits a ratty baseball cap onto his head. "You take care of my Ginny."

"Your Jenny?" Is that some kind of hand-cranked grain thingy? Or a cow?

"My Ginny," the old man says, pointing at the girl. "You take good care, you hear? She's a real special girl. Real, real special."

"Oh. Oh. Sure."

I've got no fricken clue what this guy's talking about.

When he heads off into the sweltering summer his, Ginny wraps her arm around me and says, "Woo-eee! You reek like a donkey butt in August. Let's get you cleaned up."

"I'm sorry," I say, and I'm truly embarrassed to be so sweaty, but I'm also so aroused I can't think straight.

She leads me out of the house and around back, to a barn. I can see why she likes it in here. It's considerably cooler than the house, though also musty and dusty.

"Come on now," she says as she starts unbuttoning my shirt. "Off with your clothes."

Off with my clothes? Is this what her father (or grandfather?) meant when he said to take care of Ginny? Had he put me out to stud?

Not that I was complaining.

"We're gonna git you all washed up and nice and squeaky clean," Ginny tells me as she undoes my belt. Then she points to this shower head that's sort of nailed to the wall. It's attached to a run of the mill garden hose. I've never seen anything like this set-up.

"Do you not have indoor plumbing?" I ask her.

"We're indoors now, ain't we?"

I guess she's got a point, there. Anyway, how can I argue with a buxom blonde who wants to throw me under the shower?

She tears my underwear down along with my pants, and by the time she's got them around my ankles, she's kneeling on the barn boards, face to face with my erection. I've never been so proud of a hard-on in all my life. She's a brawny girl, and still my dick looks huge in her midst. That's how turned on I am.

I tear off my undershirt and toss it aside. In all my life, I've never been so reckless with my clothing. She's inspired this in me.

After staring at my cock for a good little while, Ginny gets up and says, "I'll grab the soap." It's in a dish by the hose, and she turns on the water while she's over there."

"Go on," she says, when water starts falling from the shower head. "Git under."

I expect it to be cold, but it's actually hot.

Ginny notices my surprise and says, "The sun warms the rain barrel out there. Then we got hot water!"

Does that mean I'm bathing in the rain?

When she comes over with that soap, I don't even care. Just like she doesn't seem to care about getting her red canvas shoes wet. Or her saucy plaid shirt. Of her jean shorts. Or her breasts.

God, those breasts.

I'm melting into a pool of lust when she runs a hand through my hair. She's rough with me, runs her hand back and forth against my scalp, saying, "Come on, now. Let's get you clean."

Hard to do without shampoo. Luckily she doesn't come near my head with that yellow bar of soap. Is it white soap that's gotten dirty out here, or is it laundry soap?

When she raises my arms and rubs my armpit, I smell lemons.

She's washing me with laundry soap.

I should really care.

But I don't.

"Come on," she says. "Quick as a bunny 'fore we run out of water."

I steal the soap to wash the sweat from my ass crack, and she surprises me by finding something else to hold onto.

This girl must go long stretches of time without seeing a dick, because she wraps both hands around mine in a way that makes me think she might never let go.

"What are you doing?" I ask.

Stupid question.

"I want to play with your ding-a-ling," she tells me—and shows me. She strokes it with both hands simultaneously, stepping so close my ruby red tip slides against her perfect belly. I can feel my precum spilling across her wet skin, then getting washed away by the hot shower.

While she manhandles me, I can't move. I can't think. All I can do is stare down at her wet tits. Her light cotton shirt is soaked through and stuck to her skin, praise the lord! I can see the shape of her erect nipples poking out, but I can't see the colour and god now I'm craving the colour. She mustn't be wearing a bra. I see no trace of one. Just this soaking wet plaid shirt clinging to her tan flesh.

This is heaven, right? I've died and gone to heaven?

The water slows and she takes the soap from me. "Wash all the suds off, and make it snappy."

I'm disappointed when she lets go of my dick, but I've got a great view of her legs when she turns to put the soap back in the dish.

Feels good to be wet. The air is still warm, but I can feel it whisking water from my skin and replacing it with bursts of cool.

"Are you wearing panties?" I ask. I don't know why. Maybe because I can't see through her shorts.

She laughs and says, "Well, 'course I am! How else would I keep all that stuff down there in check?"

I have no idea what she's talking about, but I don't care. "Do you have a towel I could use?" I ask, because now I'm actually a little cold.

She picks up a tube of something and laughs as she slides it down the front of her shorts. "We ain't got no towels 'round here, city boy!"

"How do you dry off?" I ask.

"We drip-dry, 'course. If it's good enough for the washing, it's good enough for me."

So apparently they have the same rule for linens that they have for soap. Good to know.

She grabs my hand and yanks me out the barn door, and my heart jumps into my throat because we're outside! Someone could see us!

"What if your Papa comes back?" I ask.

I guess she can hear the tremor in my voice, because she says, "Papa ain't comin' back here any time soon."

My car is a good hike down the dusty road, so she's probably right.

She guides me across a lush green lawn and into the shade of a large, leafy tree. This is exactly what I'd wanted earlier, when I just about keeled over on the hike here. Never would I have imagined I'd get my wish—with a luscious farm girl thrown in for good measure.

When my bare ass touches the grass, I'm truly in heaven. The sun isn't bearing down on my skin, but its warmth surrounds me as Ginny straddles my naked thighs.

"What's that in your shorts?" I ask her.

Without looking down, she says, "Oh, we use that for the animals, whens we gotta check on something. Makes things all slip-slidey."

I can't help wondering what she's got planned for me.

"Gee, I got my shirt pretty darn wet. Mind if I take it off for a bit?"

"Go right ahead," I say, trying to sound encouraging without coming off as a sleezebucket.

She stands above me and undoes the knot, then the buttons.

A body like this—I'm telling you right now, it's superhuman. She's like some kind of angel of mercy visiting me from another plane. Her breasts are heavy without sagging. They're large but also perky in a way that seems almost nubile.

And her nipples! Those nipples! They're the colour of peaches, but with a rosy tint.

They're spectacular.

I can't speak. I can't think.

She reaches up to hang her wet shirt over the branch of a tree.

And I find my voice: "What about your shorts? They're pretty wet too."

"You men," she says, and giggles. "Always trying to in a get a girl's pants."

But she doesn't resist the idea.

The tube of veterinary lubricant tumbles to the ground when she unzips her itty bitty shorts. She pushes them down to her knees, and down go her panties, too. My dick is throbbing as I watch.

I realize, once she's naked, that her dick is throbbing too.

And to think I spent all that time staring at her boobs when this massive slab of meat was right there all along.

When I lick my lips, she steps over me so she's straddling me standing. She feeds her dick to me and I suck it like I've never sucked before. Her cock tastes like everything good, including the unmistakeable musky aroma of pussy. I ride my hand up her inner thigh until I'm close enough to touch the absolute apex.

Oh Lord, it's warm and wet. Her pussy juice is dripping down my hand while she stuffs that big dick down my throat. I choke and she apologizes, but I don't care. She can shove that thing anywhere she wants.

The same seems to go for my fingers, because when I press two of them inside her snatch, she moans and grabs my wet hair and fucks my face harder. I can't believe how much of her dick I manage to swallow. Maybe she's destroyed my gag reflex. Maybe she's magic.

Either way, she gives it to me, cock-in-mouth, and I give it to her, fingers-in-snatch, and we're both moaning and groaning. She's asking for more, but I'm in an awkward position. I can put another finger in her pussy, but I can't fuck her too fast like this. I try, but it's not working out.

She slides her dick from my throat, and her swollen shaft glistens as it leaves my lips.

I prop myself up with both hands in the cool grass while she runs her fat dick down my chest. It leaves a trail of my saliva, which cools on impact, and when she gets to my harness she doesn't hesitate. Straddling me with one knee on either side of my hips, she wraps her pussy lips around my cock and eases down.

Every inch is impossibly heavenly. I've never felt a pussy hug my dick like hers is doing right now. It's so warm and so wet that she slides down on me, gobbles me up with ease.

My whole dick is inside her. I feel her soft ass on my balls. I look down and her cock is spilling precum onto my stomach.

This is impossible. Impossibly hot. Big tits, big dick, wet pussy.

Ginny is my perfect woman.

She wraps her hands around my shoulders and rides me. Her dick whacks my abs with every go, and her butt brushes my balls. Can this really be happening?

I can't get over the soft velvet feel of her pussy. It's like another mouth. She's fucking me, but it feels like a blow job. And all the while I get to watch her beautiful breasts bouncing right before my eyes.

She's getting out of breath now and she slides off, saying, "Sorry. I need a rest."

Then, before I can say a word, she lies face-down in the green grass with her butt in the air.

"You'll have to take over," she says. She points to the veterinary lubricant and says, "Use that."

Does she want me to fuck her ass? She must, because her pussy hardly needs lubricating.

For some reason, the farm lube makes this all feel too real. I start looking around, making sure Papa isn't coming back. And who's to say they're the only ones living here? Could be that she's got incestuous brothers watching from the farmhouse.

I don't see anyone anywhere, but that doesn't stop me feeling anxious.

Luckily, my dick responds to anxiety. It pulses as I drizzle lube down this girl's crack. I watch it glint in the summer sun as it runs across her clean pink asshole, then joins the juices welling between her sweet labia. Eventually, it drips down her dick, all the way to her swollen tip.

"I need to fuck you," I tell her.

"Then dang well do it!"

I rub more lube across my erection, until it's all slick and shiny. Then I feed my hungry cock to her hungrier hole. She opens for me like a flower. I don't know else to put it. A little resistance. Yeah, she's tight. But isn't that kind of butt clench where you feel like you're going to destroy the poor girl if you fill her ass with your dick.

No. It's gentler than that. Feels not so much like a mouth, the way her pussy had. Like a hand. A firm grip. A fist closing around my shaft and then clinging to it for dear life.

"Oh Lord. Do you know how tight you are, Ginny?"

"Sure do."

Then, like she needs to prove herself, she tightens her ass muscles around my cock and I nearly blow my load.

"Now quit your yappin' and screw me up the butt!"

How can I possibly argue?

I close my hands around her perfect plump ass cheeks and imagine how her boobs feel as I drive her body against the lush lawn. Are her nipples still hard? Harder than before? Are they changing colour? Getting red like her pussy? Swollen and needy?

She wraps her fist around her cock and tugs it while I fuck her from behind. I feel the motion in her muscles. She clenches around my massive erection. How can she take it? How can she stand feeling a dick this big inside her poor sweet hole?

Her battered rosebud winks around my cock, and I just keep beating it down. My dick's never felt this swollen. It's unreal. I'm a giant inside her, and somehow her ass allows it. She's moaning and groaning, but not screaming in pain. Maybe toying with herself helps.

"God, I thought your pussy was good," I tell her. "Your ass is the hole I've been longing to fuck."

I'd thought that would come out sounding poetic, but now she's laughing at me, so I guess not. "Just keep at it," she says. "But don't come."

"Why not?"

She turns to look at me, her blonde pigtails all mussed but her full lips pouty and swollen.

"Because," she says. "I want you to come on my big ol' titties."

I almost blow my load in her butt. It's a combination of those dirty, dirty words from those sweet, supple lips and the image of actually doing it.

Now I'm telling myself to pull out of her ass, but I just keep fucking her faster, faster, faster.

What is wrong with me?

I wrap my arms around her waist and lift her off the ground.

How am I doing this?

Now I'm standing and she's in some kind of yoga pose with only her hands and the tips of her toes touching the ground. I'm fucking her so fast I can't catch my breath. I force my dick deep down in her hole, loving that I never bottom out the way I would in a pussy. Now that she's no longer pawing at her dick, I feel it flapping around down there, still hard as steel.

This is unreal. I'm telling you, nothing like this has ever happened to me in all my life. I'm ramming this stranger's asshole and she's crying out for more. Her cries are peppered with warnings not to come, but I know I won't pull out. I'm building to an incredible orgasm, and I want to plant my semen in this girl's fine ass.

"Don't do it!" she growls.

How does she know what I'm going? Can she feel it in her ass? Does she have some kind of spidey sense about oncoming explosions of sperm?

Well, she must, because as she's calling out no, no, no, I'm already halting mid-thrust, clamping hard, feeling my balls tighten at the ready, then shooting her full of jizz.

"Oh God!" I hold that pose for a moment because I can't actually move. And when I can move, it's only to collapse.

"Thanks a bunch," she says, pulling away so my spent dick slips out of her tight hole. "You knew I wanted you to come on my tits and you came inside me anyway. What gives?"

"I'm sorry," I pant, lying on my side, watching her erection whack her belly. "I got really into it. I couldn't..."

She lies flat on her back beside me in the grass and wraps her hand around her dick.

I'm speechless. Just the beauty of this moment, of this sight. She's got one knee up, one foot flat on the ground. The other one's straight. She's staring into the treetops.

"Now I'll have to do it myself," she says, and her hands moves even faster across her shaft. Up and down that fatness. Steel strength. That's no lazy cock. That's a mighty dick. Hard. Strong.

Her fist looks loose now, moves like nothing. Her skin is silk. She's got this dreamy look on her face. She closes her eyes.

She winces and I realize I'm looking in the wrong direction.

I sit up and stare at her blazing red cockhead just in time to see it blast white ropes of cum all the way up Ginny's chest. Her semen lands on one breast, then the other. More squirts paint her belly, but she puts that to use.

Releasing her cock, she sends both hands into the cream, then rubs it around her tits. Is it possible that her breasts are even bigger than before? How could they be? But they certainly look it as she slathers those big round orbs in sperm sauce.

There's nothing I want more than to stare at the stranger's tits while she rubs them, but my eyes aren't cooperating. Or my eyelids aren't. I feel them closing and there's nothing I can do. I don't want to fall asleep naked on a farmer's lawn—with the farmer's daughter here beside me.

But it happens.

And when I wake up, her sticky tits are pressed right up against my chest. My arms are wrapped around her tan body. The scent of her hair wafts in through my nose and my dick twitches.

What time is it?

I sit up and look around. The sun is setting. I race for the barn and put on my clothes, preparing myself for a quick and painful death. The farmer has surely spotted us together.

When I step out of the barn, Ginny is dressed too. She asked, "What's got into you?"

"It's late. Your Pa. He must be..."

She waves a hand and rolls her eyes. "Oh, Papa'll be long gone by now."

I don't get it. "Long gone how?"

"With your car," she says, and stands. "I bet it were a nice one, too. Yeah, I can tell by the suit and such. You got nice things." Swinging her hips widely, she walks to me and teases my shirt collar. "I should say you *did* got nice things. Now you just got me."

"What do you mean? I don't understand."

Her eyes sparkle purplish against the setting sun. She looks every bit as alluring in that top and shorts ensemble as she did the first time I laid eyes on her.

"It's just you and me now," she says. "Papa ain't coming back. Now you're my 'ol man."

"I don't understand. I need to get back, back to my life."

She smirks, but what does that mean?

"Your father stole my car, didn't he?"

"No, silly! You don't understand anything."

"That's for sure. How do you know he's not coming back? We haven't even looked. We haven't..."

She puts her warm little hand on my arm and says, "Trust me, Arthur. He ain't never coming back."

And for some reason I believe her.

And—wait. I never told her my name.

How does she know my name?

She gets up on tiptoes so her mouth is right at the level of my ear. "You're home now," she whispers. "You ain't never gotta worry 'bout nothing ever again. You're home."

A deep sense of peace pours through me, starting in my head and moving through my whole body, right down to my toes. I don't understand any of this, but I feel so good. Not worried about anything. Usually I've got money on my mind, or business bullshit, or fears of being caught naked with a farm girl.

Not now.

"This is my home?" I ask Ginny. "I live here with you? Just the two of us?"

The insatiable vixen nods eagerly. She sticks out her tongue, then giggles like a child. I feel her joy in my chest, like we're sharing emotions, and suddenly I understand something I can't yet articulate.

When she kisses me gently, then deeply, I know what pleasures I can look forward to. Her mouth and her pussy. Her fist and her asshole. And those magnificent tits! I could die a happy man in the sweet embrace of those tits.

She pulls sweetly away from our kisses and looks up at me, the sunset at her back.

"This is heaven," I tell her. "You and me together? Ginny, I'm in heaven."

She smiles coyly and bites her finger. "I been waitin' for you to figure that out."

Oh God. I get it now.

Looking at my perfect Ginny, feeling her sweet heat against me, anticipating all and anxious about nothing. She seems to think it's cute how novel I find my situation. God only knows how long she's been here.

"This is heaven?" I say to her. "I'm in heaven?"

Futa After Class

Tracy whipped around when a balled up piece of paper hit the back of her head.

"Cut it out!" she told the bad girls at the back of the room. "Some of us are trying to learn!"

"Goody-goody!" the bad girls said, disguising the word in a cough.

Miss Angelica slapped the yardstick against her desk, and Tracy's nether regions tightened. That slick slapping sound destroyed her every time.

"Tracy!" Miss Angelica howled. "What is the meaning of this?"

"I'm sorry," Tracy said, even though it wasn't her fault. "Vanna and Kristie threw—"

"No more excuses," Miss Angelica commanded, and when Miss Angelica commanded something, you obeyed.

It wasn't just Miss Angelica's demeanour her students found so fearsome. Sure she was icy cold, her voice sharp and flinty, always yelling at the class. But there was more to it. The way she presented herself was positively dominatrix-like.

She wore her long black hair slicked back in a tight bun. We're talking so tight it pulled her skin back. That must have hurt. How could she stand it?

Her skin appeared pale for someone with a golden Polynesian complexion. Hard to say whether it was makeup that lightened her appearance or if she just spent too much time indoors.

Her makeup was incredible: dark red lipstick like the mark of a vampire, thick black cat-eye liner. The bad girls called her Cat Woman behind her back, but never to her face. Even the bad girls weren't that daring.

Today she wore a tight black skirt that was long enough to be business-like, except that it was leather and slit almost all the way to her crotch at the front. With that, a silky white shirt that had mother of pearl buttons, though they weren't all done up. She left enough open that it was easy to sneak a peek at her swell of cleavage.

Her breasts were hard to ignore, especially when she wore a black bra under a white shirt. It's like she wanted to draw attention to her sexiness.

And the boots! Who could forget Miss Angelica's big stiletto boots? They could be used as a weapon, if it came to that.

With one heel, she pierced the crumpled paper the bad girls had thrown at Tracy and picked it up like a litter spike. When she unfolded it, her eyes widened and her lips pursed.

"What is the meaning of this?" she asked, showing the paper to Tracy.

It was a drawing of Miss Angelica in a cat suit. Big boobs, hairy balls and a giant erection.

Tracy felt cold all over. Even her blood turned to ice.

She turned the drawing over so she wouldn't have to look at it, then said, "I didn't draw that, Miss. I would never do something so disrespectful."

"Who would?" Miss Angelica growled.

Tracy knew exactly who would, and who did, but calling Vanna and Kristie out would only put her in the bad girls' bad books.

"I don't know," Tracy whispered.

She could feel her teacher's eyes burning a hole in her forehead, but she didn't look up. She felt so ashamed.

The bell rang and Miss Angelica said, "Class dismissed—everyone but you, Tracy. You'll stay after class."

"Yes, Miss," Tracy said, still without looking up.

She sat at her desk, trying not to cry, while everyone else filed out. Some kids poked at her or laughed as they passed by, but Tracy was used to being bullied. It had been happening for as long as she could remember. When she was little, she figured the day she turned eighteen that would all magically go away.

No such luck.

Now she was just an adult who got picked on instead of a kid who got picked on.

When the other students had gone, Miss Angelica crossed the room and closed the door.

And locked it.

"Stand up, Tracy."

Tracy slipped out of her chair and brushed her hands across her pleated grey skirt. She hated her school uniform. The skirt made her butt look big and the short-sleeved white shirt wasn't built for a girl with breasts as big as hers. She had to pin it closed with safety pins so it wouldn't pop open. And the neck was so tight! Didn't help that she had to wear the silly burgundy ribbon where boys wore ties.

"Your shirt is wrinkled, Tracy."

"I'm sorry, Miss."

"And your shoes are scuffed."

Tracy looked down at her black Mary Janes. They didn't look too bad to her, but everybody else at this school was a perfectionist. Students and teachers. They didn't understand the plights of a girl here on scholarship.

"Your left sock is lower than the right."

"I'm sorry, Miss." Tracy bent down to pull up her thick burgundy knee-highs.

"Walk to the front of the room."

She did, and Miss Angelica followed her for closer inspection.

"These safety pins are not part of your uniform, Tracy."

"I'm sorry, Miss, but if I take them out my shirt pops open."

Miss Angelica crossed her arms beneath her breasts. "They're not part of your uniform. Take them out."

Tracy did as she was told, but as soon as she'd removed the pins her breasts popped the button open, exposing her simple white bra to her teacher.

"Why haven't you purchased a larger uniform, if this one is too small?"

Feeling ashamed of herself and her family, Tracy admitted, "Uniforms are expensive, Miss."

"Your parents can't afford it?"

Tear pricked her eyes and she nodded.

She expected Miss Angelica's voice to soften, but it didn't. "Bend over my desk, young lady."

"Why?" Tracy squealed.

"The school might not believe in corporal punishment, but I certainly do."

"Why? Because of the picture? Miss, I didn't draw it! I swear to you! I would never draw something like that."

"Then who did?" Miss Angelica asked as she picked up the yardstick.

Tracy couldn't allow this to happen. She folded like a cheap suit. "It was Vanna and Kristie. They threw it at my head."

Propping herself up on the stick, like a dandy with a cane, Miss Angelica asked, "Why did you not tell me this earlier?"

"Because they'd make my life miserable if I told on them! They already make my life miserable."

No pity from Miss Angelica. "Well, now it appears it's my turn."

Miss Angelica pushed Tracy down until her face met the desk.

Then she pulled up Tracy's skirt.

"No!" Tracy cried, tugging at her skirt. "No, please, Miss! I didn't do anything wrong. Please don't pull down my panties."

Miss Angelica took a step back, and for a moment Tracy thought she was safe. Then Miss Angelica opened the desk and took a school tie out of the lost and found drawer. She wrapped it around Tracy's wrists and pulled it tight.

"Stop struggling and do as I say."

Tracy swallowed hard. "You promise not to pull down my panties?"

Miss Angelica made no such promise, only flipped up Tracy's skirt and whacked her cotton-clad bum with the yard stick. It burned through her panties, but, she suspected, not as much as it would have if her bum had been bare.

"Please," Tracy cried. "Please don't."

Miss Angelica smacked her again, and when she screamed, said, "Keep your mouth shut or I'll shove your panties in there to keep you quiet."

"You promised you wouldn't take off my panties," Tracy said.

She must have sounded as panicky as she felt, because Miss Angelica said, "Fine. If you make too much noise, I'll gag you with MY panties. How's that?"

Tracy only whimpered, because she didn't want to admit the physical reaction that idea sparked in her. The idea of Miss Angelica's panties...

The yard stick came down on her quick, and she screamed.

"I'm sorry!" Tracy said. "I wasn't ready for it. I'm so sorry!"

"You know what happens now."

Miss Angelica set the yardstick beside Tracy on the desk and sent both hands up the high slit in her leather skirt.

Her panties were black. Tracy's were white.

She hooked her thumbs around the hips and slid them down her thighs. Tracy concentrated hard, but missed seeing her teacher's mound in the flesh.

They weren't actually panties. It was a thong. And certainly not cotton. A stretchy Lycra type fabric that surprised Tracy's tongue.

She choked at first. It felt so strange to have something stuffed in her mouth. And then she began to taste the aroma of her teacher's nether regions. She'd never tasted anyone's parts before. It was the most intimate thing she'd ever experienced.

As she savoured the scent of her teacher's crotch, Miss Angelica picked up the yardstick and slapped Tracy's ass once again. This time it really hurt, but when she cried out, her scream was muffled. She realized she could probably spit the thong out if she tried, but she'd get in even more trouble for that.

So instead she bit down on the thong as Miss Angelica's yardstick slapped her ass. She could feel the tie digging into her wrists, but it didn't stop her struggling.

Until Miss Angelica slapped her thighs instead of her ass.

Tracy had never experienced a pain like this. Her thighs were bare. Did that make all the difference? Or were her thighs actually MORE sensitive than her bum cheeks?

She squealed and shrieked into the panty gag, but that didn't stop Miss Angelica doing it again.

The second time hurt even worse than the first. The sizzle of wood on soft skin wasn't worth the titillation Tracy felt. It stung too much. A centralized sting. Stuck in her thighs.

"Do you think you've been sufficiently punished?" Miss Angelica asked.

"Yes!!!" Tracy cried.

Miss Angelica yanked out the gag. "Repeat yourself."

"Yes," Tracy whispered, so as not to attract attention from anyone who might be in the hall.

She looked up at Miss Angelica, but couldn't read the expression on her teacher's face. It looked a lot like bitter hatred.

"May I go now, Miss Angelica?"

"No, Tracy. Not just yet."

She was sure her teacher would slap her ass again, but instead Miss Angelica placed the yardstick back in the tray by the blackboard, where it belonged. Her teacher also pulled out the low gym bench she often stood on when she was writing something high up on the board.

"What is the bench out for?" Tracy asked.

Miss Angelica wrenched her arm and tugged her down from the desk. Tracy remained somewhat bent over because she didn't want Miss to see how much the punishment had aroused her. But then Miss Angelica turned her around and pushed her down so she was lying with her back on the bench, looking up at the ceiling

And then looking up at Miss Angelica's crotch.

Her teacher straddled her face, hiking that cruel leather skirt up until the slit in the garment revealed the slit in Miss Angelica.

Tracy had never seen one before. It had some dark hair around it, but not much. Very short and trim.

Between the two lips, there was very pink flesh that glistened like sunlight on a peaceful lake.

Her teacher's clit was more red than pink, and it poked out between the lips, begging for attention.

"You're never done this before, have you, Tracy?"

"No, Miss."

It really didn't matter what Miss Angelica was referring to. Tracy hadn't done anything.

As Miss Angelica descended to her knees, Tracy watched the teacher's pussy coming at her. It seemed to get pinker and juicier as it approached her face.

What a sight! The pleasure of viewing her teacher's nether regions this way nearly took away the pain she felt, lying on top of her wrists, which were still tied up behind her. It made her front poke up.

When Miss Angelica got down on her knees, she was at the perfect height to splay her pussy lips across Tracy's mouth. She'd pulled her skirt almost all the way up, and now Tracy could get a full-on taste of the slit she'd only sampled when Miss put that thong in her mouth.

"I want you to make me come as quickly and quietly as possible," Miss Angelica said.

"Yes, Miss. Only..."

"Only what?" the teacher growled.

"Only I don't know how."

Miss Angelica looked quite fierce when she gazed down at Tracy. "All you have to do is lick and suck. Even a student as mediocre as you are can surely figure it out."

Tracy wasn't sure why, but the meaner Miss Angelica acted, the more she wanted to impress the woman.

So she wrapped her mouth around her teacher's mound and sucked.

Right away, Miss Angelica started to moan, so Tracy must have been doing something right. Miss Angelica also started to rock gently on her face. The teacher's pussy juice ran down Tracy's throat. She struggled not to choke, but she had to pull away to swallow.

When Miss Angelica ran both hands through Tracy's hair and gripped her head tight, that changed things up pretty fast. The woman's fingernails were fierce and Tracy could feel them against her scalp like a terrifying massage.

"Lick me, Tracy."

Tracy wasn't too confident about the licking. She wasn't sure where to lick, exactly. She tried licking inside her teacher's pussy, but that didn't elicit the same reaction as sucking. So she licked around it, licked the bottom and the sides, but that didn't do much either.

When she licked her teacher's clit, that didn't do much either. But when she tried to move on, Miss Angelica tightened her grip on Tracy's head and said, "Keep licking."

Tracy couldn't speak with her teacher's pussy in her mouth, so she just licked that tiny clit as fast and as fierce as she could manage. It was hard to do, like licking a pin over and over, but Tracy liked the way her teacher's pussy slobbered all over her chin as she did it.

"More, Tracy," Miss Angelica said, pressing her hands on either side of Tracy's head.

The pressure was painful, but at least it took her mind off the way her wrists were clanging together between the bend and her back. Or the way her crotch was throbbing so hard it might just burst through her panties.

Her teacher started riding her face like a pony, back and forth in little bursts, then sharper ones, then thrusting so hard against her mouth Tracy worried her teacher would take her head off.

"Yesss," Miss Angelica growled, ripping open her shirt and tugging down the cups of her bra.

Tracy's nether regions throbbed wildly when she got a look at her teacher's breasts. They were big and honey-golden, and the nipples were even more golden and dark. And hard!

Just the sight of those big bouncing breasts made Tracy want things she never thought she could have.

"Oh Tracy," Miss Angelica said as she grabbed both her breasts and squeezed them together. "Oh, I'm about to come all over your face."

And then she did!

Tracy had no idea women could come like this, with a wet blast of something squirting all over her mouth and face. It smelled sweet. What could it be?

Miss Angelica bit her arm to keep from screaming, and all Tracy could think was that she'd end up with red lipstick all over her top. But she'd already torn off the buttons, so maybe it didn't matter.

When her teacher sat back on her chest, Tracy's torrid arousal got the best of her.

"You got what you wanted," she told her teacher. "Now it's my turn."

She bucked her chest hard enough to drive the woman off. Miss Angelica tumbled to one said, obviously worn out from her orgasm, and Tracy took full advantage. She arched off the bench, wrangled her wrists out of the stupid tie, then stood to show her teacher what to expect.

"Tracy!" Miss Angelica said with a gasp. "What's that bulge in your skirt."

Tracy threw down her panties and pulled up her uniform to give her teacher a better look.

The wide-eyed wonder in Miss Angelica's eyes made Tracy so proud two more buttons popped off her blouse. Now her plain white bra was exposed, and so was her fully tumescent dick.

"Get up on the table, Miss. And spread your legs."

Miss Angelica scrambled up on her desk, with her skirt still pulled up over her waist and her bra still tugged down under her breasts.

Tracy had never down this before, but her arousal built her confidence. Not only did she approach her teacher, but she lifted Miss Angelica's legs over her shoulders so those dangerous boots were behind her back.

Miss Angelica looked shocked as Tracy guided her throbbing red tip toward the watery grave of her teacher's crevice. This would be her first time, a time she'd never forget, and it would be with her teacher. The meanest, snarliest, hardest teacher in the whole school!

But when Tracy planted her dick in her teacher's snatch, Miss Angelica purred like a kitten.

Tracy didn't know where to touch first. There were so many options.

She wrapped her hands around her teacher's hips and pulled Miss Angelica closer to the edge of the desk, planting her thick cock as deep as it would go.

"Oh Tracy," Miss Angelica gasped as her pussy closed tight around Tracy's shaft. "Oh, I never imagined!"

"You don't need to imagine, Miss. It's really happening."

Tracy was pretty proud of her words, and even more proud of her dick. When she pulled back and forced it in again, Miss Angelica shrieked with lust and appreciation.

"We can't have that," Tracy said, and pulled out to pick up her white cotton panties off the floor. Shoving them in her teacher's mouth, she said, "You're being way too loud, Miss. Someone might hear."

Miss Angelica offered muffled moans when Tracy stuffed her cock back inside that warm, wet snatch. It was so hot in there, and slick and tight. Tracy never knew what it would feel like to do this for real. And with a woman as sexy and scary (and old!) as Miss Angelica. Her teacher had to be... wow, maybe thirty? Thirty-five? She never imagined her first time would be with a woman that age.

But she was certainly glad.

Once she'd silenced her teacher, Tracy trapped Miss Angelica's tits between her palms. They were so round and firm and they squished really nicely when she pushed them together.

As Miss Angelica's pussy hugged her hot, hard cock, Tracy couldn't resist the call of those teacher-tits. She wrapped one arm around Miss Angelica's svelte body and plunged her face into the warm cushiony cradle of her teacher's breasts. She licked them and sucked them, and not just the nipples. She traced her tongue everywhere, even up her teacher's neck.

She bit her teacher's ear while she buried her steel rod deep as it would go inside that crushing chasm. She thrust with all her might, and her teacher just took the punishment. She slammed that pussy so hard juice splashed both their thighs.

The sensation nearly brought Tracy to orgasm, but she focused her attention on her teacher's tits.

Miss Angelica's knees closed tight around Tracy's neck as she offered muffled cries into her cotton panty gag. Tracy would have kissed that mouth if it wasn't full of underwear.

Oh well. Sucking her teacher's tits was probably even better than kissing her. Wouldn't want to mess up that gorgeous red lipstick.

Tracy didn't wear makeup, but she could taste traces of her own strawberry sundae lip chap all over her teacher's golden tits.

She couldn't imagine a better feeling than this.

And she knew, instinctively, that it was coming to an end.

Miss Angelica's divine pussy clenched tight around Tracy's cock, and that spelled the end for this erection. As soon as that teacher-snatch palpitated around Tracy's dick, she spewed her cream inside Miss Angelica's tight, willing pussy. Filled her to the brim, then pulled those panties from her mouth so she could say, "Tracy, my god! I'd never have imagined you had it in you."

"What do you think now?" Tracy asked as she pulled her half-hard dick from her teacher's slit.

Miss Angelica's legs were still over Tracy's shoulders, which brought their heads very close together when they both looked down to watch.

"Wow," Miss Angelica said as Tracy's cum-covered dick dropped from her snatch.

It was followed by loads of hot jizz, which drizzled down the teacher's asshole and eventually down the desk.

Tracy removed her teacher's legs from her shoulders and leaned back on a student desk. She put her panties back on, but they were wet from being in Miss Angelica's mouth.

Miss Angelica hadn't yet caught her breath, and Tracy had a suspicion she would collapse the second she left the classroom.

"I need some water," Tracy said as Miss Angelica folded her breasts back inside her bra.

"Yes, water," Miss Angelica said. "Good idea. Water."

"Is my punishment over?" Tracy asked.

Miss Angelica looked to the clock for answers. "Goodness, yes. Yes. For now." She pointed her finger at Tracy. "But be on your best behaviour in class, you hear me?"

"Yes, Miss."

"Because if you step out of line, and I mean even the slightest bit out of line, I'll have you on my desk every night of the week."

Tracy smirked and again said, "Yes, Miss."

Futa Science Experiment

Libby tapped gently on Robert's door. "Can I come in?"

She heard a lot of shuffling in his bedroom while he called out, "Hold on! Just a second!"

How could she wait? She'd already been home from college for three days without telling him her secret. She had to come clean, and right away.

When she opened his door, she found the man dressing hastily. His laptop was folded down on his bed and the grey-blue comforter was all mussed up. So was he. Looked like he'd been through a carwash without a car.

"What were you doing?"

"Nothing, Lib," he said, seeming all sweaty and nervous.

His sandy hair had a few greys around the temples, but only a few and they blended right in. He was very fit for his age, not that he was old.

When he looked down at his chest and boxers, Libby realized she'd been staring—and then she realized what she'd ben staring at.

The man had an erection!

She could see its massive girth through the fabric of his light blue boxers.

"Oh," Libby said as she put the pieces together: the sweat, the laptop, the messed up sheets. "Oh, I'm sorry. We can talk later."

"No, no," he said. "We can talk now. Sit down, honey."

She felt a magnetic pull toward the hall, but an equally strong pull toward his bed. So she sat on the edge while he stood around the other side.

"What's wrong," he asked.

Libby looked down at her hands, which were folded in her lap. She wasn't wearing much more than he was—just a fluffy pink robe and matching bunny slippers. Under the robe, she had on a pair of tight white panties, but they felt far too snug these days. She could scarcely keep herself inside them.

She sighed and said, "Remember after my mother died, we were sitting on the swing out back just staring at the sunset? And I started crying and you put your arm around me? And you told me you would take care of me? And I could tell you anything and you wouldn't be mad, or even if you did get mad at first you'd get over it? Do you remember all that?"

"Yes, Libby." He sat beside her on the bed and placed a confident hand on her thigh. "It's still true."

She nodded, staring at his hand, feeling its proximity to the thing she needed to tell him about.

"What's on your mind," he asked.

She shot up from the bed and said, "Something happened to me at college."

His eyes widened and he took her hand. "Did somebody... were you...?"

"In chemistry lab," she told him. "Our TA left the room."

He pulled her into his lap, into a hug, and she could feel his boner against her bum but she knew he didn't mean it like that. She knew all too well, these days, how inconvenient it was to have a penis.

"Who was it," Robert asked.

"Two boys," she told him. "And a girl."

"And a girl!"

"Yes," Libby said. "There are more girls in my class than boys. Girls are good at science. I don't know why people think we're not."

"Forget about that," Robert went on. "Tell me about the ones who hurt you."

She gazed up at the firm clench of his jaw. He obviously hadn't shaved yet today. There was a scratchy growth of stubble across his cheeks and his chin. Even a few grey ones, she noticed, now that she was looking at them close-up.

He hugged her tighter and said, "Tell me, Libby. You can tell me anything."

She didn't hug him back, just let him swaddle her in his strong arms. "Well, it wasn't their fault, really."

He leaned back. "What do you mean, not their fault?"

"They didn't mean to do it."

"Didn't mean to do what, Libby?"

She realized they must be talking at cross purposes. So she slipped out of his lap and stood before him and said, "They spilled the serum in my lap. It was an accident. The three of them were arguing over who got to pour it onto the guinea pig."

"Were you the guinea pig?" Robert asked.

"No, an actual guinea pig."

He seemed very confused.

"But they spilled it in my lap instead."

"So I guess you were the guinea pig, in the end."

Libby would have laughed, but she was building up to such a shameful revelation that she just couldn't.

"What happened, Lib?"

"Well, the teacher wasn't in the room, like I said. And I didn't have a change of clothes with me, so I just wrapped a sweater around my waist so it wouldn't look like my pants were wet, and we went on with the experiment. We had to start over, but we didn't want to fail the lab."

"Of course," Robert said. "My goodness, you are a dedicated student."

Libby shrugged. "I don't know. I guess. So we worked on the lab and by the time that was done my pants were pretty much dry. Then we got dinner, then we went to the library to do our write-up. By the time I got back to the dorm and showered, it was after midnight."

Robert didn't seem to see the significance of this.

"Well, after a few days I noticed a change."

"What kind of a change," he asked, placing his hands on her hips and then taking them away because it was sort of a strange thing to do.

She wasn't sure how to say the words. Even though they were close, they didn't talk about body stuff.

How was she supposed to explain what had happened to her?

"My crotch," she told him. "Where my lab partners spilled the serum. I noticed it felt different."

"Different how?"

"Tingly, at first." She couldn't look at him while she said it. She stared down at her fingers while she picked at a hangnail. "Then as the week went on, it started getting bigger."

He didn't say anything for a moment. Then he asked, "What got bigger?"

This was so hard to say! "My thing. Down there. What girls have."

He didn't respond.

"My clitoris," she whispered. "You know. Down there."

"I don't understand."

Libby was starting to get frustrated. She growled and said, "It started to grow. And it kept on growing! And now it's the size of a..."

She couldn't describe it. Easier just to show him.

Opening her robe, she pushed down her panties and let her enlarged clit hang between her thighs.

"It isn't a clit anymore," she told him. "It's a full-blown cock!"

Robert's eyes bulged, and she wasn't sure if it was the sight of the appendage between her legs that did it, or her use of the word cock. She never spoke that way around Robert. Not usually.

"Well," she asked. "What do I do?"

He sat on the bed, just staring at the clit that had grown into a fleshy, fully functional shaft, complete with its own mushroom head. Every so often, it was like he tried to look her in the eye, but his gaze didn't get past her bare breasts. He'd never seen them before—at least, not that she knew of. But now that he was looking, she felt strange.

"Oh great," she said as her penis lifted. "It does this. I can't control it."

"I know what you mean," Robert said, and when she looked at his crotch she saw that his dick was standing erect inside his boxers.

"My vagina's still there," Libby said. "Same as ever. Now I have this thing to deal with."

Robert swallowed hard, said nothing.

"Most days I have to tape it to my thigh or else it'll poke up like this for no reason!"

Robert nodded. "I remember what it was like to be your age."

She wasn't sure why she did this, but she pointed to his erection and said, "Looks like part of you thinks you still are my age."

He laughed, sounding nervous.

"Sorry," she said.

"No, no. It's okay. You're right."

"So what do I do?"

"Have you asked your professor? Maybe there's a serum to reverse the effects."

Libby shook her head. “I haven’t told anybody, not even my friends. I really thought it would go away after a few weeks.”

“But it hasn’t,” he said.

“No, it hasn’t.”

Her new dick throbbed so hard she could barely use her brain. Growling, she tugged the sides of her robe to keep her hands busy. “I can’t stand it! It’s got a mind of its own and it wants to fuck!”

She’d never said the word fuck in front of him, but she didn’t even care at this point. She didn’t care what he thought of her. She just wanted to relieve the tension building in her groin.

“It wants me to touch it all the time!” she told him. “I’ll be sitting in class and it’s down there going, ‘Hey, Libby. Take me out and play with me.’ What am I supposed to do?”

“Tell it to wait,” Robert said.

“It won’t wait! It’s so hard and it wants to play now!”

Robert growled and stood and grabbed Libby's robe and threw it to the ground. When she was completely naked, he slid his hands under her arms and picked her up.

Her bunny slippers fell from her feet.

He set her down, standing, on the bed, then pushed her until her back was right up against the wall. He didn’t seem to care that her toes were curling around his pillows. He didn’t seem to care about anything.

“Let me be clear,” Robert said. “This isn’t the sort of this we should do together. It’s wrong and it’s bad and it’ll never happen again. But it’s happening today.”

When he wrapped his fist around her cock, all she could say was, “Thank God!”

Kneeling in front of her on the bed, he asked her, “Has anybody else touched it?”

“Of course not,” she said. “Only me.”

His fist shuttled up and down her shaft. He knew just how to touch it to build her arousal without putting her right over the edge. “God, you’re hard.”

“I know,” she said. “It always gets like this. I put it out of its misery and it comes right back. Nothing’s ever enough.”

Robert reached down and squeezed his own crotch through his boxers. He looked like he was in pain, like his dick was so full and fat it hurt that he wasn't toying with it.

As Libby watched him clutching his cock, it struck her how wrong this was. What they were doing was totally, totally terrible.

The man who promises to take care of you isn't supposed to toy with your dick!

And he certainly shouldn't wrap his eager lips around your cockhead.

But that's exactly what Robert was doing at this very moment.

Libby's knees nearly gave out when she felt the silky warmth of his mouth tightly encircling her solid shaft. His lips slipped expertly toward her cloud of blonde pubic hair, until his nose was nearly nestled in it. He'd consumed almost her entire cock.

Was it the sight or the sensation that set her off?

She was halfway down his throat when he started sucking. How could he handle so much cock? Didn't he have a gag reflex?

Had he done this before?

Was Robert a cocksucker from way back?

This couldn't possibly be his first time. He was too darn good at it.

He moved his mouth along her shaft, leaving trails of glistening saliva in his wake. The sight of him enjoying her erection brought a swell of pleasure to her pussy. Her cock throbbed, but so did her little lips. God, she was wet. If he touched her there, he'd feel it.

But he must know how turned on she was by the hard slab of meat she kept feeding him.

Libby didn't mean to thrust. She didn't mean to shove her dick down Robert's throat. But her hips had a mind of their own. They were controlled by her cock. Her whole body was, or so it seemed. She wrapped her hands around his head, feeling his soft hair curling around her fingers as she filled this throat with cock.

"Eat my dick," she cried. "Eat it hard!"

He grabbed her ass with both hands and squeezed.

His hands, his mouth, and the sight of his face as he savoured her dick put her over the edge.

She tried to extract herself. It didn't seem proper to fill Robert's mouth with come. But she couldn't pull away fast enough.

Blasts of jizz shot from her dickhead, filling his throat. Even though she couldn't see it happening, the image was crystal clear in her mind's eye: white hot cream blasting from her dick. And he swallowed it down and hummed with pleasure.

Libby slumped down the wall. All the strength had fallen out of her body. Her muscles went slack and her butt ended up on Robert's pillows.

He didn't leave her there long.

Grabbing her ankles, he yanked her down the mattress until her head bounced on the pillow. Her boobs bounced too. So did her spent cock—it bounced against her belly as it settled in for a quick nap.

She felt far too sleepy to react physically, but her mind was firing on all cylinders. "What are you doing to me?"

"I'm sorry," he said, and he sounded it, but he also sounded too horny to do the right thing.

Libby couldn't blame him. She knew what that was like.

When she was flat on the bed, Robert parted her thighs with his knees. He was forceful about it, but she wasn't putting up much of a fight. She'd spent her seed in his throat, but that didn't mean her intrigue had fallen away.

Would he really do it? Would Robert put it in her? She was dying to find out.

He grabbed her wrists, forcing them down on the mattress. "I'm sorry, Libby. I need it. I can't explain."

"You don't have to explain," she said. "Just take off your boxers."

He looked down at the cotton fabric, the one thing keeping him from full and delicious nudity. Then he pushed them down and kicked them off.

She giggled, just lightly.

God help her, she wanted this.

She wanted Robert's cock.

Arching her hips, she offered him her swollen pink pussy.

And he took it.

Lifting her hips higher off the bed, he found her wet slit with his throbbing dick. He entered her roughly, but she didn't care. Hard or soft. Didn't matter. She'd take his dick any way he gave it to her.

Planting his cock firmly in her cunt, he moved in so close his chest touched her tits. It was a strange feeling—his hard body on the soft swell of her breasts.

Her pussy hugged his hardness so tight he struggled to move inside her. She knew by the way he grunted with every thrust. She knew by the friction his fuck-wand generated in her tight little snatch.

"Oh Robert," she moaned as his thick shaft expanded her juicy gash. "Oh Robert, it feels so big in me."

"I know what you mean, Libby."

He kissed her neck, making all her muscles hum. Her body was a Theremin, singing in time with his love.

His hands moved up her sides, scooping her breasts into his grasp as he fucked her relentlessly. She planted her feet on the mattress to give herself better leverage when she bucked to meet his every thrust.

"Yes. Pinch my tits! Feels so good!"

He quieted her with a kiss.

The second his mouth met hers, she tasted the musky sweetness of her own come on his tongue. It was a strange sensation, on so many levels. He was kissing her mouth. He was pumping her pussy. He was crushing her against the bed, and she couldn't get up even if she wanted to.

But the strangest part of all was that she didn't want to. She loved his cock. She loved his tongue. And the harder he kissed her, the more tingly she felt.

At first, she couldn't tell if the tingle was in her pussy or somewhere else. When she felt her cockhead whack Robert's belly, she realized the tingle was everywhere.

Her dick had come back to life already, God help her!

And Robert hadn't even finished fucking her yet!

As he moved between her thighs, she said, "My cock's hard again."

"I know, Libby. I feel it."

Tears pricked her eyes. "It can't be. It's too much. I can't be putting out fires in my panties all day long."

"We'll take care of it, baby." He petted her hair sweetly, and then arched so he was kneeling on the bed.

Her thighs were draped across his. Her hips tilted toward his darkly delicious groin. She had a sudden urge to run her fingers through his pubic hair, but she didn't let herself do it. She just stared at that wiry cloud of hair while he buried his shaft in her willing pussy.

Nature's nectar splashed Libby's thighs as Robert filled her snatch. He quickly built up such a reckless pace that her body bobbed in time with his thrusts. Her breasts bounded jubilantly. Her cock flapped back and forth, getting harder with every thrust.

That resilient erection whacked her soft belly, then thumped her Robert's hard abs. What a difference, hard and soft. Made her dick throb so forcefully she kicked and screamed.

"It hurts!"

"What, Libby?"

"My penis! I'm so hard it hurts!"

"Oh God." Instead of finding a solution to her problem, he worked his dick faster inside her.

He pounded her cunt.

He pummelled her poor pink pussy.

Her breasts bounced.

Her dick swung wildly.

She watched her body's motion, and it turned her on so wickedly her pussy clamped around his dick. "Oh God!"

"Yeah, Libby. That's my girl." He fucked her faster, harder, and her body jiggled like a paint can in a shaker. "Yeah Libby. I'm gonna blast my load in you sweet little pussy!"

He lunged inside her, planting his dick as deep as it would go.

His head fell back.

His back arched.

That was it. He was done.

He collapsed on top of her, breathing hard and hot on her glistening neck.

She let him have his moment, but her cock was one demanding son of a bitch. It jumped, jumped, jumped like a dog in heat. It wouldn't let up.

Libby cried, "My dick won't stop. It's so damn hard!"

He crawled off her and reached into the bedside table. Sticking his ass in the air, he passed her a tube of lube. "Only one thing left to try."

"You don't mean..."

His golden, glowing cheeks parted like two hills in a desert. "It's worth a try, Lib. I'd do anything to alleviate your pain."

Sounded cheesy, but she knew it was true. He'd do anything for her.

Even offer up his ass.

She opened the lube and splashed some onto her palm. When she worked it into her dick, God, that felt good. But it was still just her hand, and her hand could only provide temporary relief.

"Put it in me, Libby."

"Are you sure? Won't it hurt?"

"Go slow," he said. "Use lots of lube."

She squirted some down his crack. She'd never imagined a man's butt could be so beautiful, but she loved the way his pucker winked at her and sucked up some of that clear slick lube.

Kneeling behind him, Libby guided her thick dick toward his tempting asshole.

When she pressed her cockhead to his pucker, he hissed.

"Did that hurt," she asked.

"No," he said. "Keep going, baby."

She swallowed hard, then pressed forward, meeting with incredible resistance.

"Don't stop," he said.

"Your butthole's so tight."

"Keep going!"

"But doesn't it hurt?"

"Keep going," he growled. "Put it in me. Don't stop now."

Her thick shaft pulsed as she plunged inside his ass. "It doesn't fit!"

"Keep trying," he said. "It'll fit fine. Just don't stop."

She put more pressure, squeezed more lube. She thrust forward, but not roughly. Not all at once. The last thing she wanted to do was hurt the man who'd sucked her cock and fucked her fast and hard. She wanted this to feel good to him, but she didn't know how. She'd never done it before.

His butthole squeezed her dickhead. The harder she pushed, the tighter he felt. But he kept telling her to do it, so she went on pressing inside his orifice.

"Don't stop," he chanted. "Don't stop."

She felt a pop, like suddenly her dickhead was in the clear. For a second, she worried she'd broken his butt, but the way he was moaning it sounded like he wanted more.

"Are you okay?"

"Better than okay, Lib. Keep going."

"I didn't hurt you just now?"

"No, baby. Keep going."

She pressed her palms against his butt cheeks and pushed her dick deeper into his chasm. Now it felt like her cockhead was in the clear. The major tightness remained around her thick, throbbing shaft.

God only knows how that man's butthole managed to house an erection as huge as hers. It blew her mind that he liked what she was doing, but she just kept burying her dick deeper down his chute. Deeper and deeper until his hole had swallowed her to the hilt.

"Libby," he moaned. "You have no idea how great that feels."

"True," she said, since she'd never been fucked up the ass. "But it feels pretty damn good on my end, too."

"Now thrust in me, baby. Build up speed. Push and pull."

She'd already pushed all the way in, so a pull came next. The feeling of suction amazed her, as did the tightness that never went away. His ass clamped tight on her dick, and a shudder of pleasure ran down her spine and through her own asshole, making her wish she had a dick to sit on while she fucked his hole.

"Now a push, Libby. Jam it in."

She thrust, but didn't exactly jam. There was too much resistance to fuck him fast, the way he'd gone at her pussy. She just had to move it slow and steady, savouring the friction she felt as his asshole hugged her dick.

"Yes," she hissed. "This is starting to feel good."

"Good," he replied. "Keep going. It'll feel even better."

She did as she was told, launching her cock down his chute, then retracting it almost fully, but not quite. Never quite. In and out. A little faster. Picking up pace.

"You're so tight."

"Yeah, baby," he moaned. "Yeah, give it to me."

"Oh God." Libby clenched as his butt muscles locked momentarily around her shaft. "It feels so good."

She threw her hips into the motion, driving deeper, harder, burying her dick in that hot hug.

Soon a feeling passed through her that was recognizable, but on a whole different plane. She knew what it was like when she was about to have an orgasm. This felt like that, except huge and heavenly.

Her heart expanded as her dick swelled.

Her mind moved out of her head and spread out into the room.

Her consciousness was everywhere. She could see herself from up above, but she could also feel her hardness filling Robert's hole. The best of both worlds. Universal consciousness and gritty, dirty sex.

She fucked him roughly, revelling in his pleas for more, harder, faster.

The sight of her fatness filling him made her breathless. She'd expanded his hole enormously. It wasn't even puckered anymore, just a slick pink O taking everything Libby had to give.

"God yes," he groaned. "God, Libby. Give it to me hard. Don't be afraid."

She wasn't afraid. Not anymore. She rammed his asshole, sliding in and out with the help of Robert's lube stash. Her boobs bounced with every go. Her nipples tightened with arousal and all she could think was how weird it would be if he could turn around in that position and take her tits in his mouth. If his blow job was anything to go on, he'd be damn good at it.

The thought blew more than just her mind. When she pictured him sucking her tits, a tickle raced through her shaft, and immediately seized her system.

"Oh," she said. "I'm about to come."

"Come, Libby." His tone was gritty, but consoling. He wanted the pulsing, pounding arousal to pass. He wanted that for her sake. "Come, baby. Fill my ass."

The words! The hot hug of his hole! The sight of his open orifice expanding to house her huge, hard dick!

It was all too much.

Come exploded from her body like lava from a volcano. The blast was unlike any other orgasm she'd experienced. It overtook her body and mind. Every cell danced. She saw stars. The world went away and everything was black space and galaxies.

Blast after blast. Ropes of come filling Robert's hole. Her body grew weak as her essence escaped. She pulled her dick slowly from his ass, and it almost felt more difficult than going it.

Libby collapsed beside him. She couldn't catch her breath, but neither could he, so they didn't say anything for a very long time.

He got up and went to the bathroom, and Libby was jealous. She couldn't move her legs yet, or she'd have gone too. She still peed sitting down. Weird to think she could do it standing up, if she really wanted to.

When he returned to bed, he wrapped his arms around her. He hugged her front to front. Even just feeling her tight nipples against his chest and the mingle of their spent dicks made her want to do it all over again. Luckily, her body was done for now.

"We'll talk to your professor," Robert said. "We'll tell the college what happened. Maybe there's a quick fix, an antidote, something."

Libby didn't say anything right away. She held him tight and pressed her face against his shoulder.

"What's wrong, Lib? You can tell me anything."

"I know," she said. "I'm thinking if it's this much fun to play with, it might be worth keeping."

Robert pulled away, but only enough that they could look each other in the eye.

Libby should have been embarrassed saying all this, but it was hard to feel that way when she was naked in bed with a man who really cared about her.

She'd fucked him.

She'd plunged her dick in his ass.

He'd put his cock in her cunt.

He'd sucked her off!

"Even if I never play with anyone else but you," Libby said. "It might be worth keeping."

He gave her a look like what he wanted to say and what he should say were two different things. He should tell her this could never happen again, that the two of them shouldn't suck and fuck.

But that's not what he would say. She knew him well enough to know their shared desire would win out, in the end.

Futanari Pillow Fight

Sherry hugged her pillow to her chest as she entered Marigold's house. The other girls had already arrived. She could hear them being their usual rambunctious selves up in Marigold's bedroom.

"You look nervous," Marigold said, taking Sherry's overnight bag. "Everything okay?"

"I've just never been to a slumber party," Sherry admitted.

Marigold's pretty orange curls bobbed against her shoulders as she laughed. "You are too cute! How can you never have been to a sleepover?"

"I don't know. I just haven't. This is my first one."

"But you're eighteen years old! You never went to one as a kid?"

Sherry shook her head nervously.

"Aww, well that's okay. We'll make this one extra special for you." Marigold was so sweet and nice and affectionate that she wrapped her arms around Sherry and gave her a nice tight hug. Well, tight as she could with a pillow between them.

Something fell upstairs, and for a moment there was silence. Then the girls started to laugh.

Marigold shook her head. "Those two are going to destroy this house."

"It's very nice," Sherry said. "Your house."

"My parents are away for the weekend, so we can do whatever we want. Nala and Polly have already raided the liquor cabinet."

Sherry gasped. "Won't your parents be mad?"

"It's okay," Marigold whispered, like her parents might overhear if she talked too loudly. "My parents marked the bottles, so we're going to fill them with water when we're done."

"Won't your parents notice their liquor's watered down?" Sherry asked.

"They've had the same bottles for years. It's mainly just for guests. They're not big drinkers."

Sherry wasn't a big drinker either. Or a drinker at all. She didn't like to break the rules, and she truly believed underage drinking caused more harm than good.

But nobody had ever invited her to a slumber party before, so she'd just keep her opinions to herself.

"Come on upstairs," Marigold said as she carried Sherry's bag.

She could hear the two girls giggling behind closed doors, and that sound brought shameful thoughts to her head. Sherry knew she wasn't like Nala and Polly and Marigold. She had to act like them to conceal the fact that she was so very different.

When Marigold opened the door, they were lost in a swirl of wintery white feathers.

"What's going on in here?" Marigold cried.

The feathers started settling to the ground, and as they did Sherry spotted her friends holding pillows that had ripped open and spewed their contents into the air.

"What are you wearing?" Marigold shrieked. "Where did you get those?"

Nala and Polly were both wearing silky lingerie. Nala had on a strappy negligee in a shade of pink that complemented her dark brown skin. Polly wore a satin teddy with matching shorts. The sea blue colour went well with her pretty eyes and sandy hair.

Since Sherry had never been to a sleepover party, she had no way of knowing if this was unusual. In fact, it's pretty much what she'd expected.

"We got bored," Polly said.

"So we went through your mom's drawers," Nala added.

Marigold's green eyes narrowed to slits. All her freckles jammed together as she scrunched up her nose. "I'm going to kill you!" she cried, grabbing a pillow off her bed.

"Why?" Nala asked. "So what? We're wearing your mother's lingerie. We can wash it later."

"By hand," Polly added, then pointed to two more sets hanging from Marigold's closet door. "Look! We even picked out lingerie for you and Sherry."

"Hi Sherry," Nala said as she haunted the bedroom door.

When Sherry waved shyly, Nala waved back.

"Come in," Nala said. "What are you afraid of?"

Luckily, Sherry didn't have to answer that question because Marigold started shouting her head off about how gross it was that they were wearing her mother's frilly things and how she'd never do a thing like that, not even if they paid her.

Polly and Nala giggled, and the room filled with alcohol fumes. Or maybe Sherry was imagining that bit. She could certainly sense their airiness, their sheer joy, like they were anticipating something Marigold wanted desperately to prevent.

"Come on," Polly said, tossing her pillow down on the bed to grab Marigold by the arm. "Take off your clothes. This'll be fun."

"No!" Marigold shouted.

"It's like dress-up," Nala said. "Didn't you used to play dress-up when you were a kid?"

"I did," Sherry said, even though nobody was paying attention to her.

"Wasn't it so much fun?" Nala asked as she too dropped her pillow and grabbed Marigold by the arm. "It's just your mother's lingerie. It's no big deal."

Marigold dropped Sherry's overnight bag, squealing, "Yes it is! It's a huge big deal."

"No it's not." Polly grabbed at her top while she fought off Nala.

Somehow, together, the partially drunk girls managed to wrangle Marigold out of her loose-fitting shirt. Underneath, she had on a plain white bra, much like Sherry's. Her breasts were considerably larger than Sherry would have guessed, since she usually wore heavy sweaters and oversized shirts.

"Wow," Nala said, taking one boob in each hand and balancing them like the scales of justice. "You've got big tits, Marigold. I never would have guess."

"Big Irish boobs," Polly said, ripping the straps down Marigold's shoulders and pulling down on the bra until both breasts popped out.

Nala grabbed them and held them up like a pair of trophies. "Wowee! I can't believe how pink your nipples are."

"Aww look," Polly said. "She's got freckles on her tits."

"That's so cute!" Nala replied.

"Shut your gobs," Marigold said, swatting at them and missing. "Leave me alone!"

"What?" Nala asked. "We're admiring your body. We think your boobs are beautiful."

Polly looked to Nala, then grabbed the waist of Marigold's pants. "Let's find out if her pussy's just as nice."

"No!" Marigold screamed, holding her pants so Polly couldn't yank them down. "Get your hands off me, you lesbo pervs!"

Sherry's heart hurt when she heard Marigold calling them lesbos. If Marigold knew the truth about her, she'd never have been invited to this sleepover party.

"What about you, Sher?" Releasing her grip on Marigold, Nala took one step closer to the door. "Come into the bedroom. You don't need to hide."

Sherry stepped inside, but held her pillow closer to her chest.

Nala closed the door behind her. "You brought your own pillow? That's so cute."

"I've never been to a sleepover before," Sherry confessed, even though that would probably be thrown back in her face soon enough.

"Awww, that's okay." Nala took the pillow and placed it on the bed while Polly took the stretchy purple negligee off its hanger and jammed it over Marigold's head.

"Hey, look at that," Polly said. "Your boobs barely fit inside this thing. You must have a bigger chest than your mother."

Marigold covered her face with both hands. "Please don't make me think about my mother's chest!"

Polly wrapped her arms around Marigold so their breasts pressed together. "Oh my God, your boobs are so plump and juicy!"

"Get off me!" Marigold said, pushing Polly away so hard she fell back on the bed.

Sherry was sure Polly would scream and shout, but instead she just laughed and said, "What about Sherry's boobs? What do they look like?"

"Let's find out," Nala said, grabbing the hem of Sherry's knitted sweater. "Arms up over your head. That's a good girl."

"You don't have to listen to them," Marigold cried. "They're drunk lesbo jerks."

Little did Marigold know Sherry had always dreamed of being taken by drunk lesbo jerks. Well, maybe not jerks. But certainly drunk lesbos.

Nala lifted her sweater very gently over her head, then said, "You're wearing an undershirt instead of a bra?"

"Her boobs are too small for a bra," Polly commented. "No offense."

Sherry smiled weakly.

Nala touched her finger to the sweet little rosette sewn into Sherry's undershirt. It was meant for a child, but Sherry had always been bony and small, quite the opposite of Marigold, who was bouncy and bountiful. Nala and Polly were somewhere in between—not skinny, not fat. Practically perfect.

When Nala had lifted Sherry's undershirt over her head, all the girls simply stared at her chest.

"What?" she asked, and looked down at her mosquito bite nipples and her barely-there boobs. She covered them with her hands. "They're tiny. I know."

"It's okay," Nala said, and swiftly shooed her hands away. "They're cute. They're like little-girl boobs."

"Are you sure you're eighteen?" Polly asked with a laugh.

"Almost nineteen," Sherry said. "My body just doesn't know that, I guess."

The girls laughed faintly as Nala grabbed the last negligee off its hanger. This one was white and made of stretchy lace, like a tiny little dress.

"Take your pants off," Nala said as she fitted the lace dress over Sherry's head.

Fear gripped Sherry's heart, and she said, "Marigold didn't have to. I shouldn't have to either."

Without answering, Nala took a step back and just looked at her. "Wow, that fits you better than I thought it would."

The lace clung tightly to Sherry's body. She could feel the cool fabric against her nipples, and a streak of arousal moved through her body.

How she wished she could simply tell the girls the truth, and take off her bottoms and see what would happen next.

"You don't have to take off your pants," Nala said, sneakily picking up her pillow. "We'll do that for you."

All at once, Polly and Nala launched a feathery attack on Sherry and Marigold. They weren't at all prepared. Feathers went flying as they grabbed for their pillows. Sherry couldn't see anything but white as she whipped hers out in front of her. She made contact with Nala's shoulder before Nala whacked her in the face. That strike knocked her onto one of the two twin beds. Maybe Marigold used to share this bedroom with her sister? That's what Sherry was wondering when she felt a tug on the hem of her pants.

Shrieking, she said, "Stop!"

She tried to sit up while swinging her pillow in every direction, but she was soon attacked by another pillow, right in the face. Heaving herself forward, she fell on top of Nala on the floor, with her crotch right up against the girl's chin.

Sherry panicked and tried to get up, but Polly struck her from behind with a wrecked pillow. The blow landed hard enough to propel Sherry onto the other bed. She landed there face-down, and Nala whacked her butt with a pillow, giggling wildly.

When Sherry lifted her head, she saw Marigold coming at Nala with a pillow of her own. Nala noticed too, and ducked out of the way. Poor Marigold ended up crashing into Polly, and they both squealed on impact. Those two went at each other roughly while Nala yanked down Sherry's pants. Sherry had become so engrossed in watching Polly pummel Marigold that she hardly noticed at first.

"I'm doing it!" Nala called to Polly. "I'm getting this girl's pants down."

"No!" Sherry cried, grabbing for them before realizing she was still holding her pillow. She tried whacking Nala in the face with it, but no luck. Before she knew what was happening, her bare butt was sticking out for all the world to see.

"Look at this," Nala cried as she stood and spanked Sherry's ass with the pillow. "Look! I'm smacking her tiny little butt."

Sherry's heart hammered her ribs as she kept her thighs pressed tightly together. Hopefully no one would notice anything out of the ordinary with so many feathers flying around the room.

Polly said, "It's your turn, Marigold. Get these pants off. Now!"

"No!" Marigold cried, like she was in actual physical pain. "No, you can't! Please, Polly! Please don't!"

Sherry turned just in time to watch Polly yank down Marigold's panties, revealing something even Sherry didn't expect to see.

"Oh my God!" Polly squealed. "Marigold's got a dick!"

Marigold's rosy glow faded to the whitest shade of pale Sherry had ever seen. "I told you I didn't want to take off my clothes."

Nala burst out laughing. "No wonder! You're a freak."

"Haha," Polly said. "Marigold's a freee-eeak!"

Marigold started to cry, and Sherry wouldn't stand for it. Rising to her feet, she turned so the girls could see her front. "If Marigold's a freak, then so am I!"

It was pretty much the bravest thing she'd ever done, and she braced herself for torment.

But Nala and Polly's jaws just dropped and they looked at each other like they were wondering if maybe they were the weird ones.

Sniffling, Marigold sat up on the other bed. "You too?" she asked. "You never said."

"Either did you," Sherry told her.

Marigold nodded. "I thought I was the only one."

Polly looked back and forth between their two dicks, which were reacting very positively to this room full of girls in silky lingerie. "Do you ever... have you ever... you know, like, used them?"

Just then, a floating feather landed on Sherry's throbbing cockhead and all the girls laughed. This time, the laughter didn't seem mean. It was just a funny thing that happened, and Nala leaned forward to blow the feather away.

As Sherry's shaft clenched, Polly giggled. "Nala just gave Sherry a blow job!"

"Haw-haw," Nala replied, sneaking a peek at Sherry's swollen dick. "At least I'm not a total prude who's too scared to even touch one."

Polly's jaw dropped. "Are you talking about me?"

"Who else?"

"I am not too scared!"

Sherry bit her bottom lip to keep from smiling. She thought she knew where this was going, and she didn't want to knock the wheels off.

Nala kneeled on her pillow and leaned against the mattress. "Have you ever got a blowjob, Sherry?"

Sherry could feel her cheeks turning bright red. "No. Never."

"Do you want one?"

Her eyes bugged so hard she worried they'd fly out of her head. "Ummm..."

"It obviously works," Nala said, wrapping her hand around the base. "Look how hard you are already, and that's just from me blowing a feather off your tip."

"Mine works too," Marigold piped up. "Look! See how big it is?"

Polly glanced at it, but seemed suddenly embarrassed and shy.

"You can touch it if you want," Marigold told her.

"Oh. Yeah, I..."

"She's seriously never touched one," Nala said, in a critical tone.

"So?" Polly shot back. "Either have you. Stop acting so high and mighty."

Pumping Sherry's erection in one hand, Nala said, "At least I'm not afraid of a dick."

"I'm not afraid of one either," Polly said, and inched her fingers up Marigold's thigh.

"Oh God," Sherry whimpered. She didn't mean to draw attention to herself, but what Nala was doing felt so good she wondered how long she'd hold it together.

"What does it feel like?" Nala asked.

"Good." Sherry folded her pillow in half and smooshed it against her face.

"Just good?"

Sherry nodded.

"Well, maybe this will feel better than good." Getting between Sherry's thighs, Nala leaned in and licked her tip. "How's that?"

Sherry moaned into her pillow.

"More?" Nala asked.

Sherry nodded, hugging her pillow tight.

"I can do it too," Polly said, though she didn't sound totally sure of herself. "I bet I can make Marigold come before you make Sherry come!"

"You're on," Nala said before dropping her face in Sherry's lap.

Sherry was not prepared for the sensation as Nala wrapped those full pink lips around her swollen shaft. Once Sherry felt the full wet warmth of Nala's mouth, Nala slid her lips down Sherry's dick about halfway to the root. When her lips met her fist, which was still closed around Sherry's root, it was like every kind of heaven.

"I can't do this!" Polly cried. "I'm too scared to touch it."

Nala bobbed out of Sherry's lap, letting her cock pop out from between those beautiful lips. "Haha! Told you."

Polly climbed up on the other twin bed and buried her face in her own pillow. Her head was down, but her butt was up in the air. She reached back and tore down those silky blue shorts. "Can you just put it in me, please?"

Marigold gasped. Her dick straightened like a soldier.

"I thought you were scared," Nala said.

"Scared to touch it," Polly said, speaking into her pillow. "Not scared to... you know..."

"Get fucked in the butt?" Nala asked.

Polly arched up. "Not in the butt!!!"

She hid her head again after she'd said that.

"Well?" Nala said to Marigold. "What are you waiting for? Polly wants your P in her V."

Marigold swallowed hard and nodded. She looked positively terrified.

"You've never done it before," Sherry said. "Have you?"

"Have you?" Marigold pleaded.

Sherry shook her head.

With a deep breath, Marigold climbed up on the bed and kneeled behind Polly's exposed ass. Her butt was flawless. Marigold obviously thought so too, because she traced both hands around that expanse of soft, supple flesh.

Nala couldn't take her eyes off this scene. As much as Sherry wished the girl would wrap those luscious lips around her swollen shaft, she understood the appeal. At least Nala hadn't let go of her erection, and was still absentmindedly stroking it.

"Put it in her pussy," Nala cheered. "Do it, Marigold! Jam it in!"

"Don't jam it in," Polly said into her pillow. "Put it in, but don't jam it!"

Marigold's big breasts swelled as she guided her erection toward Polly's pretty pink pussy. Even from across the room, Sherry could see how wet the girl was. Polly's blonde pubes were the sweetest she'd ever seen. Marigold's were curly and orange, just like her hair. She wondered if Nala's were dark like hers, or darker. Probably the same colour, just a different texture. She'd have to wait and see.

Sherry's long black hair was braided behind her back, and she liked the way it felt when it whacked her like a rope. She liked the way her breasts looked too, inside this stretchy white thing that belonged to Marigold's mother. Her nipples were so hard they showed through the lace, and she wondered if Nala had noticed how sexy she looked, but Nala's eyes were locked on the scene across the room.

"Gentle," Polly pleaded as Marigold pressed her fat tip inside the girl's tight hole. "Oh God, Marigold. It's too big!"

"No it's not," Nala said. "It'll fit. Just keep breathing."

Polly hugged her pillow. Sherry noticed her thighs tensing as Marigold forced deeper inside.

"Oh God," Polly cried. "Oh God!"

Sherry's cock pulsed against Nala's palm, and Nala jumped. "Somebody's eager."

Embarrassing, but true. "Please suck it," Sherry begged. "Only if you want. But please do it. I'm so turned on."

"Yeah, I noticed." Nala turned so she could still watch the other girls even while she wrapped her lips around Sherry's shaft.

When she started sucking again, Sherry's entire body felt weak. Nala was sucking her life force. It felt so good, but it turned her arms to jelly. She just sat on the bed, trembling while Nala's mouth moved down her dick.

So warm! So wet! So tight with sweet suction.

Marigold urged her erection harder into Polly's poor little pussy, and Polly squealed into the pillow. "Oh God!" Her blonde locks were everywhere. Her face was lost beneath them, even when she came up for air. "Thank God you've got a cock. Thank God my first time is with you."

"Better a friend than some sleazy guy who just want to get in your pants!" Marigold said, panting with every thrust. She was holding onto her mother's blue teddy, and tugging it so hard Polly's lovely breasts fell out the front.

Her nipples teased the bedspread, and Sherry could practically feel the sweet scratch and tickle. It made her dick throb and grow in Nala's throat, so much so Nala gagged and pulled away.

"Girl, I can't take much more!"

"Sorry," Sherry said. "I didn't mean it."

Nala glanced over at the other bed and got a scheming look in her eye. "Follow me."

She walked on her knees across the floor, then climbed up on the other bed and yanked down Marigold's tight purple negligee. Marigold shrieked as both her breasts popped out. "What are you doing."

"This," Nala said, then wrapped her lips around one of Marigold's nipples.

Sherry's dick clenched when she saw Marigold's blissful reaction. She never imagined something like this could happen in real life: four friends getting together for a simple slumber party, and it erupts into an all-out orgy? Who could have predicted something like this?

As Nala suckled at Marigold's breast, she opened her knees wider where she kneeled on the bed. The moment Sherry got a peek at the pink pussy beyond that silky negligee, she sped across the room to surprise Nala from behind.

Nala shrieked when Sherry fed her needy cock into that warm, wet slit. She knew Nala had done this before, but that didn't stop the girl from squealing like a stuck pig as Sherry plunged into that tight chasm.

"Sherry!" Nala screamed. "You're inside me?"

"Yes!!!" Sherry moaned, holding Nala's negligee like a set of reins. "God you've got one hot little snatch!"

Sherry had never said anything quite so raunchy, but Nala obviously liked hearing it. Her pussy clamped around Sherry's dick. The sensation reminded her of Nala's mouth, and just thinking about getting sucked off brought her dangerously close to orgasm.

"Fuck me harder," Nala cried before wrapping her arms around Marigold's body and her lips around Marigold's nipple.

Marigold's boobs looked even bigger than before, and Sherry found it comforting to know a girl like her could sport such large and luscious breasts. She'd always felt a bit embarrassed by her own, since they were so small. But what difference did it make when she could use her dick to make a girl like Nala grunt and groan and buck back against her hips?

"She's gonna blow," Marigold said, gazing down at Nala.

"So am I," Polly said. Her head was still buried in her pillow, just like her body was buried under Nala's. She'd practically disappeared, except where her butt bobbed up for Marigold to work diligently at her snatch.

"I don't want to come until you do," Marigold said to Polly. "But I'm not sure I can help it!"

Sherry couldn't blame her, with one girl hanging off her breasts and another offering up a perfect pink pussy.

The four of them moved like clockwork, making the bedsprings sing and the floorboards creak. Sherry fucked Nala and Marigold fucked Polly. Nala sucked Marigold's tits while Polly screamed into a pillow.

Out of nowhere, Sherry picked up a feather-spewing pillow. She struck Marigold's back while she fucked Nala's swollen centre.

Marigold laughed, so Sherry kept going, kept striking her head, her back, her butt. Then Nala got a turn. Then Polly. She whacked everyone with the pillow, sending feathers up in the air while the four of them worked toward a collective climax.

Sherry's cock had never felt so huge, never been so hard. She almost couldn't believe this was real life when she rammed her dick as hard as humanly possible into Nala's snatch.

Too hard.

So hard Nala tumbled forward, toppling the girl pile at the worst possible moment.

Orgasm was upon them. All of them. Once Sherry had planted the entire length of her shaft inside Nala's swollen pussy, her muscles all locked and she spewed her essence deep inside her friend's slit.

But the two of them had already landed hard on Polly, flattening the poor girl against the mattress. That caused Marigold's cock to pop out of Polly's pussy just at the moment when her first rope of cum streamed from her body. That hot streak of cream landed on Sherry's naked ass and drizzled down her thigh. Burst after burst followed, until her butt was covered with Marigold's jizz. It was hot and sticky and smelled like sex.

And when she slithered off the bed, Marigold's mother's tight white lace soaked it up like a towel.

"Sherry!" Marigold squealed. "You got cum all over my mom's negligee."

"I'm sorry," Sherry said, and really meant it. But actually, it felt weird and wonderful when the lace garment hugged her cum-slathered butt. "I'll wash it, I promise."

Polly pulled herself out from under the other two and whimpered, "After all that, I didn't even come!"

"Sorry," Marigold said. "I tried. I thought you were right there with me."

She rolled over and rested with her back on the pillow she'd been screaming into, her knees slightly parted. "I almost was."

Marigold sat at the edge of the bed while Nala pushed Polly's legs apart. "I can make you come. Now problem."

Polly's eyes widened. "How?"

"How do you think?"

Bowing between the girl's long white legs, Nala extended her velvety pink tongue and licked Polly's pretty pussy.

"Wow," Marigold said as she moved to the floor alongside Sherry. "That looks so delicious."

"Sounds it too," Sherry said, listening to the slurpy sounds Nala made as she licked and sucked Polly's pussy. "I can feel my thingy twitching already."

"Oh yeah?" Marigold asked, stealing a glance at Sherry, then returning her gaze to the rug muncher and the rug. "Hey, why did you never tell me you had one?"

Sherry swallowed hard as Marigold made her big breasts accessible. "It's not the kind of thing anyone talks about. I didn't want anyone thinking I was weird."

"Well, I don't think you're weird."

Marigold grabbed both Sherry's hands and placed them on her breasts.

That did the trick. Didn't matter that Sherry had just blown her load. She was hard again already. And she moved closed behind Marigold so they'd both know how turned on she was.

Marigold moaned softly while Sherry squeezed her tits from behind. They were so soft and supple Sherry had to battle her jealousy while Marigold parted her legs. "I don't know if you have both," she said. "But I do."

She took hold of Sherry's erection and guided it between her legs, where a warm, wet slit waited. Sherry's cockhead popped easily inside, and she concealed her surprise in a satisfied growl. While she fondled her friend's fleshy breasts, she slid further into that sweet, slippery pussy.

Sherry fucked her friend relatively quietly while they watched Nala suck Polly's clit. Without a pillow covering her face, Polly was an air horn without an off switch. She kicked her legs in the air and screamed Nala's name and hugged her breasts while her nipples played peekaboo inside the blue satin number. Her hair was everywhere, a blonde explosion. It was the sexiest sight Sherry had ever laid eyes on.

And the whole time, Sherry took Marigold from behind, thrusting at an even pace, thinking how nice it would be to sleep side by side in one of these little beds. She wouldn't even have to wake up. Not fully. She'd just wrap one arm around Marigold's body and squeeze those sleepy breasts and plant her morning wood inside a tight, loving pussy.

Marigold moved one of Sherry's hands down her belly and said, "Look what you've done to me."

When Sherry's hand met Marigold's erection, she almost pulled away. She'd never touched one before, other than her own.

But now that she'd started, she was pretty sure she'd never stop.

As he palm shuttled up and down Marigold's dick, Sherry thrust her own deeper inside the sweet swell between the girl's legs. Marigold smelled like freshly cut grass and summer laundry. That's the smell Sherry would go on to associate with her first time: the smell of laundry and grass, the feel of Nala's lips around her throbbing shaft, the sound of Polly filling the rafters with squeals of joy.

And the sight of fluffy white feathers floating through the air.

The Perfect Maid

Reg raced home from the office at Aunt Cordelia's insistence. She sounded eager to see him, but wouldn't say why over the phone.

"Auntie?" Reg called out as her burst through the front door. "Aunt Cordelia?"

Nobody answered, but he heard the tip-tap of high-heeled shoes on marble floors. That couldn't be Aunt Cordelia. He knew the sound her shoes made against the floor. He knew the sound of her slightly dragging gait.

He'd been living with the woman since he was seven years old. He knew her better than he'd like to admit.

But this woman before him... this was not Aunt Cordelia.

"Hallo," she said, with an accent of some sort. "You are Red?"

"I am Reg," he said. "And you are?"

"The maid."

"No you're not," he replied, even though she was superbly attired in a frilly black skirt and tight, low-cut shirt ensemble, topped off with a white apron and antiquated maid's cap.

She also wore fishnet stockings and dangerous heels.

Reg said, "Phillipa is the maid. Where's Phillipa?"

"Not here," the woman said, fluffing her ostrich-feather duster.

"Where is my aunt?"

"Not here."

"But she telephoned me just now. She told me to come home."

The fake maid shrugged. She was up to something. He could see it in her eyes.

"What?" he asked. "Who are you really?"

"Kitty. The maid."

"Kitty the maid?" he asked flatly. "You're Kitty the Maid."

She nodded.

This maid did not look like a Kitty. Well, perhaps she did. But she looked like she'd been given that name by some kind of pimp or strip club owner.

"Why are you looking at me that way?" she asked.

He hadn't realized he'd been looking at her any way, but of course he had. How could he not look at her? That petite frame. The poufy skirt, the skin-tight blouse, the open front revealing just a hint of a lacy bra.

And that face! What a beautiful, fabulous face. If you passed her on the street—without the maid's uniform, even—you'd turn to get a second glance. She looked like the kind of girl you'd see representing Thailand in a Miss Universe pageant. Or so he imagined. He'd never actually watched one. But the full pink lips, the dark almond eyes, the hair swept back beneath that silly maid's cap... she was stunning. Perfectly stunning.

"Who hired you on?" Reg asked.

"Miss Cordelia."

"Ah. But why would she hire you when we already have Phillipa?"

Kitty began a shrug, but let it fall halfway, and said, "Miss Cordelia thought perhaps you were developing an unhealthy attachment to Phillipa."

Reg felt his heart clench and his blood drain into his toes. He felt like an icicle standing in the grand foyer of a millionaire's mansion.

Kitty seemed to think his reaction to this provocation was cute. She giggled, and that melted him a bit. Then she went on to say, "Your aunt hired me to provide you some relief."

"Relief?" Reg asked, feeling hardly relieved at all.

"Yes. She took Phillipa to the country house on holiday."

"I'm not sure how much of a holiday it'll be for Phillipa," Reg said. "She'll still be cooking and cleaning—just in a more rustic environment."

When Kitty turned to walk away, Reg noticed that her fishnet stockings had seams at the back.

Stockings with seams! Oh happy day!

He followed her into the drawing room. "Where are you going?"

"Your aunt hired me to clean. So here I go, cleaning."

"Can I watch?"

"Watch me clean?" she asked. "Of course. You're the boss."

Reg was accustomed to being called the boss, but he never really felt like the boss. Here at home, his aunt took control of finances as well as household matters.

And at work? Well, he had a corner office, of course, but he mostly used it to practice his golf putt. Every so often he offered input on some matter or another, and the others smiled and nodded, but his ideas were never implemented.

Sometimes he wondered if they only kept him on because his grandfather had built the company from the ground up.

Often, as he stared out his 27th story window, he admired his parents for taking off without him to farm cocoa in warmer climes. Must be more exciting than sitting behind a desk getting paid through the nose to do absolutely nothing.

He was probably getting paid right now, while he sat on the settee, watching Kitty the Fake Maid step up onto the library ladder to dust the old books.

"Careful," he said. "Don't want you to fall."

She reached farther afield with the stretch of a ballerina. Just look at those long, limber legs, those glorious, gracious arms. Just look at her crinolines picking up to reveal a stunning set of garters! It wasn't often you saw a woman with seams in her stockings and garters as well!

He could feel his body reacting.

It was strange to think his aunt had orchestrated this encounter, but his aunt liked Phillipa and surely didn't want to lose her. Reg had to admit, he'd chased off his fair share of housemaids.

It wasn't lechery, of course. It was love! He fell in love too easily.

Really, he had not much else to do.

But lust certainly factored into things, especially as he stared up Kitty's crinolines while she dusted the bookshelves. This was certainly more entertaining than staring out the window.

"How am I doing, Mister Reg? Is this a good job?"

"A very good job," he told her. "But why don't you get down from there? That ladder is dangerous in those heels."

"It's fine," she replied. "But Miss Cordelia said there would be a reward for a job well done."

Kitty turned around on the ladder to look at him.

"Miss Cordelia said that you would give me a reward."

Reg could hear his heart beating and, for a moment, could hear nothing else. "What sort of reward?"

She set her duster down on the bookshelf and hooked her heels firmly around the bottom rung to steady herself. She didn't have to lift her skirt because the crinolines did that for her.

Kitty did, however, shift her black lace panties to one side, giving Reg a clear view at the stunning specimen which lay beneath.

Hard to believe this was the woman Aunt Cordelia selected for him. Hard to believe his elderly maiden aunt was able to assess his preferences and his desires so neatly.

Reg raced across the drawing room, letting his knees land on either side of her feet on the rung of the ladder. There was scarcely room for the two of them. Her ankles knocked together and she shrieked, then giggled, then ran her hands through his hair.

"You like?" she asked.

"Very much," he replied.

Her impressive cock twitched, like it had hardness in its sights and, with his mouth, Reg could get it there.

"Do you mind very much?" He didn't want to just wrap his lips around a stranger's dick without asking permission first. That would be such a terribly classless thing to do.

"Go ahead," Kitty said, with a tease in her voice.

Reg wrapped his thumb around her lacy panties and pulled them fully to one side, expecting an ample set of balls to descend. But Kitty had nothing of the sort! Rather than balls, she possessed a sweet set of labia, which unfolded gently as a flower to reveal juicy pink flesh, nectar of the gods.

Inside his pants, Reg's shaft turned to steel. It was so hard his trousers frisked him roughly as he bent toward Kitty's cock and kissed the fat, round tip.

"Oh, Mister Reg!" she cooed. "I love a man who starts it with a kiss."

He kissed her again, this time on the side of her shaft. The skin was incredibly soft, but her cock grew incredibly hard as he kissed it and kissed it and kissed it some more.

"Feels so great," she said, still running her hand through his hair. "Now suck it, Mister Reg! Suck the tip!"

She seemed so excited, and her emotion ramped up his arousal so much he worried he'd come in his pants. But he put that concern out of his mind when he opened his mouth to let her in. Not too wide, mind. He wanted her to feel his lips as her tip passed between them, like a train hitting low-hanging branches as it chugged by.

He loved the sensation of her throbbing pink head entering his mouth.

He loved that feel of soft skin on soft skin, both sites so sensitive they gasped in unison.

Of course, the gasp led him to open his mouth wider, let her in deeper, faster. But she didn't gag him with it. She was gentle. She was kind. She planted her cock just far enough inside his mouth that he could suck it without feeling overwhelmed.

It felt good, just sitting there on his tongue. Felt even better when he closed his mouth around the shaft. That's when he really tasted the scent of her skin. He tasted her sweetness and her musk.

And she returned the favour by hardening incrementally as he sucked, until her cock filled his throat in a surprisingly enjoyable way.

He held the ladder. She did too, though only with one hand. With the other, she tickled his scalp, tickled his neck, behind his ear.

Her touch was so soft, yet its impact was so extreme. He sucked her harder, faster, bobbing his head inside that cacophony of crinolines. She was like some kind of superstar with strange fashion sense. Could she sing? He'd put her on stage, turn her an easy million. She had the looks. That's for sure.

"Yes, Mister Reg," she said, in this high-pitched whining voice that sounded quite desperate.

She started bouncing on the ladder, which worried him even though it was locked in place.

"Mister Reg, I'm going to come in your mouth!"

With that much warning, she did indeed come. She filled his throat with warm cream, so sweet and thick he wished he'd had a better taste before swallowing it down.

Her hand left his hair and her wrist met her forehead in a classic "woe is me" pose. Her eyelids fluttered and she said, "I think I'm going to faint!"

She collapsed over his shoulder.

He rose just fast enough to catch her waist and carry her Viking style to the settee. But not quite on the settee, because her knees ended up on the rug, and her face and upper body lay sprawled on the seat.

"Are you quite alright?" Reg asked. "Can I get you some water?"

"Yes," she said, and he rushed to the kitchen, wondering where the water was kept. He found it eventually, and brought a glass to Kitty. He held it against her pretty pink lips and poured, but she was on an angle and much of it spilled on Aunt Cordelia's settee.

Kitty took the glass and sat on the floor and drank and sputtered and drank some more. She almost didn't look like a flesh-and-blood human. More like some kind of cartoon character. Huge eyes, huge breasts.

"What happened?" Reg asked.

"I came too hard," she said, handing him the glass.

"Goodness."

She untied her apron and took off her top. "Maybe this uniform is too tight."

Reg sat beside her on the floor, gazing at her glorious breasts.

The lace of her bra was black and rose-patterned, and the slight golden tone of her skin glowed through every hole like a ray of sunshine. The heaviness of her breasts impressed him greatly, and he savoured the sight of her rosy-brown nipples, which he could easily see through the lace.

He wondered if she would take off the bra too, but she didn't. She kept the skirt on as well, and the crinolines, and the garters and the seamed fishnet stockings.

Though she did manage to take off her panties. It turned out they tied together at the hips for easy removal.

Resting her head on the settee, she raised her bum in the air. Her crinolines shot out in a circle around her bare bottom, making it look like a strange black flower with a juicy pink middle.

Then she reached for Reg's crotch and traced her hand gently the length of his hardened dick. Her fingers played it like a flute, dancing in one direction, then the other.

He loved how much she seemed to enjoy touching him, even over his trousers, and he was yet more delighted when she unzipped his fly to find him in the flesh.

His cock jumped out of his pants and into her waiting hand like it had a mind of its own.

She giggled and, at first, just watched it jump and twitch. It was cute, the way she smiled at it. Reg felt as though he'd given a sick child a toy and succeeded in brightening her spirits.

He put the glass on the floor behind them and then set his cold hand on her warm forehead. "How are you feeling now?"

She nodded and smiled. "Better."

Then she closed her fingers around his cock and slowly began to stroke him off.

"Oh my," he said. "Your hand is so soft."

"It can be hard," she said, and pulled his dick a little more roughly. "But I prefer soft." She went back to that.

"So do I."

She smiled sweetly as she pumped his dick, then asked, "What do you want now?"

In a way, he just wanted to sit here on the floor and allow this girl to fondle him lovingly. But if he came on her wrist, he'd live to regret it.

"I'll do anything for you," she cooed.

Oh, that just about brought him to climax right there!

He was somewhat surprised to hear himself say, "Take off your bra. Let me see those fine breasts."

Kitty looked surprised, too, but not insulted.

She sat back on her heels (her actual heels, not her shoes—they'd fallen off when he'd carried her to the settee) and reached around to unclasp her bra. The second she did, the straps snapped forward and so did the clingy cups. It was like an underwear slingshot repelled by luscious skin. She dropped it on the rug and all that was left was this topless maid in crinolines and fishnets.

"Clean something," he said, staring at her full and yet still perky breasts.

Kitty looked around, and he still stared at her tits when she turned. "Clean what?"

"The windows," he said. He gave her his pocket square and said, "Use this."

"Ahh."

She tiptoed to her shoes and slipped them on her feet.

Then she walked to the large window, which faced out on the back gardens and pond. Unless gardener was in today, nobody should be hanging around back there.

Kitty reached up to scour the window in circles with Reg's square. He could just imagine the feel of cold glass pressing against her big breasts. In a way, he wanted to run outside to see what her soft cock looked like pressed up against the glass and surrounded by crinolines.

Flattened dick. Flattened breasts. Skin pressed against a clear, cold window pane. She didn't seem to mind exposing herself to the world, or at least the back garden.

Reg's cock hardened as he strolled across the room. Hardened and bounced, he should say. His heat-seeking missile knew just where to land.

He trapped his new maid against the window and lifted her crinolines. She gasped as he guided his throbbing dick into her salivating slit. He didn't push it straight in, either. He rubbed his fat tip up and down her chasm, feeling the strength of her pussy trying to suck him in.

"You want it so bad," he said, whispering the words in her ear. "My naughty maid is almost naked and she wants my huge hard cock in her cunt."

"Oh yes, Mister Reg!"

She squirmed and he teased her a little more, pressing just his tip to the mouth of her pussy. "Look at you, pressing your parts to my dirty windows. Look at you, showing off for all to see."

"Only for you, Mister Reg! I'll do anything for you."

"Will you scream when you come?" Reg asked as he jammed his cock right up inside her snatch.

She did him one better and screamed right then, and it seemed authentic because he lifted her right out of her shoes. "Oh, Mister Reg! I didn't expect that."

"Expect what?" he asked.

She stammered, "I knew it was big, but if feels *so* big! So *huge*! It's stretching me out inside."

He loved every word, but he loved her body more, and he slid his hands between the window and her front.

He grabbed her breasts roughly as he thrust inside her, deep as his dick would go.

She screamed and he went at her again, another violent thrust as he manhandled her tits.

"Yes, Mister Reg! Yes, harder! Harder!"

She'd asked twice, but that certainly wasn't necessary.

He filled her full of dick and growled as he played with her tits. They were so big that flesh pushed out between his spread fingers. He worked her so hard her pussy spilled juice down his balls. He'd never encountered a woman so wet, and he loved knowing he'd inspired her arousal.

Kitty stood her ground in those dangerous heels, but forced her bottom back into the saddle of his hips. The more he gave, the more she took, the more she wanted, the more she pleaded with him to fill her full of cum.

"Yes, Mister Reg! Yes, fuck my pussy! Fuck it fast!"

Holding tight to her precious tits, he drove his dick in her like a machine.

He'd never fucked like this before. His body had never been so driven to provide pleasure. But for Kitty, he'd do anything. She wanted him to come, and that's what he'd do.

Squeezing her breasts tight, he blasted his load deep inside her snatch.

His muscles stiffened for a moment, trapping Kitty in his arms against the window.

He wished they could stay like that forever. Then all the world would be able to see Kitty's unfathomable breasts through the glass. And her soft cock and her splayed lips and her crinolines.

What a magical moment. What a beautiful girl.

When Reg released his hold on Kitty, she moved across the room in an extended sort of fall. He wondered what she was doing until she reached for her water glass. She took an extended sip, and then laid face-up on the rug.

Every time she panted, her breasts rose and her nipples peaked. Her cock wasn't hard, but it had been pumping juice against her thigh while he fucked her.

Reg lay down at her side and wrapped an arm around her naked belly. He pulled her close and she didn't push him away.

"How long did my aunt hire you for?" he asked.

"She didn't say. Only said I start today and if you want me, you keep me."

"My own personal maid?" he asked.

She nodded and giggled. "Maid for you."

"Made for me."

Kitty sighed and so did Reg. He'd never napped on the floor of the drawing room before, but now was as good a time as any to start doing new things.

Futa Cheerleader Car Wash

The girls brought their sparkly signs to the roadside and waved them high above their heads.

"Car wash! Charity car wash! Support your local team!"

Most of the vehicles that drove on by were in need of a good scrub, but those weren't the ones that stopped. In fact, despite the girls' tight little uniforms, despite their bouncing breasts, despite their short skirts flapping up every time they jumped, five minutes went by before anyone even slowed down.

He drove a red convertible. He had a tan and a dark moustache, dark sunglasses.

"Charity car was?" he asked. "What charity would I be supporting?"

"The local team," Blondie said, leaning over the passenger side to give the guy a good look at her cleavage. When his eyes fixed on her boobs, she asked, "What's your name, big fella?"

"Warren," he replied.

"Warren," the other girls chuckled.

"Sounds like a rich guy name," Asia added. "Are you a rich guy, Warren?"

"Well, I don't know about rich..."

Erin tossed her orange curls behind her shoulder and took a step toward the car. "But I bet you've got a spare buck or two for the team."

"Which team is this?" he asked, without removing his gaze from Blondie's spectacular cleavage.

The girls giggled and said, "The cheerleading team, of course!"

"These are our old uniforms," Asia said.

Erin told him, "The day I turned eighteen, it's like I burst right out of mine!"

"Me too," Blondie said.

Asia nodded. "Me three. We need to fundraise for new ones."

Blondie bent even lower over the side of Warren's car, so her breasts swung heavily, barely held in check by her cheerleading sweater.

As her tiny cross sparkled in the sun, Warren nodded and said, "You seem like nice girls. I'd be happy to help you out."

They told him to pull up behind the concrete building so they could work in the sun, but away from the dusty road.

Carrying their handmade signs, they ran behind him and caught up soon enough.

It was quieter here, away from the road. Behind them was an industrial lot, but nobody worked there on the weekends. They couldn't be sure that no one would pull in to use the coin-operated car wash, but if so many drivers had passed up the opportunity to get washed down by three gorgeous cheerleaders, what chance did a concrete building stand?

"Want me to put the top up?" Warren asked.

"No," Erin said. "Leave it down."

"Want me to get out? I saw a coffee shop back there a ways. I could come back when you're done."

Blondie stood with her hip bones pressing into the driver's side door. "You're not going anywhere, Mister."

Asia climbed on his hood with a huge soapy sponge and started washing it on her hands and knees. Her full, fleshy breasts swung with every circle of the arm.

She'd barely gotten started when Erin came over with a sun-warmed bucket of water and dumped it over Asia's back.

Letting out a scream, Asia turned to Erin. "You brat!"

She threw her sopping sponge at Erin, and it smacked Erin's top with a wet squelching sound.

"You girls certainly like to have fun," Warren said as the sponge fell to the gravel ground, leaving Erin's sweater soaked through.

Asia remained kneeling on the hood when Blondie emerged from the concrete building, tugging a garden hose behind her. "You girls want to get wet?"

"Nooo!"

Erin and Asia both screamed and held their hands up in front of them as Blondie squeezed the trigger.

"Maybe I should put the top up," Warren said as shimmering water cascaded like a rainbow from the leggy blonde to the girls by the car.

Erin raced for another bucket of water and threw that at Blondie. The wall of water hit her with such force it drove her back. The spray arced high, like a fountain, and everybody felt it strike them in huge, hard droplets.

Warren slid to the passenger side, then opened the door and slipped out.

"Where do you think you're going?" Erin cried.

"Yeah," said Asia. "We're not done washing your car yet."

"You seem to be more interested in washing each other," he said.

Blondie dropped the garden hose in the gravel and walked over to Warren. "Don't you want to stay and watch?"

Erin walked up close behind her, so the two were almost touching. "We like being watched. Isn't that right, Asia?"

"No," Asia said, bending low on all fours on the hood. "We love it."

Warren swallowed hard as Erin's hands slipped around Blondie's bare midriff. He'd have thought the move would shock the blonde, but instead Blondie turned her head and parted her lips just slightly.

Just slightly enough for Erin to slip her tongue inside.

Their saliva sparkled in the sunlight as they kissed. They made kittenish little mewling sounds, too. It was like living in a dream.

This is what girls did together? Rounded up unsuspecting men to watch as they made out?

"Get back in the car," Asia said while Blondie turned her back on him and her front on Erin. "We're going to show you a drive-in movie. Except not a movie. A live action performance."

Warren wasn't sure how he ended up in his car. He didn't remember his feet moving or curling his fingers around the handle or opening the door. His mind was entirely preoccupied by the barely legal beauties kissing as they backed up against the side of his front end.

"Ooh, you're getting me all wet!" Blondie complained.

"Is that a problem?" Erin asked.

Asia jumped down to grab another sudsy sponge. She leapt back up and stood on his hood in bare feet. Then she squeezed the suds over Blondie's head.

The two girls were so into their make-out session that neither of them seemed to notice the soap running slowly down Blondie's side. When it reached her bare arm, she shrieked, as though she thought it were some kind of bug.

When she saw what Asia was doing, she scooped up the soap with her opposite hand and threw it back. "Brat!"

"You're the brat," Asia said. "You two always start together and then nobody kisses me."

"You want to be kissed?" Erin asked. "Where?"

Asia's eyes widened. She eased down until her skirt met the hood of Warren's car. "You mean I've got a choice?"

"You bet," Blondie replied.

Erin grabbed Asia's ankles and gave them a tug. The girl fell flat on her back on the hood with her legs spread. Erin then ran her hand up the girl's thigh, under the girl's cheerleading skirt. Cupping that mound of arousal, she said, "We could kiss you here."

Blondie covered Asia's mouth. "Or we could kiss you here. Make your choice."

With Blondie's palm muffling her words, Asia pointed down, then up. "First there, then there."

"You slut," Blondie teased, and slapped Asia's wet boobs inside that sopping sweater. "You choose a pussy kiss before a mouth kiss?"

"Isn't she a slut?" Erin asked Warren.

In a daze, he stammered, "I... I..."

"Sluts don't deserve cheerleading sweaters," Blondie said, and tore off Asia's tight wet top. "And sluts don't deserve bras, either."

Asia arched slightly and reached both hands behind her back. When she undid the clasp, both cups sprang away from her skin, revealing her big breasts in all their glory.

"Look at these tits," Blondie said—maybe to Warren, maybe to Erin. Maybe to Asia herself. She pulled Asia closer so she could smack those beautiful breasts together, making them bounce and recoil off one another.

The girl had no tan lines. Her skin was consistently golden, and her nipples boasted a pinkish-peachish colour that darkened as they puckered in the sunlight.

These cheerleaders sure liked taking chances! Anyone could catch them out here, between the carwash and the industrial park. But they didn't seem to care. Like they said: they wanted to be watched.

And with bodies like those, who could blame them?

Warren adjusted himself. His jeans had grown tighter than they'd ever been.

"Are you sure you want your first kiss down there?" Blondie asked, and flicked Asia's nipples violently enough to make the girl shriek. "We could start here instead."

"You want to kiss my nipples?" Asia whimpered.

"We want to kiss you everywhere," Erin said. "But it's your choice where we start."

Staring up at the sky, Asia swallowed hard. Then she rolled up her wet skirt. "Start down there."

"Down there," Erin laughed. "She can't say what it's called."

"I can so!"

"Then say it," Erin teased as she grabbed Asia's purple panties with both hands. "Say the word!"

Blondie hovered close to Asia's breasts, like she could hardly resist the pull they exerted on her mouth. She extended her tongue so close the two pink parts almost touched. But she pulled away when Asia said, "My pussy first!"

The other girls laughed and Blondie backed off as Erin pulled down Asia's panties.

With Asia lying flat on the hood, Warren had a perfect view when the girl arched her hips to let her friend remove those purple panties.

A perfect view of her sweet pussy.

Black hair, but not much.

Juicy pink slit that opened wider as she parted her legs for the other two cheerleaders.

"Wow," Blondie said. "What a pretty puss."

"Yeah," Erin echoed. "Wish I had one."

"I wish you did too," Blondie said.

"Then who would fuck you senseless?"

"True." Blondie tilted her head and her blonde locks tumbled to one side. "Then I wish you had both, like me."

"Oooh, yeah!" Erin ran her hands under Blondie's belly top, clutching those big breasts and growling. "Your tits are making me so hard!"

"Your hands are making me so hard!"

Asia cleared her throat. "Hello! You were supposed to kiss my clit!"

"Right," Erin said. "But, god, now all I want to do is fuck. I'm so hard it hurts."

"Well, lick my pussy first!" Asia said.

The other two leaned forward in their tight little uniforms, both sticking out their tongues in anticipation. When their heads hit together between Asia's legs, they looked at each other and both said, "I'm going first."

Blondie rolled her eyes and waved Erin in. "Age before beauty."

"Shut up. I'm only three weeks older than you."

Asia covered her eyes and cried, "Would you both just kiss my cunt! Kiss my tits! Kiss anything! Just kiss me!"

Blondie crawled up her body until she was beside the girl on the hood, her head at the level of Asia's breasts. While she brought the nearest one to her lips, Erin plunged that freckled face between Asia's thighs.

The nearly naked girl spread out on the hood of the car lurched when her friends licked her. "Oh my GOD!"

"Your pussy's so sweet," Erin said. "Tastes like honey and mangoes. So, so sweet."

Blondie nodded as she traced her tongue in circles around Asia's nipple. "Your nipple's sweet too. And salty. It's both."

"Stop talking," Asia begged. "Just lick me!"

The girls went at their friend, devouring her flesh like food. Their velvet tongues sparkled in the sunlight as they licked and lapped. They really seemed to be enjoying themselves.

Erin dug her nails into Asia's thighs to keep them apart.

Blondie sculpted the girl's tits like clay pots.

Their efforts were obviously working, because Asia's whines turned to groans, and then moans and then grunts! She grabbed Erin's curly orange hair and arched her hips, driving her pussy at the girl's face. Erin shrieked, but didn't fight her friend off. Didn't even try. Just kept licking and sucking that slobbering cunt.

"You're gonna make her come!" Blondie cried.

"You both are," Asia said, and Blondie got back to work, sucking tits like she was getting paid by how hard the girl climaxed.

And hard was an understatement.

Asia cried out so loudly Warren said, "Shush! Shush! Someone's going to call the police if they hear you screaming like that!"

But the girls paid him no mind.

Erin and Blondie kept at Asia's pussy and breasts until the girl flipped over on the hot hood.

"Ouch!" she cried when her sensitive nipples met the surface.

Blondie raced to the garden hose and sprayed the car and her friend with cold water to give her some relief. Then she turned the hose on Erin, who screamed, especially when Blondie aimed the flow at her crotch.

"Too much!" Erin said, covering the tent where her skirt clung to her hardness.

"Gosh, that sun is hot," Blondie said, dropping the hose in the gravel. "I'm sweating through my top."

So she pulled it off and threw it on the ground, easy as that. Then she undid her bra and tossed that down too.

Blondie's breasts were unfathomably gorgeous. Her skin obviously wasn't as naturally golden as it seemed, because she had distinct tan lines. She'd obviously soaked up the sun in a bikini. That way, her sweet pink nipples had been protected from harsh UV rays. They remained fresh and rosy, perky and bright.

Her breasts bounced as she made her way between Asia's legs. "Are you going to flip so I can eat your pussy?"

Asia was still breathing hard, struggling after a spectacular orgasm. "My clit can't take any more. You'll have to fuck me."

"You're the boss," Blondie replied, seeming not the least bit disappointed as she rolled up her skirt and pushed down her panties.

Out leapt an erection of staggering proportions. Its tip was every bit as pink as Blondie's nipples. Her panty zone was every bit as pale as her untanned tits. She had a few sweet curls of blonde pubes, like doll's hair, which gave her dick a distinct personality.

"What are you waiting for?" Asia asked. "Stick it in me, Blondie. After Erin's tongue, I need a good fuck."

"What's that supposed to mean?" Erin asked.

Setting her cheek flat on the hood of the car, Asia said, "It's like a meal: your tongue was the main course and Blondie's dick is dessert."

Blondie slapped Asia's bare ass with her massive erection. "Fuck that! My dick is the main course. Erin's tongue was an appetizer."

Erin pushed Blondie from behind, driving her dick unexpectedly through the valley of Asia's butt cheeks.

"Hey!" Asia squealed. "I didn't say put it in my butt!"

"I'm not," Blondie said. "Keep your pants on. I just slipped."

"Well, don't slip again!"

"It was my fault," Erin admitted. "I'm just getting itchy, over here."

"So take off your top," Blondie said.

"Not that kind of itchy."

"Well, take off your top anyway."

Asia laughed until Blondie pumped her thick slab of meat between the girl's legs. Then her eyes widened and she melted against the hood of the car. "Ohhhh..."

"You like that, huh?"

"Ohhhhh...."

Blondie pulled back and then launched her dick inside Asia's pussy again.

"Ohhhhhhh...."

"Is that all you've got to say for yourself?"

Asia swallowed, then lifted her head slightly. She gave up, didn't say anything, just moaned while Blondie plunged that spectacular dick inside her again and again.

Meanwhile, Erin followed her friend's suggestion and took off her top.

She hadn't worn a bra. Never did. Her mosquito bite tits didn't warrant covering. But the one thing they did have going for them was how incredibly long and pointy they became when she was aroused.

Like right now.

Her nips stuck way out in front of her, and she tugged on them as she watched one friend fucking the other.

In fact, when she tugged on her tits, she felt it in her dick.

So she pushed down her panties and rolled up her skirt and let her dick guide her toward the nearest pussy, which happened to belong to Blondie.

She was sort of jealous of Warren's perspective. From where he sat, he must be able to see Asia flat on her back and Blondie's full breasts waving in the air.

When Blondie leaned forward, her tits smacked Asia's. The sound of boobs slapping boobs ricocheted off the concrete blocks that formed the car wash wall. And that sound was soon joined by the crunch of gravel under Erin's feet.

Blondie obviously wasn't expecting it, because she shrieked when Erin rammed her.

Well, maybe her brain wasn't expecting it, but her pussy sure was. When Erin stabbed it, it burst like a water balloon, blasting her with wet hot pussy juice. So much pussy juice it soaked Erin's thighs and ran slowly down her skin.

"Holy Jesus, give a girl some warning!" Blondie said.

"Sorry."

But as soon as the castigation had left Blondie's lips she'd turned back to Asia, rutting between the girl's legs, giving her a very filling meat course.

Erin wrapped her arms around Blondie's front as she thrust in her friend's tight cunt. She found those breasts that inspired jealousy in every heart and squeezed them roughly.

When Blondie didn't react strongly enough, Erin dug her nails in. That gave her some satisfaction, because Blondie shrieked and elbowed her. "Cut it out! Jesus! You trying to kill me?"

"My nails aren't going to kill you," Erin groaned.

"Well, stop!"

So Erin moved down to Asia's big breast, which meant kind of pressing Blondie flat between them. That way she had Asia's tits scooped up in her palms and Blondie's against the back of her hands. Best of both worlds.

And Blondie must have liked it more than she was willing to admit, because her pussy clamped tight around Erin's huge hard-on.

"God, I love dicking you," Erin growled.

"I love dicking the little one," she said of Asia.

"I love dicking her too. We should both dick her at once."

"No!" Asia squealed. "I told you to stay out of my butt."

"Who said anything about your butt?" Erin asked, pulling her erection from Blondie's cunt and guiding it forward, following the straight line of her friend's swollen shaft.

"I don't think it'll fit," Blondie said.

Erin bent slightly. "We'll make it fit."

Blondie pulled out just enough that Erin could stick her dickhead into the mouth of Asia's pussy.

"What are you two doing?"

"Don't scream!" Warren pleaded. "If someone calls the cops we'll all get hauled in."

"We're both gonna fuck you," Blondie told Asia. "So shut up and relax."

Asia breathed in hard, then closed her eyes. "Okay. It's worth a shot."

Erin held Blondie tight, so their bodies were one. They thrust together, driving both their dicks inside Asia's snatch.

The girl was obviously trying to relax, but no barely legal pussy was built for two cocks.

They stretched her and she screamed, and Warren kept saying, "Shush! Shush! Shush! Don't make so much noise!"

"Oh God, she's so tight," Erin moaned.

"Tighter than your asshole," Blondie added as their dicks throbbed together inside Asia's snatch.

This time, when Erin fondled Blondie's tits, she didn't complain. In fact, she sighed and moaned and said, "Your nipples are stabbing me."

Erin would have laughed, but she was concentrating too hard on fucking Asia's tight cunt.

Asia buried her head in her hands and said, "You two are so biiiiig!"

"We know," Blondie replied. "And you're so smaaaaall."

Erin was getting close. Her balls swung freely and fiercely, and she could feel Blondie's slit leaking pussy juice all over her root.

Two pussies in such close proximity! How could she hold back?

Her dick swelled as it prepared to blast a load in Asia's cunt. She warned them both she was about to come, and then came mid-warning.

"Jesus Christ," Blondie said. "I feel your cum all over my cockhead. I'm gonna... I'm gonna... Oh Christ Almighty!"

She blasted her load too, filling Asia with a second load of jizz.

They both pulled out and Asia stayed put. Then they waved Warren over and said, "You gotta get a look at this."

He stepped awkwardly out of the car. It wasn't easy walking on three legs.

But it was worth the sight of that young cheerleader's swollen cunt leaking rivers of cum down her labia and her legs.

"Want to hose her off?" Blondie asked, and he thought maybe she meant... until he realized she was holding the garden hose.

"Oh," he said. "Sure."

He didn't really expect three hot cheerleaders to take him on, but he sort of hoped they would. But that was okay. It was enough just watching. Anyway, he had an on-again off-again girlfriend he wouldn't mind paying a visit. She'd be at work right about now, but it wouldn't be the first time they'd fucked upright in a bathroom stall.

Blondie handed him the hose and he blasted it at the gravel first, just to see how hard it would be.

"Blast her cunt!" Erin said, grabbing his hand and aiming the hose at Asia's posterior.

Erin's piercing nipples brushed his arm and he nearly jizzed his jeans.

"No, you're only getting her butt cheek," Blondie said, and approached from the other side.

Now her big boobs were brushing up against his other arm while she helped him aim and, god, he couldn't keep it together much longer.

He shot the hose at the cheerleader's pussy, and the sound of the soaring water changed when it entered her cunt. He was actually washing her friends' cum from the inside out.

"Lower," Erin said. "Get her clit."

Erin moved the nozzle in his hand, and Asia shrieked.

Then rolled.

When she was on her back, she lifted her legs in a V and screamed, "Yesssss!!!"

"You're making her come!" the girls said, both hugging him so hard their very different breasts played against his sides.

They jumped and squealed, which made him shoot water up Asia's chest and splash her face, for which he apologized profusely. The other girls helped him aim again, and Asia grabbed her ankles and howled.

Warren's hand went numb and he dropped the hose. Asia was still screaming as she slid down the hood. The other two rushed over to catch her before her butt landed on the gravel.

"Oh boy, that was intense!"

Warren could see the throbbing outline of his dick through his jeans.

He needed to get off.

He needed to get gone.

Rushing to his car, he asked, "How much to I owe you?"

"We really didn't do very much," Blondie said.

Erin nodded as they propped Asia up. "Yeah, call it a freebie."

Warren pulled a wad of cash from his wallet and tossed it in the air as he drove off, calling you, "You deserve it."

The girls laughed as bills fluttered in the air.

The guy was gone before his money hit the ground.

"Wow, those are fifties," Asia said, still gasping for breath.

Blondie brought over their folding chairs and set them up in the gravel. If there's one thing they could all agree on, it was that they deserved a breather.

Asia pushed off her skirt. "Tan time."

"Good idea," Blondie said, and took off her skirt too.

Erin followed suit. "Hey, next time let's be church girls raising money for bible camp."

Blondie covered her cross. "Blasphemy."

"I like it," Asia said. "Or nuns."

"Not nuns," Erin tsked. "Nobody wants their car washed by nuns."

"You're right. Not nuns."

Blondie slid her cross between her lips and sucked gently. When it fell out, she said, "Okay, fine, we'll be church girls."

Erin stretched her arms out over her head and sighed. "I love summertime!"

The girls all smiled and sighed as they lazed in the sun, fifties fluttering at their feet.

Fucked by the Futa Traffic Cop

THIS STORY STARTS THE same way as every other story about getting pulled over by a sexy cop in the middle of the night. Doesn't end the same way, though.

You'll find out soon enough.

It was late and I was lost, driving down this remote stretch of highway at two in the morning, wishing I could read that map by the light of the moon.

Not that it would do me a lick of good. I didn't know where the hell I was.

So when those flashing lights came up behind me, I gotta admit: I was relieved.

No sirens. I knew I wasn't speeding. Cop car made a beeping sound to indicate I should pull over, and I did.

No sweat.

You shoulda seen this gal getting out of the cruiser: blonde hair swept back in a bun, uniform so tight I thought her boobs would pop all those buttons down the front of her dark blue shirt. Slim body, not too tall. And then the typical gear around her waist: the billy club and gun, radio and cuffs.

She was a sight to behold.

The traffic cop strutted her stuff toward my vehicle as I rolled down the window to greet her.

I said, "Evenin' ma'am," beating her to the punch.

She said, "Officer Paine, to you."

"Evenin' Officer Paine." I took my map off the passenger seat. "Maybe you can help me. I can't seem to find where I'm going."

Taking two steps back, she drew her gun and said, "No sudden movements!"

I'd never had a gun pointed in my face. You can't imagine how truly terrifying it would be, especially when ya done nothin wrong.

How could I convince her I was innocent as they come?

I let the map flutter against the steering wheel while I raised both hands. "Hold up now, Officer. I ain't done what you think, whatever that is. I'm just a lost soul trying to find my way in the darkness."

She slowly brought her gun down and slid it back into the holster. "Lost, are ya? Most men wouldn't admit a thing like that."

"I'm not like most men," I said.

"I'm not like most women," she told me.

"I can see that."

She cocked her head and got a mean look in her eye. "What's that supposed to mean?"

"Nothing," I said, feeling nervous, sweating bullets. "Only you got a real forceful personality. You tell a man what to do, he's gonna do it. That's for sure."

"Are you sayin you wouldn't normally do what a woman tells ya?" she asked in a gruff, flinty voice.

"Me? Oh, I always do what I'm told, ma'am. Like I said: I'm not like other men."

"I see."

Officer Paine stuck her head inside my window so fast I nearly jumped. She took a deep inhale, which made me mighty conscious of when I last showered.

Then she said, "You been drinkin tonight?"

"No," I said. "I ain't much of a drinker, in all honesty."

"I see."

She didn't seem to believe anything I said to her, so I tried asking again for directions.

I don't think she was even listening to that bit, because she opened my door and said, "Step out of the vehicle."

My heart wouldn't quit pounding like a drum, but I did what she asked. I stepped out and said, "What's this about, Officer?"

"You ever walked a line?"

"Well, no," I told her. "Like I said, I ain't much for the drink."

"You're gonna walk one tonight," she said, taking a slim metal flashlight from her holster to illuminated the yellow line.

"Isn't this a little dangerous?" I asked. "Stepping out in the middle of the road when a car could come streaking by at any moment?"

"Ain't been any vehicle but yours down this stretch all night."

Made me wonder who she hoped to catch speeding camped by the side of a deserted highway.

"Git," she growled, flicking the light at the line. "I thought you said you listened to women no question. I thought you said you ain't like other men."

"That's true," I told her. "More than you know."

"Well then do as I tell ya and walk that line." She then sneered, "Unless you're too drunk to walk it straight."

"I swear I ain't been drinking," I told her, but that obviously wasn't good enough. She squinted her dark eyes at me and her fingers wriggled at her side, just over the holster where she'd lodged her gun.

She flicked the flashlight again and I hopped to it.

I'll be honest with you: I'm not what you'd call a daring man. I don't go out of my way looking for adventure. So traipsing into the middle of the road in the middle of the night didn't get me all riled up the way it would for some.

Fact is, I was shakin in my boots as I put one foot in front of the other.

Officer Paine stood a damn sight back. If a truck came barreling down the highway at top speed, it wouldn't be her in danger. And me? I'd be flat as a pancake.

Least I wouldn't be worried about finding my way in the dark.

"Good enough," the officer told me.

I crossed the empty lane quickly. Being in the road like that got my heart racing, and I couldn't slow it down.

As I approached my vehicle, Officer Pain picked up the map off my seat and stared down at the white powder I'd spilled there earlier.

"Well, well, well," she said, like the cat that got the canary. "What have we got here, Mister Upstanding Citizen?"

"Oh, that." Don't know why I felt so nervous. There was a simple explanation. "That's sugar substitute. I spilled the packet when I was putting it in my coffee."

"Sugar substitute?" she said, sounding like she didn't believe a word.

"I watch what I eat."

She raised her brow. "Sure you do."

"If you taste it you'll see. It's sweetener for my coffee."

"Lab tests will verify that," she said coolly. "If what you're saying is true."

Grabbing my arm, she pulled me around to the front of the car and forced me down. The hood was warm against my face, but not hot. Warm enough that I could feel it through my shirt, though. Good thing I'd been through the car wash, or it would have got my clothes all dirty.

Mind you, I'd been driving along dusty roads all day.

"I want to see both hands behind your back," Officer Paine instructed.

That's when I heard the metallic shriek of handcuffs.

My heart beat a mile a minute.

"Am I under arrest? Please, you can't arrest me, Officer!"

"Why's that?" she asked, like she was enjoying this. Like arresting me was sweet as taffy and she just wanted to take her time with it.

"I'm not drunk," I said. "I wasn't speeding. That white stuff's nothing more than coffee sweetener. I'm a law-abiding citizen! I don't deserve to be arrested!"

"That's for me to decide," the cop growled. "In case you forgot, I'm an officer of the law. If I see fit to dish out a little discipline, that's my prerogative."

I didn't think that was strictly true, but what choice did I have once she got those cuffs on me?

That was the first time I'd ever felt the sharp metallic clink of cuffs around my wrists. I expected them to be cold, but they weren't. I guess they got warmed up, being so close to her body... which was undeniably arousing.

With my chest down flat on the hood of my car, I couldn't get up. Couldn't move, 'cept wriggle side to side. Even then, it sure put a strain on my shoulder.

"Are you taking me to the station?" I asked.

Her voice sounded different when she said, "The choice is yours."

It came out more like a purr than a growl, and that made me real suspicious of what she was up to back there.

"I could take you to the slammer," she went on. "Lock you up for the night, 'til we run some tests on that white powder."

"If you taste it—"

She cut me off. "Orrrrr we could come to some sort of... agreement?"

"What kind of agreement?" I asked, feeling more innocent than I had in all my adult life.

Officer Paine reached around and found my belt with both hands.

"What are you doing?" I shrieked, sounding very far from masculine.

She unbuckled it masterfully, then released the latched and unzipped my fly. God only knows how she managed without being able to see what she was doing. The only lights illuminating the scene were her vehicle's headlights and the swirling, silent police ones on top of the cruiser.

I'd never felt so apprehensive.

My pants hit the road with a swift thud, thanks to my wallet and pocket change weighing them down. Officer Paine was only interested in my body, it seemed. She stroked my hardness and cooed like a dove.

"Someone's raring to go."

She bucked against me, and I felt her night stick bump my butt.

"I can't explain it," I told her. "I don't know why it's like that."

"You're excited," she said.

"No, no, I'm not excited."

"Why sure you are." Her voice went all high and fluttery for a second. "You like it when a woman takes charge. I got you cuffed, got your trousers down by your ankles, and there ain't nothing you can do about it. I decide what comes next."

That wasn't the whole truth, but she had no way of knowing.

Although I had a feeling she'd come to find out sooner rather than later.

"So," I asked her, "What comes next?"

She laughed, but it was more like a cackle. Officer Paine was damn sure pleased with herself as she pushed my underpants down past my knees.

"Oh please," I begged. "Just toss me in the slammer. I'll take my chances."

"You're no fun," she teased, wrapped one hand around my balls to play with them.

She cooed and hummed as she jingled my bells, and the more she did it the harder my dick grew against the hood of my car. I lifted myself up as best I could and I shook my shirt around until my dick was against my skin, sticking straight up. That way at least I had a layer of cotton between my hard-on and the vehicle.

Officer Paine stopped rubbing my balls and I knew we had a problem. She let go and said, "What's this? I got something wet all over my hand."

"Yes, I... meant to tell you..."

My heart went off like an old alarm clock, but there weren't no button to stop it.

I arched my back and turned my head just enough to spot Officer Paine grabbing hold of her flashlight.

"No," I said. "Please."

She shone the light on her palm. "What *is* this stuff? It's all glossy. Feels like..."

I couldn't watch, mostly because my back wasn't strong enough to stay arched that way. I collapsed on my car as she crouched behind me. I could feel the heat of her light shining on my balls... and then her fingers moving between them, parting them slowly.

"My lordy-loo!" she squealed. "You got one just like me!"

I started to turn too fast, not remembering that my wrists were cuffed behind me. I fell back down on the hood of the car and asked, "What do you mean just like you?"

"You got a pussy between your balls!" she said, shoving two fingers in the wet crease between them. "Ain't that a laugh, because I got one too!"

"A p—" I found I was too shy to say the word *pussy* in front of a person of the female persuasion. "You've got one too? Well, so do most gals I know."

"Sure, I s'pose. But most gals ain't got one 'a these!" She dropped her trousers, pushed down her underpants, and let a huge slab of salami slide between my cheeks. "See? We're the same. I got a pussy 'n a pecker, just like you. Well, ain't that a hoot!"

A cold sweat broke across my brow and I wriggled against my cuffs.

"What's your problem, citizen? You resisting arrest all 'a sudden?"

I didn't need to see her hard-on to know how huge it was. I could feel its girth between my butt cheeks.

She reached for her night stick and I guess I could have kicked at her when she was bent over like that, but what next? Run for it with my dick out and my pants around my ankles?

Officer Paine held me down against the hood of the car, with that night stick across the small of my back. "You're acting mighty strange."

"Not really," I reasoned. "Wouldn't anybody act this way?"

"It's like you're nervous or something."

"Nervous?" I cried. "Of course I'm nervous! A cop's coming at me with a schlong the size of her billy club."

She slid her cock down the crease of my balls, where they parted to make way for my hot, ready hole. "What's 'a matter? Don't tell me you ain't never been fucked."

My heart hammered the hood of my car. "I... I... I've put things in there."

"But you ain't never been fucked by a cock," she teased. "You got a sweet virgin pussy all juiced up and ready for the taking."

My knees shook. My legs trembled.

"Aww, don't you worry, pup. Officer Paine'll be gentle."

Her cockhead found my crease easy as pie. She heaved her night stick toward my ass like a rolling pin as she pushed her dick inside me.

I always thought it would hurt, if it happened. Though I never expected to get fucked by a cop... or by anyone with a cock, for that matter.

If you didn't look too closely, you might never know I had a pussy hidden between my balls. I'd been extra careful in my dealings with women. Never let them look down there or feel around too much. And most 'a my girlfriends seemed pretty okay with that. I suppose I'd always dated the kind of girls who would lie back and let me get on top and do my thing. That was the only kind of sex I'd ever had.

Until that night with Officer Paine.

She'd found my cunt no problem at all. She'd found it and stuck a dick in it, and I was shivering head to toe because I never imagined it. What an experience! She had me spread across the hood of my car like jam on toast, and she was rolling my ass with that night stick, rolling me out like biscuit dough.

And all the while she fucked me from behind like it was goin out of style.

So much for gentle. If this was her version of gentle, I'd hate to see what rough sex meant.

She rammed me with that hot rod, over and over again. Once she'd planted her dick in my snatch, I knew she'd never want to take it out. And, truth was, I didn't want her going anywhere.

Sure I was scared. Who wouldn't be, getting fucked by a cop on the side of the road? Middle of the night. Remote section of highway. Anyone could come by at any moment. Gang 'a bikers could bang me all night long and nothing I could do with those cuffs keeping me in place.

One dick was more 'an enough to start. And the more she slammed her hips against my ass, the more glad I was that she had such big damn cock. Because the friction it built inside my wet pussy, I tell you, that was some mean heat!

Like I said, I always worried it would hurt... and sometimes it did, but not the way I thought it would. I thought when she put it in me, my knees would buckle and I'd fold over in agony.

That's not how it happened.

She stretched me to my limits, damn straight, but the only thing that hurt was when she smashed her body clear into mine. Because, when she buried her dick balls-deep in my cunt, that motion compressed my nuts between my legs, and that pressure bordered right on the edge of pain.

The officer rammed me over and over again, dragging that night stick up the curve of my ass and then starting over at the small of my back. Every time her body smacked my balls, that sharp slap hurt a little less and felt a little more like the pleasure of being fucked.

"I'm gonna come in your damn pussy," she hollered as something hard like a pebble smacked my ass.

"What was that?" I asked.

Officer Paine wailed as she hammered my cunt. "I'm breathin too hard, sugar dumpling. My boobs are bustin my uniform clear to kingdom come!"

The harder she fucked me, the more buttons flew off her shirt. When I turned to get a look, it was hanging clear open and her clean white bra glowed bright against the night sky.

Her breasts were pale and huge, but I loved her plain white brassiere best of all. She wasn't some nasty cop who went around fucking everyone she could find. At heart, she was just an innocent southern girl taking on a man whose pussy had never been fucked.

I bucked back against her, feeling her hip bones bang my ass. She must have liked that, because she cried out. My body reacted to her shrieks, locking on her cock, milking her shaft until she shimmied and shrieked and howled at the moon.

"Oh yeah," she cried. "Yeah, baby. That's right. You want my cock to explode inside you."

"Yes!" I replied, and that one word seemed enough to make her come.

I turned to catch the expression of pain and bliss cross her face. Her brow furrowed, then all that tension dissipated. Her bottom lip trembled. She praised the Almighty Lord before pulling her dick from my snatch and flipping me over on the car.

"You'd better be hard, because I'm ready to go!"

She pushed and pulled me until I was sitting on the hood of my vehicle, both hands planted flat behind me, my legs hanging down, not quite touching the road. Officer Paine tried stepping out of her panties and trousers, but she couldn't shake out of them with her boots on. Had'ta bend down and unlace them.

After all that hassle, she had on nothing but her buttonless shirt, gleaming white bra, and cute little bobby socks.

Her dick hung at half-mast, still dripping cum when she climbed into my lap like a bunny. She didn't seem so intimidating with her arms wrapped around me and her tongue lost inside my ear.

"Oh I can't wait to wrap my pussy 'round your cock," she said.

"Well, have at it," I told her. "Don't let me stop you."

"So you want it too?"

"More than you, I bet."

"Doubt that," she said, pulling my dick out from under my shirt.

Her grip was forceful as all get-out, and I told her, "I ain't gonna last long."

"I ain't gonna need long," she told me.

Dropping down on my dick, she took me into her pussy like her body was my home. I'd been inside other gals, but it never felt like this before. Officer Paine's pussy was not just hot and tropical, but her big balls tickled my shaft and bobbed against my thighs.

She had such a sense of fun about fucking me. She bounced on my lap like my cock was a toy. She loved it. That much was clear.

My heart raced from more than just the excitement of making it with a stranger. Officer Paine didn't feel like a stranger anymore. In fact, I don't think I'd felt so close to anyone, even after knowing 'em for years.

"Yes," I whispered, breathin in the scent of her hair. Everything about this girl turned precious as she bounced in my lap.

"You like my sweet pussy, sugar pie?"

"I love it," I told her. "I could eat a slice of you every dang day and never get tired of it."

She hugged me tight, and that's when I realized she was holding me in place. If not for her strength and her feet pressing down on the bumper, I'd have slid down the hood four times over by now.

"You are such a darling man," she said, her pussy tightening around my dick like a juicy coil. "Why truly, I ain't never met no one like you!"

"I've never met anyone like you either," I told her, and every word was true.

She squealed as she moved in my lap. Clearly, she couldn't get enough. She worked my cock hard until all I could do was give in to the pressure.

I warned her, "I'm about to come."

She egged me on with her body and her mouth. "Then come, sugar pie! Fill my cunt with cream!"

Her pussy clung tight to my cock, and I released a torrent inside her.

All at once, I felt weak.

When she jumped out of my lap, I slid down the hood, but she was there to catch me.

I lay face down on my car, utterly spent, my pants around my ankles while Officer Paine unlocked my cuffs.

It took a while before I found the strength to roll over. When I did, she was dressed in her trousers and boots, with her shirt tucked in but hanging open. All the buttons were gone.

"What you gonna do about that?" I asked.

She gazed down at her big breasts. "I got safety pins in the cruiser. That'll do for now. Fat chance I'll see another vehicle down this stretch before my shift ends, anyhow."

I put my clothes on and got back in my car, but I didn't want to leave her. I didn't want to go. I don't suppose she wanted me to leave, because she leaned against the door and we shot the breeze for a long time, talking about nothing in particular.

Finally, she asked where I was headed. She offered to help me find my way.

"Truth is, I'm supposed to meet the girl my folks want me to marry."

She swallowed hard. Didn't look pleased. "You're getting married, eh?"

"My parents think I'm too old to still be out gallivanting. They found a girl for me to settle down with."

"And you ain't never even met her?"

"That's right."

"Wouldn't you rather marry a girl you actually done met?"

"Well sure, but what kind a girl would settle for me?"

"Settle? You're crazy! Any girl'd be lucky to marry you."

"None 'a the ones I met seem to think so."

She looked down at the road and said, "I ain't married neither."

"Now that I find hard to believe."

"It's the truth."

"You're pullin my leg, Officer Paine."

"I ain't!"

She beamed at me like a schoolgirl, and I knew what I wanted to ask but I couldn't get the words out.

Lucky for me, she stepped up and said, "We fit together pretty nice. How's about you and me get hitched?"

"I'd like that," I told her. "I'd like that a whole damn lot."

Camp Futa

THE GIRLS WERE PAIRED up two by two when they arrived at camp.

Melody thought for sure they'd be sleeping in a cabin, not on the cold hard ground. At least she got to share a tent with Vix.

Of all the girls at Camp Futa, Vix stood out the most. Melody wasn't sure why. Vix was tall but plain, with long sandy hair she wore in two braids. Melody watched her all day, especially during the beach volleyball game. The navy blue camp shorts fit all the other girls loosely, but they were tight around Vix's athletic thighs. She even looked good in the plain cotton T-shirt they all had to wear.

With her curly golden locks, Melody was used to being Belle of the Ball. At camp she felt totally out of place. Her press-on nails kept popping off and the instructors made her leave her jewellery in the safe.

The take-home list told campers not to bring necklaces, rings or bracelets for insurance reasons, but Melody rarely followed instructions.

Yet one more reason she didn't fit in at camp.

All the other girls did as they were told. They didn't mind collecting firewood or chopping vegetables. They were happy to help.

Melody even overheard one girl calling her "spoiled" behind her back, while another girl called her a snob.

She'd never been an outcast before. It was strange. She didn't fit with any group here.

Vix, on the other hand, was friendly with everyone. She didn't hang out in just one clique. She moved easily from group to group, and whoever she sat beside seemed happy to see her.

At mealtime, Melody asked one girl why everyone liked Vix so much.

The girl said, "Why? Don't you like her?"

"I do! I like her a lot!" Melody said.

"So why wouldn't everyone else?"

That was the end of that conversation.

When it came time to get ready for bed, Melody changed in the washroom facility. She didn't like undressing in front of other girls because one of her breasts was bigger than the other. It was the sort of thing she could cover up with a bra, but not bare-chested.

Once she'd put on her nightie, she covered it with a robe and slid on her satin slippers. She held her camp clothes in front of her chest to make sure nobody got a glimpse of her breasts.

As she walked from the washrooms to her tent, she heard other girls tittering about her pink robe and her slippers. She heard them saying she didn't fit in.

When Melody unzipped the tent, Vix was already cozied up inside her sleeping bag.

"Can I turn the lantern on?" Melody asked.

Vix grumbled, "Why?"

"I haven't scoured my face with toner yet, or applied my evening lotions. It's never too early to prevent wrinkles, you know."

"You can't use lotions out here." Vix clicked her teeth. "The scent will attract bugs."

"Oh." Melody didn't like bugs. She certainly didn't want to draw any into their tent. "Well, I guess I can skip it just for one night."

"Six nights," Vix reminded her.

"Right. Six nights." Six too many, but Melody didn't want to say so in front of Vix.

Vix obviously enjoyed camp or she wouldn't still be coming at her age.

Melody was only here as some kind of punishment.

Her parents didn't think she was well-rounded enough, and it didn't seem to matter that they had no legal right to boss her around. They said if she didn't come to camp, they wouldn't pay her allowance anymore—and that would mean she'd have to get a job! As if!

Vix fell asleep pretty much right away.

Melody didn't.

The woods were boring, and also kind of scary. She could hear all kinds of weird insect noises, but what if there were bears out there? What if she fell asleep and a bear ripped through their tent? By the time she woke up, he'd have ripped her to shreds!

The later it got, the colder the night became.

When they set up their tent, Vix told her the sleeping bag she'd brought would never do.

Vix's bag would keep a person warm to -30 degrees Celsius.

Melody figured that was overkill. It would never get that cold during the summer.

But it certainly felt that cold now.

Melody shivered inside her sleeping bag.

She couldn't get warm.

She just got colder and colder and colder, until she couldn't stand the chill.

"Vix?" she whispered. "Vix, I'm freezing. Can I get in with you?"

No response.

Melody reached over in the dark and shook Vix by the shoulder. "Can I get in your sleeping bag? I'm cold."

Vix made a noise, like a groan or a grunt.

"Are you asleep?" Melody asked.

She'd been turned away, but now she rolled onto her back.

"Are you awake? Can I get in? I'm so c-c-cold!"

Vix made another sleepy noise that sounded like a word, maybe "Okay"?

Or maybe that was wishful thinking.

Melody didn't really care, at this point. Her toes were like popsicles. She needed to share Vix's body heat, and also Vix's super-warm sleeping bag.

The air inside the tent felt frigid against Melody's bare legs. She tucked them quickly into Vix's bag, even though it didn't look big enough for two people.

When she tried to squirm inside, she soon discovered there was a tie at the top, to keep it tight around Vix's neck. Melody released that tie and felt Vix's body head escape like a sauna cloud. Felt nice against her cold, cold flesh.

She'd hoped to sleep beside Vix, like spoons, but with Vix on her back it was clear Melody would have to lie directly on top of her.

Great.

"Mehhh," Vix moaned as Melody wriggled down the bag.

"Shhh," Melody said. "It's just me. I'm cold, that's all."

Her nightie rode up as she slid down her tentmate's warm body. How dreadfully embarrassing.

Then she realized... goodness gracious, Vix slept in the nude!

As she felt her way down Vix's naked body, her thigh nudged something strange. It felt like a stick, but fleshy.

Why would Vix have a fleshy stick in her...

"Oh my!"

When Melody reached down to touch it, Vix groaned.

"I'm sorry!" Melody squealed, sure she'd get in trouble for touching another girl's private parts.

VERY private parts!

If Melody was scared the other girls might notice her breasts were two different sizes, imagine how Vix must feel. Melody hadn't asked around, but she doubted very much the others had something like this between their legs.

"I'm sorry, Vix," Melody repeated, but she didn't stop stroking her tentmate's hardness.

She'd never touched one before.

Never even seen one, actually.

This was better—just finding it and touching it while Vix was still asleep. She kind of hoped Vix wouldn't wake up. But she also kind of wished Vix would.

Melody was too old to still be a virgin. She wanted to try sex, but not with a boy.

This couldn't be more perfect.

Melody let her weight sink slowly onto Vix's body. Her nightie had been pulled up so high that her breasts were fully exposed. They were so cold that her tentmate's smaller ones felt hot.

Sizzling.

Melody could feel her own nipples pressing forcefully into the heat of Vix's flesh. It was such a good feeling that she felt it not only in her breasts, but between her legs as well.

She spread her thighs across her tentmate's thighs, but it was too awkward to keep stroking like before. Instead, Melody let her pussy lips splay around Vix's thick shaft. She almost wished she could see it, but she was also glad she couldn't.

It might be scary. It felt really big.

Melody's clitoris throbbed when it touched Vix's erection. She'd never felt so swollen and engorged in all her life. In fact, she didn't think about sex very often... but she was certainly thinking about it now, while Vix's body pulsed in time with hers.

There was something incredibly naughty about feeling their breasts pressed together. Having their private parts lined up should have felt naughtier, but maybe that just seemed more like the way "normal" people were supposed to have "normal" sex.

Vix and Melody were far from normal, with Melody's weird-sized breasts and Vix's big thingy down there.

They were different, and that made them the same.

"Are you awake?" Melody asked.

Vix didn't respond. She was breathing pretty heavily. Definitely asleep.

Was it wrong to get inside another girl's sleeping bag and rub your naked body against her naked body without waking her up first?

Probably.

That was probably one of the wrongest things a person could do.

But Melody was doing it.

She stroked her clitoris slowly up and down Vix's shaft and felt her juices dripping from her body to coat the other girl's hardness. The wetter Melody got, the better it felt to rub against Vix.

How could she sleep through this? It felt amazing to Melody. Maybe Vix was dreaming of sex stuff. Her shaft kept getting harder and harder, throbbing against Melody's clitoris with every pass.

As Melody pressed her breasts against Vix's, she found she was too turned on to just rub on the outside. She wanted to feel Vix's hardness rubbing her on the inside too.

This was a big deal. But she wanted it. She couldn't stay a virgin forever.

What about Vix, though? It should be a big deal for her too, especially if she'd never done sex stuff before. What if she woke up in the middle and freaked? Melody would get kicked out of camp for sure.

But maybe Vix wouldn't be mad. It felt so good to rub together. Maybe Vix would just go with it.

So Melody raised her body up from Vix's just enough that her tentmate's hard part met the entrance to her virgin vagina. She'd prepared for this moment. She'd prepared by shoving things up there at home. Not for pleasure. Just because she didn't want it to hurt when she had her first time. How embarrassing would it be if she cried?

With her fingers, Melody nudged Vix's hardness toward her juicy wet opening. She hoped it would slide right in, but it wasn't that easy. Melody's vagina was still pretty tight. She had to work it in by lowering her body toward Vix's.

That hard part entered her like a missile ready to explode.

It felt huge.

Melody whimpered and bit her lip.

Vix made noises too. Growling noises and groaning noises, grunting noises even. But Melody was pretty sure the girl was still asleep.

Sweat beaded across her brow and down the small of her back. She wasn't just getting warm—she was getting hot.

Melody pushed down harder, gobbling up her tentmate's hardness with her soft, wet vagina.

This was her first time.

They say you always remember your first time.

Would she always remember this moment? In a sleeping bag with a girl she barely knew, who was still asleep even though they were having actual penis-in-vagina sex right now?

"Why aren't you awake?" Melody whispered, though she couldn't decide whether she wanted Vix to wake up or not.

This way, Melody had to do all the work. It would be kind of nice to have sex with someone who would flip her and take over, but maybe that would happen next time.

This time, it was all her.

She moved on top of Vix, stroking her clitoris against the girl's soft belly. Her vagina swallowed that hot cock again and again.

Cock!

Well, that's what it was. A penis. An actual penis was in her vagina! They were having sex for real, unless Melody was dreaming all this.

What was Vix dreaming of, she wondered? What was going through the girl's mind as Melody pressed her boobs against Vix's boobs? As Melody greedily gobbled her cock?

Some girls did it with their mouths. Melody had always thought that sounded gross, but she wasn't so sure anymore. She could almost imagine herself going down on Vix.

She could definitely imagine Vix going down on her.

Straddling the girl, she thrust her hips, feeling like she was doing a pretty good job. Vix felt so huge inside her that the friction increased with every stroke.

She never thought she'd lose her virginity at camp. Thank goodness she was assigned to the same tent as a girl who slept naked.

A girl with a nice big cock.

Little thrills ran through Melody's body as she made love to her sleeping tentmate. It felt amazing to have another girl's cock between her legs. She was so hot and wet and sticky down there the sleeping bag grew humid.

She was sweating all over.

A dizzy sensation came over her.

Suddenly, her body started moving without her. She forced herself at Vix even harder, smashing her clitoris against the girl's belly, grunting in time with her tentmate's moans.

She hoped no one else was awake. She hoped no one else could hear them moaning as she buried Vix's cock inside herself harder and harder with every thrust.

It wasn't good enough to stroke off on the girl's belly, so she slammed her boobs down on Vix's boobs and planted her hand between their bodies. She touched herself roughly, so roughly her whole body tightened around her tentmate's pole.

"Yes, yes, yes!" Melody growled. She rubbed herself harder, faster. Her fingers were wet from her juices. "Yes, yes, yes!"

Suddenly, she felt something she couldn't describe. It was like colours exploding inside her eyes, and bombs going off in her belly... but in a good way.

She had to stop stroking when her vagina locked around Vix's hardness.

For a while, she couldn't move. Her body planted itself against her tentmate's as they breathed roughly together.

Finally, Melody had to get up. She was just too hot inside that sleeping bag.

It wasn't until she'd worked her way up the other girl's body that she realized Vix must have climaxed too. She only knew because the part that used to be hard was now soft. When it slipped out of her vagina a lot of gooey stuff came with it, spilling across Vix's belly.

Melody scuttled out of the girl's sleeping bag, careful not to wake her.

Vix remained fast asleep. Would she realize what had happened the next morning, when her belly was wet with goo? Or would it have dried by then?

The cool night air came as a relief to Melody's overheated flesh. She was happy to get back inside her own bag. The insects and animal noises were no match for her tiredness, but before she fell asleep she found herself wondering what she would do if Vix asked her about all this. If Vix said, "Did you crawl into my sleeping bag and put my penis in your vagina?" how would Melody respond?

Maybe she'd said, "I did, and I want to try it again. I want to try it with you on top. I want to try it side by side. I want to try it in a scissory way, and I want to try it on my hands and knees. And I want to take you in my mouth and I want to feel your mouth on me. And I want to try it all before this week of camp is up."

They had a lot to try in only six nights.

Dr. Futa Treats Her Patient

STELLA LEANED BACK on the padded bench and set both feet in stirrups. "It's been aching night and day, Doctor. Please... tell me what's wrong!"

Dr. Futa stood between Stella's legs, snapping on latex gloves. "Where exactly is this ache?"

"Down there," Stella said quickly, hoping she wouldn't have to explain any more than that.

Wearing only a paper gown and no panties, Stella felt totally exposed. She'd never let anyone look between her legs.

Not even a doctor.

But if she was going to let anyone look down there, at least it was a pretty doctor. Dr. Futa had honey-brown skin and long black hair that shone like the jewels embedded in her gold necklace. Dr. Futa wasn't very tall and definitely wasn't thin. She had luscious curves and big breasts that were amply visible thanks to a low-cut neckline.

Most of the other doctors in this facility wore scrubs. The nurses all did. But Dr. Futa had on a slinky black dress dotted with a subtle tan pattern. If it wasn't for the white lab coat and the stethoscope around her neck you'd never know she was a doctor at all.

"According to your notes," the doctor said, "You've never been in for a pelvic exam."

"I'm sorry," Stella said.

Dr. Futa's smile warmed her heart. "No need to feel sorry, my dear. I only wonder why. By your age, most young women have come to see me at least once."

"I didn't think it was necessary."

"Why not?"

Stella stared at the ceiling, feeling her cheeks go red. "Because I've never had sex."

"Ahhh. So you've only come in today because of... the ache?"

Tears pricked Stella's eyes as she nodded. "It won't go away. It never goes away. I'm in college now, Dr. Futa. I go to lectures and the ache is there. I go to the library and the ache comes with me. I come home to my dorm room and the ache is inside me. What can I do?"

With the toe of her shoe, Dr. Futa wheeled over a stool and sat between Stella's parted legs. "Your labia appear quite glossy and engorged. I'm going to touch them with my finger. Tell me if you feel any pain."

When Dr. Futa gently touched Stella's lower lips, the sensation was too much to bear. It was the same feeling she got when she pressed her thighs together too hard or when she yanked on her panties with too much zeal. Electrical pulses shot through her, making her cry out.

"Oh Doctor," she said. "What can I do?"

"You feel pain when I press here?" the doctor asked, touching her again.

Who says lightning doesn't strike twice? It did for Stella, sending those same bursts of electricity through her veins. She bit her bottom lip so she wouldn't scream.

"Describe it," Dr. Futa said. "Describe your pain."

She did it again, and Stella said, "Feels like someone poked me with a cattle prod!"

"And this?" the doctor asked, pressing one finger at the apex of Stella's aching lips.

If the other had felt like being poked with a cattle prod, this was like being hooked up to a car battery. Or sitting on an electric fence! Stella had never felt anything so powerful. She gripped the padded bench and pressed her stocking feet into the stirrups.

Dr. Futa rose from her stool to ask, "Stella, my dear, I must ask you a personal question."

"Okay." Stella stared at the ceiling.

"You are not sexually active?"

"No! I'm not married yet."

"You are a virgin?"

"Yes, of course!"

"And tell me honestly, Stella: do you ever touch yourself?"

Stella felt the colour drain from her cheeks. "You mean... down there?"

"Yes, my dear. Self-love. Self-pleasure. Masturbation."

That word embarrassed Stella so badly she almost choked. "I would never do a thing like that. It's sinful and wrong."

She could feel the doctor staring at her, but Stella didn't look back. Not even when Dr. Futa said, "I believe I know the cause of your ache."

"That's a relief. What's wrong with me, Doctor?"

Stella made the mistake of glancing into Dr. Futa's eyes in time for her to say, "You are an extremely sexually frustrated young woman."

"No! Sex is bad! It's wrong!" Tears spilled from Stella's eyes, racing to her temples and disappearing into her hair. "Please, Doctor. There must be another explanation."

"I'm afraid not, young Stella. If you don't want to live with your ache, there is a very simple solution."

When Stella adjusted her position on the padded bench, the paper sheet crackled beneath her. "You don't mean..."

"It's something you can do on your own, with no cost to you."

"No. I can't. I'll take a pill instead. What can you prescribe, Doctor?"

"I can only prescribe self-love, my dear. It's very simple."

Stella's little heart tremored. "But I can't, Dr. Futa. It's wrong. It's bad."

"To touch yourself is wrong and bad?"

"Yes!"

Dr. Futa could obviously see that she wouldn't get anywhere with this approach. Stella was set in her convictions. So she said, "What if your ache is resolved by another's hand?"

Stella felt a familiar throbbing sensation between her legs. "But whose?"

"Do you have a special friend?" the doctor asked.

"Certainly not. I'm concentrating on my studies."

"I see."

Taking a deep breath, Stella asked, "Can you do it, Doctor?"

Dr. Futa's eyes widened. "It would be most unusual."

"But you're a medical professional," Stella reasoned. "So if you do it, it's a medical procedure just like surgery or anything else. Then it won't be wrong and I won't have to feel bad about it."

The doctor seemed reluctant to resolve her problem this way, and asked, "Are you certain this is what you wish?"

Stella nodded. "I can't go on like this, doctor. My body aches every second of the day. I need you to help me. Please?"

The doctor gazed down at her hands in skin-tight latex gloves. She sighed. "If you're sure this is what you want."

"I can't live with the ache, Doctor. I can't concentrate in class. I can't even read a book. The words blur before my eyes. Please, you have to help me!"

Dr. Futa nodded solemnly. "Very well, Stella. I will do my utmost to resolve your ache."

Stella closed her eyes, preparing herself for the procedure. She could feel the doctor's warm hand against the inside of one of her thighs. Even that slight sensation made her heart storm.

"I'm afraid I'll have to ask a nurse to prepare the site," Dr. Futa said. Kicking the stool away, she stepped back, took off one of her gloves and dialled the phone on her desk.

Moments later, a pretty young nurse with dark skin and sparkling eyes entered the room, wheeling a stainless steel tray. On it was a metal bowl full of soapy water, shaving cream, a regular razor like you'd get in a drug store, and also an electric razor like they use for buzz cuts.

"What's going on?" Stella asked.

Her heart pounded as the friendly young nurse plugged the electric razor into the wall. "We just need to prepare the site so the doctor can carry out her procedure."

Dr. Futa smiled kindly.

As soon as the nurse turned on the electric razor, Stella jumped. She dug her nails into the sides of the padded bench, because she suspected that as soon as that buzzing contraption touched her skin she'd lose it.

Thank goodness the razor made so much noise. It drowned out the sounds of her pleasured cries as the nurse slid it between her legs.

The nurse started with her inner thighs, and the doctor kicked a wastepaper bin underneath to catch the falling hair. Stella couldn't see what was happening down there because her gown was in the way, but she could feel that razor buzzing all around her most sensitive spot. It came so close to her ache that she cried out repeatedly. The void kept clenching, like it was trying to lock down on something that wasn't there. Again and again it clamped and released, and Stella had to bite down on her forearm to keep from screaming.

When the nurse had finished with the electric razor, she picked up the regular one and swished it around in the water. She left it there on the tray while she picked up the shaving cream canister. She squirted some onto her hand and the smell wafted up to Stella's nose.

It smelled like lemons.

The nurse rubbed the shaving cream between Stella's legs while Dr. Futa watched. She seemed to be avoiding the slick and aching parts of Stella's body in favour of the surrounding areas. That was a bit of a tease, and it even made Stella squirm to try to get the nurse's fingers to "accidentally" brush her pink, engorged flesh.

While the doctor looked on, the nurse shaved between Stella's legs in quick, precise strokes. The whole procedure made Stella very nervous. She didn't budge for fear of being cut.

Luckily, that part was over soon enough. The nurse pressed a warm cloth between Stella's legs, and the heat made her moan.

"Too hot?" the nurse asked.

Stella whimpered. "It's fine. Keep going."

As the nurse washed away errant bits of hair, Stella whined like a puppy. She kept thinking naughty thoughts and wanting to say naughty things. But she didn't allow herself to say anything at all. It would be too wrong.

Dr. Futa thanked the young nurse, who smiled at Stella and left, closing the door behind her.

The doctor pressed the lock on the handle, and then put on a fresh glove. "We're ready to begin."

"Good," Stella said. "I feel like I'm going to explode. The ache is worse than it's ever been."

"We'll have it resolved soon enough," the doctor said, stepping between Stella's legs and pressing her palm against Stella's smoothly shaved mound.

"Oh my sweet lord," Stella said. "Oh, I'm sorry for taking the lord's name in vain. It won't happen again."

"Say whatever you wish," the doctor told her. "I won't hold it against you."

Dr. Futa cupped her hand around Stella's mound and mashed the outer lips around the inner ones, squeezing.

"Oh, Doctor!" Stella whimpered. "Oh, I can't tell you how amazing that feels."

"Good," the doctor replied as she released her grip. "Nothing wrong with your reflexes."

Stella swallowed hard. "Was that the procedure? I don't think it worked."

"Oh, my dear girl," the doctor said. "We haven't even started."

Dr. Futa traced her gloved fingers up from the base of Stella's slick slit, up toward the throbbing bud at the top. When she reached that dangerous spot, she started to rub it in slow circles.

"Oh, Doctor! Oh, the ache is getting worse!"

"It has to get worse before it gets better," the doctor said.

"When will I be cured?" Stella asked as she squirmed on the paper.

"You'll know," the doctor assured her. "You'll feel your body releasing the ache and it will be like nothing you've ever experienced."

In a way, Stella hoped that wouldn't happen soon. She hated to admit it, even to herself, but she was enjoying the doctor's delicate touch. She liked the way Dr. Futa circled her fingers around and around that aching, slippery flesh. Oh, it felt so good Stella wanted to scream.

But she didn't. She held it in.

And the ache increased.

It grew at the apex of her slit. Grew so big and fat and swollen Dr. Futa said, "Oh my!"

"What?" Stella asked when the doctor stopped touching her. "What's wrong?"

"You have a very rare condition," the doctor told her.

"What?"

Her swollen bud felt huge, and when the doctor folded down her gown, she realized... her bud HAD grown huge! She was no longer looking down at a flat mound of flesh. She now had a growth extending between her legs. And though she'd never seen one before, she knew instinctually that she'd somehow grown a cock.

Stella screamed.

"Hush!" the doctor said. "This happens, in some women."

"No it doesn't!" Stella hollered, staring at the huge erection jutting out in front of her. "I've never heard of other girls spontaneously sprouting a..." Her cheeks grew hot and prickly as she whispered, "Penis."

"I assure you, my dear, this happens to some women when they neglect their self-care for too long."

"You're lying," Stella said. "Make it go away. Just make it go!"

"I will," the doctor said, wrapping her hand around Stella's throbbing shaft. "I will resolve your ache in no time at all."

The doctor shuttled her fist up and down Stella's swollen dick. Slowly, at first.

Stella said, "Make it go away!"

So the doctor picked up pace, stroking Stella's cock hot and fast. The latex gloves stuck to her hot skin, so the doctor reached for lubricant and squirted some on Stella's dickhead.

"Cold!" Stella shrieked.

"I'm sorry," the doctor said, and when she traced that slippery stuff down Stella's shaft, all was forgiven. Her hand slid so swiftly up and down that throbbing dick that Stella couldn't prevent her hips from thrusting, thrusting, like she was making love to the doctor's hot hand.

The ache increased. It became a wondrous, swirling motion, like a vortex in Stella's belly.

Now Stella understood what the doctor meant. The ache had to get worse, and it did. It hurt so bad Stella's mind swirled. But it wasn't a bad hurt, like if you stubbed your toe or cut your finger. It was a good hurt like... well, she couldn't think of anything else that felt this way. She just kept thrusting into the doctor's hand, watching her inexplicable dick ride Dr. Futa's fist. It looked so hot, and she felt so guilty for thinking so.

This was supposed to be a medical procedure, not a sexual experience. Just relieving and ache.

"Release," the doctor said, stroking harder and faster. "Release your ache, my dear."

"I'm trying!" Stella cried. "I don't know how!"

"Don't think. You mustn't think. Just let it happen, my dear."

Stella drove her feet into the stirrups, thrust her hips in the air, and surrendered to the pleasure the doctor had granted her.

"That's right," Dr. Futa said. "Almost there. Almost..."

Stella growled and grunted and released her ache into the world.

It emerged from her body as a white rope, which flew into the air before cascading back down to land on her belly.

Another spurt emerged from the head of her dick, and another and another. These ones didn't fly so high. They shot up and fell back down and settled on her skin as she set her bum back down on the bench.

The doctor backed away while Stella's magical dick grew smaller and smaller, until it was no bigger than it had ever been: just a bud at the apex of her slit.

The procedure weakened her to the point where she couldn't keep her eyes open. She apologized to the doctor and said she must sleep.

Her eyes closed and darkness descended.

When she awoke, she found herself in a room she didn't recognize.

Dr. Futa was there at her side.

"Where am I?" Stella asked.

"This is our recovery room for day surgery patients."

"Did I have surgery?" Stella asked, feeling suddenly alarmed.

The doctor chuckled. "No, dear. But you were very sleepy and I didn't have the heart to wake you."

Stella looked around. There were other beds in the room, but no other patients. She was alone with the doctor in this dimly lit place. "What time is it?"

"After six," the doctor said. "Everyone else has gone home for the day."

Stella's heart swelled. "But you stayed?"

"Of course. I'm your doctor. It's my duty to take care of you."

Everything that had happened that day returned to Stella's mind, and she felt a host of emotions, from embarrassment to relief.

The ache returned, but it was only an echo inside her body.

"I'm concerned about you, my dear. What will you do the next time your ache reaches a tipping point? Will you take matters into your own hands?"

"Do I have to?" Stella asked. "Can't I just come back to you and you can take care of me?"

Dr. Futa's beautiful face grew fretful. "I know it shouldn't, but it has an effect on me. I'm a medical professional. I should be able to handle it. But..."

"But what?" Stella asked. "You can tell me, Doctor. I'll help you if I can, after you've helped me so much."

The doctor stood up, and that's when Stella realized her lab coat was buttoned all the way up. It hadn't been before. Dr. Futa undid the top few buttons, and Stella was shocked to see bare breasts underneath.

"Dr. Futa, what happened to your dress?"

"I want to show you the effect you've had on me, my dear." She kept unbuttoning the coat until it hung open, revealing the very condition Stella had developed earlier that day. "After I treated you, this began to grow. It grew all afternoon until it was full and fat as you see it now."

Stella swallowed hard. Before today, she'd have been shocked. But not after it happened to her.

If it could happen to Stella, it could happen to anyone.

"I want to help you," Stella said. "Just like you helped me."

"This is so unprofessional..."

The ache tingled between Stella's thighs, and she felt a slick stream of wetness down there. "It's okay, Dr. Futa. You helped me so much."

It's like a switch had been flipped inside Stella. Now that she'd experienced sexual release, it's all she wanted. And not just for herself! For the doctor, too.

She was lucky to have such a beautiful doctor, with big bouncy breasts and that yummy cock between her legs.

"I just had a thought," Stella said. "What if I never get married? I might go my whole life without having sex. I don't want to die a virgin."

"You've got plenty of years ahead of you, my dear."

"I could get hit by a bus when I walk out of here, doctor. And then I'd never have experienced the joy of sex. You were the first one to touch me. I want you to be the first one inside me, too. Will you deflower me, Doctor?"

Dr. Futa's eyes widened. Her cock jumped.

Stella pushed down the heavy white sheet that had been put over her. She untied her paper gown and threw it on the ground. "Look at me. I'm naked, Dr. Futa. I've never been naked in front of anyone before. Only you."

The doctor's cock hardened like a steel rod. It was all big and veiny, just like Stella's had been.

Stella pulled her feet up onto the low hospital bed she'd been moved to. She dug her heels into the thin mattress on either side of her bare bottom, exposing her juicy centre to the doctor. "I never thought I'd be like this. I was always such a good girl, and it almost drove me insane. If you hadn't resolved my ache, just imagine what would have happened to me. I'd have gone crazy!"

"I don't know about that," the doctor said.

"Doesn't matter now." Stella parted her pussy lips with her fingers. "Look how slick I am, Doctor. No need for that slip-slidey stuff you used in the office. You can just stick it in me right now. I'm ready."

"But you were so adamant," the doctor said. "You said you wanted to wait until marriage."

"That was then," Stella said. "Now that I know how good it feels to be touched, I want to find out what it's like to get fucked."

She'd never said that word in her entire life.

"Fuck me, Dr. Futa."

"Oh, Stella. I shouldn't..."

"That's what I thought before you relieved my ache. Now I know better." Stella stuck one finger inside her very tight pussy and drew some slick stuff up to her clit.

Once she started rubbing there, she teetered on the verge of orgasm almost right away.

"Put that dick in me, doctor. Make me come."

The doctor's cock had a mind of its own. It stuck straight out, like it was pulling Dr. Futa toward Stella's ready cunt.

Dr. Futa stepped closer, wearing nothing but that unbuttoned lab coat and her bejewelled golden necklace. Even in the dim light, her black hair shone.

"I can't help myself," the doctor said. "I'm sorry."

"Don't be sorry," Stella said. "Just stick that dick in me and drive it hard."

Stella thought she was ready to lose her virginity. And, mentally, she was. But physically?

When the doctor traced that glistening cockhead up and down Stella's slit, her whole body trembled. "Oh yes. Put it in. Fuck me with your big cock, Dr. Futa."

"Oh, my poor dear girl," the doctor said as she drove her dick into Stella's virgin hole.

Stella couldn't have anticipated the pain if she'd tried.

It wasn't the same hurt as when the doctor relieved her ache. That had been a happy sort of pain.

This was not happy pain.

This was screaming pain.

It was pain that shot through her like a hot knife.

She felt it everywhere.

She thought she was going to die.

"Oh God," Dr. Futa moaned, opening her lab coat so her large breasts pressed against Stella's much smaller ones. "Oh thank you, my dear. Your pussy is so warm, so wonderfully wet."

Stella planted her face in the crook of the doctor's neck so the woman wouldn't see how much pain she was in.

Dr. Futa hugged her harder, driving those hot tits against her much cooler ones. And that felt good. In fact, if it wasn't for that swirly arousing sensation, Stella might have pulled away then and there.

But she wanted more. She hugged the doctor back, pushing her tiny tits against those bouncy big ones.

"This is most unprofessional," the doctor said. "But, please my dear, may I kiss you?"

"Yes!" Stella said, surrendering to the doctor's embrace.

It was her first kiss. Ever.

And it couldn't have been better.

When the doctor's tongue first entered her mouth, that did feel a little strange. But she let it happen, and it started to feel good. The good feeling travelled through her entire body, swirling between her legs until her tight cunt welcomed the doctor's hot dick.

As the doctor traced her hands around Stella's naked skin, Stella wrapped both legs around the doctor's waist. She wasn't sure why she'd done it, but it made things much easier. Suddenly the doctor could thrust in her pussy with no trouble at all.

They moved together as they kissed. Stella bucked her hips while the doctor thrust inside her.

Where had the hurt gone?

She'd felt so much pain not long ago, and suddenly she couldn't find it. Not even the slightest twinge of that sharp stab remained when the doctor climbed into bed with her, straddling her small body while they continued to kiss.

This was sex.

This was the kind of sex Stella had heard about, except it was usually a man on top. Stella was actually glad her first time getting fucked wasn't with a man. She couldn't even picture that. It would be too weird.

But with her trusted doctor, she didn't even mind the pain she'd experienced, because that pain had led to this pleasure.

The doctor moved inside her. They were both so wet down there that their parts made sticky squelching noises. If she hadn't been so aroused, she'd have found them funny.

She loved the way the doctor's big breasts weighed down on hers. They were so smooshy and fleshy and warm and wonderful that Stella drove her tiny tits up for more pressure. All the while, Dr. Futa thrust that hard cock between her legs, mixing her insides like a dessert spoon in a thick milkshake.

It felt so good Stella moaned in the doctor's mouth.

She could feel release coming, but it was different this time. When she'd been the one with the cock, release felt sharp and centralized in just one part of her body. Now that her doctor had the dick and it was deep in her pussy, release felt as big as a swimming pool. It was hot and wet and swirling and delicious.

Dr. Futa drove faster, then slower, in jerky smashing strikes. When Stella cried out, the doctor stopped all together, clinging to her body, shrieking, then panting. Stella wondered if that's what she'd sounded like when she had her cock release.

She thought about those ropes of arousal filling her void.

Streaks of cum. Jets of sticky white stuff. Filling her body. She trembled under the doctor's warm weight.

When the doctor fell asleep on top of her, she felt that once-swollen dick retract from her pussy and disappear altogether. It was an odd sensation.

She couldn't move, but she didn't want to. When she'd woken up after her first ever release, Dr. Futa had been there by her side. When the doctor woke up, she wanted to be there too.

Stella had a feeling the ache would never go away completely. Maybe they should set a standing appointment to work it out together, passing their mysterious cock back and forth, using it on each other every week.

Maybe more often than that...

Pregnant by her Futa Friend

WHEN MY PHONE RANG at 12:34, I knew it was Becca. She had a lot of crises, and always in the middle of the night.

I hadn't even said hello when she wailed, "He broke up with me, Corrine! He broke my heart! Why???"

Not this again.

Rolling out of bed, I said, "Hold tight. I'll be right over."

The short drive to Becca's house gave me a moment to think about what I should say.

I knew what I wanted to say: *he broke up with you because you've only gone out four times and already you're talking about babies*!

Becca didn't understand how desperate she came off. Her biological clock was ticking so loudly it alerted everyone in the vicinity. I'm surprised Frank made it to four dates with her.

Most guys didn't.

It's a shame, because Becca was a beautiful girl. She looked younger than her 37 years—tall, thin, gorgeous. Blonde hair and good skin. I think that's why she never had many close friends. Other women were intimidated by her good looks.

Anyone self-assured enough to stick around eventually got driven off by her neediness, though. It wasn't only men's attention she demanded.

When I got to Becca's little house, she was standing in the doorway, backlit by interior lights. I couldn't see her face clearly until I'd walked up the front steps.

"Oh, Becca!" I said, wiping her cheeks with both thumbs. "You need to start buying waterproof mascara."

The girl was a mess.

She hadn't taken off her date dress, which was shiny red and tightly fitted. Sometimes I wondered how she pulled off a strapless dress. It's not like she had the boobs to hold it up. That was the only area where I had her beat, though I never showed off my assets.

Becca's dress was very short. She liked to show off her legs, and I could understand why. They were long and pale and looked perfect when she'd fitted her feet into high heels. She'd kicked those off, but her bare feet were quite attractive, too, with the nails painted the same scarlet red as her dress.

"Come on," I said, leading her to the couch. "Tell me all about it."

She clung to me like a koala. Despite being taller than me, she managed to bend down low enough to rest her head on my breast. Good thing the top I threw on was old, because her makeup would stain it for sure.

"He said... he said... he said I was too much woman for him!!!"

"Too much?" I asked as her tears soaked through my bra. I'd been called too much woman as well, but I doubt for the same reason.

"I want too much, he said. More than he's got to give!"

Big surprise.

"But I don't!" Becca said. "I don't want too much. I only want a baby, Corrine. That's all. I don't even need the guy. Once he's made his deposit, I can raise my child alone. I don't need him at all."

"You didn't say that to Frank, did you?" I asked, knowing perfectly well what the answer would be.

Becca sniffled as she raised her head from my breast. Sure enough, she'd left traces of makeup all over me, but she was too self-involved to notice.

"Think I shouldn't have?" she asked.

"Oh, Becca!" I hugged her warmly, but she stiffened in my grip.

"We shouldn't," she said.

"Shouldn't what?"

She batted her lashes, which were glued together with wet mascara and tears. "You know."

"No..."

"We shouldn't... you know..." She glanced down at my crotch and raised a brow.

I smacked her bare thigh. "Becca! Gross!"

"What?"

"Did you think I was coming on to you?" I cried, shooting up from the couch.

"Well," she said. "I know you like girls, and I know you've got... *that*..."

She reached for my crotch like a zombie grasping at brains. I smacked her hand away and said, "No touching!"

"Why not?" she whined. "Don't you think I'm pretty?"

The sad thing was, even with a face full of smudged makeup and eyes full of tears, Becca was one of the prettiest women I'd ever known.

"Of course you're pretty," I told her. "That doesn't mean I'm going to sleep with you. We're friends, Bec. Nothing more."

"But we could be more." She scooched closer and grabbed my hand. "There's no reason not to be."

"Have you ever slept with a friend, Becca? There are plenty of reasons not to."

She whimpered like a puppy.

"That's not gonna work on me, Bec."

She stuck out her bottom lip and made a pouty face.

"Is this what you tried on Frank? Because I'm beginning to see why he dumped you."

Oops.

Becca wailed for real, throwing her head back and opening her mouth wide like a Peanuts character.

"Sorry, sorry, sorry, sorry!" I threw my arms around her as she cried. "Oh Bec, I shouldn't have said that."

"He dumped me because I'm awful!" she sobbed.

"Some relationships just don't work out. It's not your fault."

That was total BS, but what are friends for?

"It *is* my fault," she said, rising from the couch and dragging me along with her. "It's *all* my fault."

"You're a little intense on the baby thing, that's all."

When she got to the bathroom, she pulled me inside and turned on the shower.

"Good idea. You get freshened up. I'll wait outside."

She stepped into the shower without even taking off her dress. I was lucky to detach my arms from around her waist beforehand.

"What are you doing, Bec? Your dress! You're ruining it!"

"Who cares?" she moaned. "I'll never need it again. I'm never going on another date for as long as I live."

"Maybe a break from dating wouldn't be the worst idea in the world."

The shower struck her mid-chest. She scooped water into her hands to splash her face. Her hair was done up in curls. She managed not to get it wet while she scrubbed her face with both hands.

"I'm just gonna wait outside, okay Bec?"

"No!" she cried, like a toddler. "Stay with me! Stay!"

I grabbed a towel off the rack. "I'll turn around so you can take off your dress, okay?"

"What's the point? It's already ruined."

"Okay, well... whatever you want."

I heard her zipper go down, then heard the dress fall in a heavy wet heap.

"You'll feel so much better when you're squeaky clean," I told her.

When she didn't answer, I worried she might have a razor in there. That's the only reason I turned around.

"Ah-ha!" she said. "So you DO want to see me naked!"

"Becca..." I didn't want to admit it was a suicide-watch sort of thing. Anyway, she was only holding a bar of soap, not a razor. "Just don't be too long, okay? My hair's getting frizzy with all this steam."

"I love your hair."

My hair was nothing special, just a bronzy mess that I kept pretty short. Becca was the one with the nice hair. She always said it was too thin, too fine, but I thought it was great.

When she turned off the water, I held out a bath towel so she could step right in.

I didn't mean to look at her naked body, but how could I not? It was right there in front of me.

She held my gaze as I wrapped the towel around her nudity. I could still see it, like I suddenly had X-ray vision. I could see right through her towel. See her small, pale breasts with their little peach nipples. See her dainty curls of blonde pubic hair.

God, she was beautiful.

I stepped quickly out of the bathroom and Becca said, "Where are you going, Corrine?"

"It's late. I should get home."

"Don't go!" she cried, following me out and grabbing me by the wrist. "I'm not done with you yet."

"I know you've been through a lot," I told her. "But I work in the morning."

"Please," she begged. "You're the only friend I've got. Everyone else thinks I'm annoying."

I thought she was annoying too, but I was still her friend.

"Ten minutes," I sighed. "Why don't you put your pyjamas on and get into bed and we'll talk for a bit?"

Hopefully she'd fall asleep the second her head hit the pillow.

I tried to stay outside her bedroom while she changed, but she pulled me in for that too. I turned to face the door and I didn't spin around until she said, "Okay. You can look now."

She hadn't put on a pair of pyjamas.

She'd put on a negligee instead: white lace with pretty pink ribbons. I could see her peachy nipples through the stretchy lace. She obviously wanted me looking, because she just stood there modeling her lingerie.

I didn't know what to say.

Becca leaned back on her bed and opened her legs, giving me an unobstructed view of her pussy. The colour matched the pretty pinkness of those ribbons on her negligee.

Two soft rose petals parted to reveal a glossy interior.

She wanted me to look.

"Tell me the truth," she said. "You think I'll make a good mother, right?"

"Sure," I said. "Of course, Becca. You've got so much love to give."

Flipping onto her front, she crawled to the edge of the bed on all fours. "Please, Corrine. You're my last chance."

I forced a laugh. "Last chance? Bec, Frank's not the only fish in the sea. You'll meet someone else."

"Not before my ovaries shrivel up and die!"

"Becca, no!"

She was looking at me like a tiger about to pounce. She knew what she wanted, and she wouldn't take no for an answer.

"Please," she said, but her voice didn't sound kind or sweet. "Please, Corrine."

"No, Becca." I had to be firm with her. "I'm sorry. I'm leaving."

"You can't!" She jumped off the bed and cut me off at the door.

"Becca, I'm not going to father your child."

"Why not?" she asked, getting this crazed look in her eye. "You don't need to be involved. I just need your swimmers, Corrine. You're the only one that can help me."

As she said all this, she wrapped her hands around my wrists and held them tight.

So tight it hurt.

She forced me against the bed, pressing her nearly naked body against mine.

When I felt her breasts on mine, the sensation shocked me. Her body looked so soft, but her breasts felt hard. Not like mine. My big tits were cushiony and comforting. Her nipples poked me like needles, stabbing my chest while she pushed me down on the bed.

"You like girls," she said. "I'm a girl."

"Yeah, but we're friends," I told her. "*Just* friends."

She obviously didn't care. I could say anything and it wouldn't change her mind. She knew what she wanted and she wouldn't quit until she got it.

When my back was flat on her bed she straddled my hips and rode her hands up my belly. "I've never done this before, you know. It would be my first time."

"With a woman, you mean?"

Becca nodded greedily. "Don't you want to be my first?"

When her hands met my breasts, I couldn't say no. She squeezed my tits and that pleasure resounded in my crotch. I was already aching down there from seeing Becca naked, but now I knew nothing could ease the pain except the hot hug of my best friend's naked pussy.

"This is stupid," I said as she pushed up my clingy top. "We can't. We're friends."

"It's okay, it's okay." She pushed my top up to my neck, revealing my sturdy cream-coloured bra. "Just get me pregnant tonight and we'll go back to being friends tomorrow."

When she tugged on the cups, releasing my big breasts and dark nipples, I thought I might faint. The cool night air felt so good on my skin. Becca's warm gaze on my tits felt even better.

"We can't do this," I whispered.

She bent down until her mouth hovered just above my breast.

She looked up at me as she extended her tongue, and my whole body went weak.

I knew I should fight her off, but I couldn't.

The way her curls framed her face, she seemed so innocent, like an angel. But her eyes blazed like she'd been sent to me straight from the devil.

"Don't," I pleaded. "Once you start, I won't be able to—"

Becca licked my nipple, sending a shudder straight to my core. For a girl who'd never done this before, she knew exactly what she was doing.

When she wrapped her mouth around my nipple, I couldn't help moaning. Nothing had ever felt so good. Her sweet lips suckled my tit, pulling gently, warming my cool skin.

"Please," I begged. "Please don't do this, Becca."

But she knew what her mouth was doing to my mind. I was possessed by her beauty and ability. The more she suckled, the more my resolve wore down. I tried to wriggle away, but my body wouldn't move.

I lay beneath her, letting my best friend suck my breasts.

She wasn't doing any of this for my benefit.

She wanted me to put a baby in her.

And, goddess help me, that's what I would do.

I pulled off my top while she ripped down my jeans. She left my underwear to me, like she was afraid what she'd find even though she knew what to expect.

Her expression changed once I'd taken off my panties. She stood with her back against the wall, just staring at it.

I could have left, if I really wanted to. I could have picked up my clothes and dressed in the hall and slipped out to my car and forgotten all about this night.

"Can I touch it?" she asked.

It jerked in her direction, like it understood her words.

She laughed. "Is that a yes?"

My breath shook in my lungs. I knew she was using me, but I didn't care.

She took a step closer, extending her fingers, then drawing them back.

This time I was the one to laugh. "You're scared."

"No I'm not!"

To prove her point, she wrapped her hand around my shaft.

A little too hard.

"Sheesh, Becca! Start slow!"

"Sorry." She eased up and rubbed me with just her fingertips, sending tingles all the way to my toes.

"Oh my god, how are you so good at this?"

She giggled. "I don't know. I always liked touching them. And sucking them."

My erection throbbed in her hand.

"Guess you like that too," she said.

I nodded. I couldn't deny it.

She bent at the hips and locked on my eyes while she wrapped her lips around my tip.

If I thought it felt good when she sucked my nipples, this felt... I don't know! I don't even have a word for how incredible it felt when she went down on me, burying my shaft in her warm, wet mouth.

She stroked my base with her fist while she suckled the upper three quarters of my hardness. She burbled with pleasure, and I knew she wasn't faking. I knew her too well. If she just wanted to get knocked up, she'd have sat in my lap without any of this other stuff. She'd have made me come as fast as humanly possible, just to extract my seed.

But she wanted more than that. She wanted to make this a night we'd never forget.

Her mouth was amazing.

I loved how enthusiastic she was about giving me a blow job. She moaned around my girth as she sucked, and it made me feel so sexy I giggled.

She reached for my hands and placed them on my tits, so I guess she wanted to watch me play with them. I squeezed them together and pinched my tight nipples and twisted them around to bring more urgent pleasure to my crotch.

"Oh Becca," I cried. "Oh God, you almost made me come!"

My hardness popped out from between her lips. "Uh-oh! Better get down to business!"

She jumped on the bed and set one knee on either side of my hips. When she inched her body down, I could see my straining erection through the white lace of her negligee.

I watched my body disappear into that cluster of sweet blonde hair.

Not that I needed to watch. I felt every moment of pleasure as my tip met her slick centre and popped through the tightness of her opening.

I couldn't get over how wet she was. Blowing me must have really turned her on. Or maybe it was sucking my tits that got her so aroused.

Either way, by the time she swallowed my shaft, her pussy felt full and throbbing and ready to go. I bet her parts were pulsing as hard as mine, maybe even aching for release.

I hoped I could hold out long enough to make her come.

Her thighs were thin, pale, like marble. I couldn't resist sliding my hand up her leg, then brushing my fingers across her bare belly. I'd never touched her like this.

Her skin reacted to mine. She gasped with every pass.

She reached for my breasts and used them to steady herself while she rode me. I always imagined she was the kind of girl who would just lie there and let her partner do all the work.

But look at her now! Straddling me, bouncing on my mass, squeezing my tits together hard enough to make me scream.

"Are you coming?" she asked, her voice high up in her register.

"Soon, if you don't stop playing with my boobs."

She didn't stop.

In fact, she played with them more.

So I brushed my fingers toward her cloud of pubic hair, finding her sweet clit with my thumb.

"Oh God!" she cried, clamping her pussy muscles around my shaft. "Oh my good God, Corrine!"

I sent the ball back to her court and asked, "Are you coming?"

Her pussy fluttered around my erection.

I'd felt versions of this, but never so pronounced. Her body trembled around mine, tight, hot, wet.

She slammed her body down on mine and I rubbed her clit faster with my thumb. She panted like a dog, which was actually really cute, but it wasn't until she pinched my tits and twisted that I exploded with pleasure.

She picked herself up and dropped herself down on me over and over again, and the friction did me in.

"I'm coming!" I cried, since she was so interested. "Oh my god, Becca, don't stop!"

She twisted my tits harder. It hurt, but in a good way.

So I pinched her clit between my thumb and the side of my index finger, and I yanked that all around.

Becca's eyes bulged. "What are you doing?"

"I don't know!"

"Well, keep doing it!"

I'd never pinched a girl's clit before. I don't know where the idea came from, but apparently it was working. She bounced harder on me, and then dropped her weight down and grunted. I'd never heard a noise like that. It would have been funny if I wasn't having an orgasm at the time.

Maybe it was wishful thinking, but I doubt I'd ever spilled so much seed. She'd be leaking with the stuff once she rolled off my spent shaft.

But she didn't roll off me right away.

She rested on top of me, hugging me, feeling precious in my arms.

Now that we'd been to bed together, I had this weird sense that I had to take care of her. I guess I always felt that way, emotionally, but now it was physical too.

Becca could very well be carrying my child. I needed to defend her from the elements.

"Corrine?" she said. "Thank you for coming."

"I care about you, Becca. I wanted to make sure you were okay."

She hugged me harder, and I hugged her back.

"But I should probably get up and go. I have to work tomorrow, and then I'm thinking we should discuss a few things."

She tightened her grip around me. "Don't go. Call in sick to work. Stay here with me."

"What for?" I asked.

She arched up to look into my eyes. "What if it didn't take? We should try again, don't you think? At least three or four... or six or seven times."

I had to admit, I was surprised to hear her say all this. Had she been hot for my body the whole time we were friends?

"I guess we could try again," I said. "Anything's better than working."

Becca gave me a playful smack on the arm and I smiled.

Imagine Becca my babymama.

Imagine Becca my wife!

Wow. Things could get real serious real fast.

But when we got under the covers to cuddle, I couldn't complain.

Futa Geek Girl Gets It

AMARINDA WOULD NEVER forget the moment Carli walked into that study room.

She always reserved one of the carrels at the library when she was tutoring, because they had doors you could close and windows with blinds. They were pretty close to sound-proof, too. A lot of the students she worked with had trouble concentrating and were distracted by people on cell phones.

The library wasn't what it used to be.

And girls weren't what they used to be, either. That was among her first thoughts when she spotted Carli's floor-length gown.

They'd been introduced by phone, but this was their first face-to-face meeting. After introducing herself, Amarinda found herself captivated by the contrast of Carli's pale white skin and jet-black hair. Amarinda had black hair too, but hers wasn't a dye job. Carli hadn't coloured in her brows, which were a very pale shade of corn yellow—that was obviously Carli's natural shade.

"What are you staring at?" Carli growled.

On the phone she'd been so polite. Maybe because she'd been sitting in her guidance counsellor's office at the time.

"That's an interesting outfit you've got on," Amarinda said. "Very lacy. Almost looks like a wedding dress."

"It *is* a wedding dress," Carli said. "I dyed it black. Looks way better this way."

"And the safety pins?"

"It was ripped in places. But some are just there for fashion."

Obviously Amarinda didn't have the same grasp on "fashion" as this girl. She only had a few years on eighteen-year-old Carli, but that gap seemed cavernous.

"Come in. Sit down. Close the door behind you and we'll get started with your tutoring session."

Carli stepped into the study booth and dragged the door closed behind her. The last person in here had closed the blinds, and Amarinda hadn't opened them, but Carli glanced at her suspiciously. "Doesn't this place seem a little claustrophobic? It's so cramped."

True, there wasn't much space between the one wall and the other, but the room only housed two chairs and a long desk, which butted up against one wall.

"It serves a purpose," Amarinda said while Carli pulled her messenger bag over her head and tossed it on the desk. "Why don't you tell me what you need help with?"

"I don't need help with anything," Carli shot back. "I'm smarter than pretty much every kid in my class. Hell, I'm even smarter than my teacher."

Amarinda smirked. "I see."

Carli fell in a heap on the second chair. "Stupid Mr. Anders keeps failing me even though I'm always right about everything."

"This is your science teacher?"

"Biology, yeah." Carli unlatched her bag and pulled out a test with a big red F on the front.

At a glance, Amarinda could see how the girl had earned herself a failing grade. "You didn't answer any of the questions."

"Flip to the back," Carli said, then flipped through the pages herself. "There. See? I wrote a whole essay. And it's brilliant!"

"But there aren't any essay questions on this test. Look, you didn't fill in the short answer sections or draw any of the diagrams or—"

"The questions were all stupid and easy. Any sheep could just baaah back what the teacher wants to hear. Just read a few lines of my essay. It's amazing."

Amarinda wouldn't be able to outwit this bright young woman. Sometimes being exceptionally intelligent didn't count for much, certainly not in high school.

So Amarinda glanced over the essay Carli was so proud of. She'd written this in place of labelling the male and female anatomy charts. Her essay was adamant that Mr. Anders's course was overly simplistic because it didn't explore the true diversity of human sex organs. She included statistics, cited her sources, and even provided anatomy charts with labels of her own.

"This is very impressive work," Amarinda said.

Carli beamed momentarily, before returning to a scowl. "So then why did Mr. Anders give me an F on my paper?"

"Because you didn't answer any of his questions."

"But his questions are stupid!"

"That doesn't matter," Amarinda said. "In university you'll be able to express yourself more freely, but you'll never get into university if you flunk out of high school."

Carli's expression hardened, and just when Amarinda thought the girl would scream and shout, she instead burst into tears. "I already failed a bunch of courses last year. I'm the oldest kid in most of my classes. Not even a kid! I'm a legal adult and I'm still in high school."

"You're obviously smart enough to pass with flying colours. My suspicion is that you're just too stubborn."

All at once, Carli's sobs ceased. Her expression turned stony. She looked Amarinda straight in the eye and said, "What did you call me?"

"Stubborn," Amarinda said simply. "You could easily have passed this test, but you chose not to."

"Because I would just be telling the teacher what he wanted to hear!"

"Yes, I know. That's what school is."

"But I'd be perpetuating the myth of well-defined sexes when I know for a fact even physical sex is non-binary. I know for a fact not everybody has just a penis or just a vagina."

The tears gleaming in Carli's purple-grey eyes told Amarinda everything she needed to know. "You know... from experience."

Carli's voice cracked when she said, "Yes!"

Amarinda didn't usually show her students physical affection even when they cried, but she took a chance on Carli. Moving her chair close enough that their knees touched, Amarinda put an arm around the girl's shoulder. Carli took it one step further, wrapping both arms around Amarinda's neck and sobbing wet tears onto her skin.

"If they taught the real facts in school, nobody would think I'm a freak. They'd know I'm one version of normal. Normal isn't just this or that. Sometimes it's this *and* that."

"I'm so sorry," Amarinda said as she softly stroked Carli's hair. "If it means anything, I don't think you're a freak."

Carli pulled back and sniffled. "You don't?"

"Of course not." Amarinda smiled warmly. "Like you wrote in your very well-executed essay: *there is considerable diversity and divergence in human sex organs*. And you're right that they should teach this stuff in schools. But you won't change the world by flunking out."

Carli laughed through her tears. "I guess you're right about that."

"So ask Mr. Anders for a make-up test and this time tell him what he wants to hear. You don't need me."

Carli's eyes widened. "Yes... I do."

Amarinda's heart beat a little faster. She could tell, from the look in Carli's eyes, that the girl wasn't talking about improving her studies.

"Carli," Amarinda said. "I think perhaps we should give up our study space to someone who needs it."

The girl bit her luscious pink lip, and that one small move shook Amarinda's resolve. Those stunning grey eyes pleaded with her, begged her to stay. And she understood why. She understood the need, the want, the desire. Because she wanted everything Carli did.

"We can't do this," Amarinda said without pulling away.

"Yes we can!"

"But I'm your tutor."

"My tutor, not my teacher."

"Still..."

"And, anyway, you said I don't need your help so I hereby fire you. You're not my tutor anymore."

Amarinda realized, in that moment, that she'd set her hand on her student's hip. She gasped and pulled it away. "Oh god, I'm sorry!"

Carli caught her by the wrist and said, "It's okay. I'm an adult, just like you."

"But I'm older," Amarinda said. "I should know better."

She couldn't resist those lips. Leaning forward, she kissed the geeky Goth—her favourite kind of student because they tended to be so smart. Of course, Carli had the added benefit of a body Amarinda couldn't pass up.

"Have you ever done this before?" Amarinda asked as she moved down, kissing Carli's long white marble neck.

Carli gave a laugh. "Who'd want me?"

"I want you," Amarinda admitted.

"Oh god!"

Amarinda's fingers moved behind Carli's back, seeking out a zipper on that black wedding dress. Carli got it for her, and pulled it down while Amarinda slipped the gown from the girl's pale shoulders. Amarinda kissed them both, and kissed her chest when the girl stood, letting her dress fall to the floor. She stepped out of it wearing knee-high Doc Martens and a gorgeous silk slip.

"Wow." Amarinda traced her fingers gently up the cream-coloured slip. Up the girl's slim side, up her belly, up to her breasts, which were barely a handful.

When Amarinda cupped the girl's sweet breasts, Carli said, "Your turn."

If only she'd worn more attractive undergarments. Nothing she owned could compare to Carli's vintage slip, but that didn't seem to matter. When she pulled off her heavy sweater, Carli's eyes bulged. Amarinda had quite large breasts, which looked fantastic in a sturdy black bra.

She stood from her chair and pushed her jeans to the floor, slipping off her shoes and socks all in one go. Her panties were hot pink, which made Carli laugh. They didn't match the bra, but at least they were memorable.

"We shouldn't be doing this," Amarinda said once more, not because she thought it would have any effect—only because she felt like she should. For a tutor, sleeping with a high school student was very poor form. But she had a feeling Carli wouldn't tell anyone.

When Carli hooked her thumbs beneath her slip and tugged down a pair of panties, Amarinda became senseless with lust. She pressed the girl against the wall, using only her belly and her breasts. Carli gasped with surprised, but didn't fight when Amarinda planted a forceful kiss on her lips.

"God, you're gorgeous!" Amarinda sighed.

Carli laughed incredulously. "You're the gorgeous one."

"I'm a nerd," Amarinda said as her slick hair escaped from its ponytail.

Carli wove her fingers through Amarinda's hair. "I'm a geek."

Amarinda tugged Carli's crunchy braids and the strange ribbons and clips she wore. "It's been so long, for me."

"At least you've done it before. I never have."

"I'm older."

"I'm not a kid anymore."

Amarinda couldn't say why those words turned her on so hard, but she kissed the girl with yet more force and tore the straps of that silky slip down her shoulders. Carli's breasts weren't big enough to hold it up. It fell to her waist while Amarinda struggled out of her bra.

When their breast met skin to skin, it was like coming home to a place you've never been. Amarinda's brown tits were huge, but Carli's were cute with hard, peachy nipples that poked into Amarinda's dark ones. They kissed harder, wrapping their arms one around the other, hugging so their tits would touch. More than touch: their breasts smashed against each other, so hot Amarinda could feel the gusset of her panties growing slick with juice.

She couldn't resist seeing what was happening under Carli's slip. Goodness knows she could already feel it.

Falling to her knees on the library's industrial blue carpet, Amarinda lifted Carli's slip. The girl's cock popped up, making a beeline for Amarinda's ready lips. She couldn't resist. Letting the slip hang over the girl's marble shaft, Amarinda took her first lick.

"Ohhh!" Carli groaned, stifling the sound by biting her forearm.

"You have to be quiet," Amarinda whispered. "There's no lock on that door."

The idea of a librarian intruding upon them made her heart race. She was a regular at this library. She knew many of the people who worked here, and they often recommended students to her for tutoring. They wouldn't know, at a glance, that Carli was over eighteen. They'd probably call the police!

Backing away from Carli's beckoning cock, Amarinda shook her head. "We can't do this here."

Carli's bottom lip trembled. "But... I thought you liked me."

"I do." Amarinda reached for her bra, but it seemed to have disappeared. "It's just... if we get caught it would be ruinous for me. They'd never let me set foot in this library again."

Much to Amarinda's surprise, Carli wrapped both hands around her head and said, "Then we'd better do this quick."

The girl pulled Amarinda's face swiftly toward her crotch. Resistance was futile. The truth was that Amarinda wanted that luscious cock in her mouth.

It tasted amazing. She would suck it all day if she didn't have other clients later on.

Stifling her cries, Carli whispered, "That feels so good. You're getting me so wet!"

Amarinda had already forgotten that Carli had more than just a cock. She explored with her fingers, feeling around where she expected balls to be. Instead, Carli had pussy lips and a wet, juicy slit. She pressed two fingers inside and Carli whimpered.

"Be gentle," Carli whispered.

This girl really was a virgin!

Amarinda had never finger-fucked a virgin pussy, apart from her own. It was a big responsibility, and a huge pleasure. Carli's cunt was swollen and tight, and so sopping wet that pussy juice drenched Amarinda's hand.

Felt so good to suck the girl's dick and fuck her sweet pussy at the same time.

Obviously felt good to Carli too. The girl bit her bottom lip to keep from squealing, and Amarinda could see the pain of not being able to scream creasing her brow.

Carli clung to Amarinda's hair, bringing her closer, forcing that firm dick deeper down her throat.

Even when she sputtered and choked, Amarinda still loved sucking cock. She loved the pleasure it brought the virgin geek girl. More than that, she loved the friction she felt against her closed lips. She also loved the way Carli's cunt clamped down on her fingers with every plunge.

"I want more," Amarinda whispered as she rose from the floor and pushed down her panties.

When she hopped up on the desk and spread her legs, Carli's eyes bugged. "Wow. You've got a big clit."

Amarinda blushed. "You really think so?"

"Yeah!"

"Not as big as yours."

"No, but..." Carli's pale cheeks turned red as she pushed down her slip. "It's still pretty big."

"Thanks," Amarinda said with a smile.

Her clit was nowhere near the size of Carli's cock, but she always wondered if there was someone in the world who could turn her on enough that her dick would grow to a fuckable size.

Now she thought perhaps Carli was that girl.

Wearing nothing but her big black boots, the nearly-naked Goth girl pulled a chair between Amarinda's parted legs. She sat and stared.

A knot developed in Amarinda's stomach, and she said, "You don't have to... if you're nervous."

"Nervous," Carli repeated. "I am nervous... but I still want to."

She bowed toward her tutor's clit as Amarinda leaned her bare back against the wall. If someone opened that unlocked door, the first thing they'd see would be her big brown boobs.

The second thing they'd see would be the student between her legs.

She tried to say "We shouldn't be doing this," but the words wouldn't leave her lips.

Carli glanced up with a fearful look in her soft grey eyes. "Will you tell me if I'm bad?"

Amarinda's heart swelled. "Honey, you won't be. Geeks give the best head."

A glorious smile crossed Carli's lips as she bowed between Amarinda's legs. Her first lick was cautious, but that was always the way with a virgin. They were afraid of everything they'd never done.

It was only natural.

Amarinda had been the same way.

The more Carli went at it, the stronger her little licks became. As she caressed Amarinda's clit, it swelled and grew. Carli traced her tongue round and round in circles, and then, totally without prompting, took it in her mouth and sucked.

Amarinda groaned against her better judgement. She thought she saw a shadow cross in front of the door and kicked at the second chair. "Prop that under the handle," she instructed her student.

Carli did as she was told, angling the chair back so it would keep the door closed if someone tried to enter.

When Amarinda's gaze turned to her own crotch, she was shocked by what she saw. "It's never gotten that big before. I almost wonder..."

"If you could fuck me with it," Carli said, finishing her thought.

Amarida slipped down from the desk and seated herself in Carli's abandoned chair. She backed it up against the wall so she wouldn't topple over, then smacked her thighs with both hands. "Climb on board. Let's see if we can take you for a ride."

Carli giggled nervously. Even with the strange black hair and the big boots, she didn't seem so intimidating anymore. She seemed more like a manga character, a virgin princess who'd never sampled the pleasures of the flesh.

"Like this?" she asked, straddling Amarinda, standing so close her little nipples touched her tutor's lips.

Amarinda sucked those sweet tits, fondling her swollen clit with one hand and fingering her student with the other. Carli obviously couldn't handle this much arousal. Her knees buckled and she began to tumble. Amarinda extracted her fingers from the girl's wet cunt, but held her clit steady.

She guided the girl's slim body, helping it to land in the perfect place.

Amarinda's clit had grown to the size of a small cock.

Carli gasped as Amarinda's big clit filled her unpenetrated pussy, but she didn't scream the way a good girl would if she were slammed with a monster cock.

A starter cock. That's what Amarinda had. A starter cock, perfect for deflowering virgin pussies.

Sweet, untouched virgin pussies.

The very idea made her clit throb. She could feel it growing inside her student's cunt, getting firmer and larger, stretching that virgin vagina.

"You love this," Amarinda growled.

"Shhh," Carli hissed, but when Amarinda forced her clit all up inside that girl's pussy, she groaned and said, "Yeah I do. I love it."

Carli was easy to fuck, even from below. The geek girl was skinny and light as a feather, easy to bounce—especially on a lap as pillowy and wide as Amarinda's.

"You're gonna make me come," Carli whimpered.

Amarinda wrapped her fist around Carli's cockhead. "Don't you dare!" Tossing the girl aside, she bent over the desk, stuck out her butt and parted her legs. "Not until you've fucked me first."

Carli seemed apprehensive, like she didn't know where to begin.

"Just stick your dick where it's wet," Amarinda told her student.

Carli took one step closer.

"You're overthinking it. Let your cock do the walking."

The Goth girl made a pained sound. She covered both eyes with her hands and said, "Fine!"

Blindly, she thrust forward. Her cock found its way between Amarinda's thick thighs, but not inside her cunt.

"See?" Carli said. "It's harder than it looks."

"It sure is," Amarinda replied as she caught the girl's dick and rubbed.

Carli whimpered as her tutor nudged her dickhead into a less virginal but still fairly inexperienced vagina.

"Oh my god," Carli groaned. "It's so hot and tight and... oh my god!"

"Don't tell me you're coming already."

"Soon!" Carli warned, wrapping both arms around Amarinda's back to play with her big tits.

When the girl teased her tits, Amarinda's toes went numb. She felt an extraordinary burst of pleasure between her thighs, and moved her hand to her neglected clit. It didn't feel as big as it had when it was inside the girl's virgin pussy, but it was still wet with Carli's juices.

Amarinda played with her big clit while Carli moved jerkily behind her.

"I'm so bad at this!" the girl whined.

"Just keep going. You'll get better."

"But I'm gonna... I'm... oh god!"

Carli's whole body trembled while Amarinda rubbed herself wildly. She was so close to coming inside Carli's cunt that it didn't take long to get that feeling back. She stroked off rapidly beneath the desk while the dick in her pussy swelled and pulsed.

"God, you're like a tree trunk!" Amarinda growled.

"Feels so... feels so..."

"God!" Amarinda squeaked. "I can taste colours!"

"What?" Carli said, and when she laughed her cock throbbed wildly.

Her whole body started gyrating, like her dick was a jackhammer and she didn't know how to use it. She hammered Amarinda's cunt in imprecise stabs. With one thrust, she'd come out and jab Amarinda's thigh. With the next, she'd jet back in and hammer the tutor's depths.

"I can't stop it," Carli cried.

"Shhhh!" Amarinda said, then squeaked, "Neither can I!"

Amarinda's knees knocked. Her calves trembled but her thighs locked. When she came, she had to use Carli's trick of biting her arm. Otherwise she'd have screamed until her throat went raw.

As she came, her cunt locked on Carli's cock so it couldn't get out. The girl was trapped inside, and she bit into Amarinda's back to stay silent. Well, not totally silent. She still made puppy-ish whimpering noises while her cream filled her tutor's pussy.

They stayed like that, locked together while their bodies trembled with wave after wave of orgasm.

Amarinda's cunt was full. Her fist remained wrapped around her clit, which pulsed so hard she'd have thought it would get bigger. But it didn't. It got smaller, just like Carli's spent cock, which slipped wetly from between Amarinda's thighs.

"Oh god, I can't catch my breath," Amarinda said. "Where are my clothes? We need to get... oh god... get dressed."

"Do you have another student?" Carli asked as she picked up her panties and put them on.

"I'm afraid I do."

Cum leaked down Amarinda's thigh while she crumpled against the desk, her ass in the air, her legs inexplicably supporting her despite the weakness in her muscles.

Once Carli had put on her slip, she picked up her tutor's panties and lifted Amarinda's feet off the ground, one and then the other. She pulled those hot pink undies up and then went for the black bra.

Amarinda took over dressing herself, since it wouldn't be easy for a girl with small breasts to put on her bra for her. "You're an amazing kid. You know that?"

Carli's expression fell. "I'm not a kid." She grabbed her gown roughly off the floor.

Finding her jeans and sweater, Amarinda said, "You're right. I don't know why I said that."

"Because you want to minimize what just happened between us," Carli said, right on the mark. "If you say I'm just a kid, then you don't have to see me again, when really all you want to do right now is take me out and buy me dinner and talk and talk... then take me home and fuck and fuck... then cuddle all night long."

Every word was true. Still, Amarinda tensed.

"I've never had a real adult relationship," Carli said as she pulled on her black wedding dress. "But I can see myself with you. I can see a future together."

Amarinda put on her sweater and fastened her jeans before saying, "Carli, you're still in high school."

"So what? Take me out on a date. Let's see if our brains are as hot for each other as our bodies are."

There was a knock at the door, and Amarinda jumped while Carli rushed to zip up her gown. She grabbed her messenger bag, pulled the chair away, and opened the door.

Dante stood outside the study room, ready for his tutoring session.

Carli stormed past him, saying, "You've got my number—and I've got yours."

Dante stepped into the study room and dumped his books on the desk. "Smells funny in here."

Amarinda opened the blinds and watched Carli storm through the library. "Get out your homework. I'll be right back."

She raced through the stacks, catching up with Carli on the steps outside the building. The weather had turned and Carli looked cold wearing nothing but black lace and silk.

"Okay," Amarinda said. "You're right."

"I know I'm right. I'm always right."

"But I won't take you out until you pass that make-up test."

Carli rolled her eyes, but also smirked. "Piece of cake."

Amarinda lowered her voice. "And I won't sleep with you until you've earned that high school diploma."

The geek girl's expression fell. "What? That's not fair! You know I'm smart enough."

"I know you are. Now you need to prove it to your school. Answer the questions they ask. You can be a know-it-all in university."

Carli's lips pursed. "I'm not a know-it-all."

Amarinda raised an eyebrow.

"Okay, maybe sometimes."

"Think of it this way: now you've got something to look forward to when you graduate."

"But you're still gonna take me out on a date," Carli confirmed.

"Saturday. I'll take you to a see this local theatre group—really intellectual stuff. You'd like it."

"And dinner?"

Amarinda smiled. "You're so demanding."

"That's how I get what I want," Carli said simply.

Amarinda wanted so badly to kiss the girl in front of everyone but knowing she shouldn't. "How do I get what I want?"

With a shrug, Carli said, "All you have to do is ask."

That geek girl couldn't graduate soon enough, because there was so much Amarinda wanted... and she was going to ask for it all.

Futa Girls Repopulate the Planet

AFTER FORTY DAYS, THE answer was clear: we were the last six people on earth.

First we turned to social media. If technology was still functioning, you'd think survivors would take to Twitter, to Facebook—anything to get the word out. Technology isn't a message in a bottle. You don't have to wait twenty years for a response. If anyone was out there, you'd think we'd hear back instantly.

But we didn't. We heard nothing. The bunker had saved us when so many had perished.

We were numb when we first came out. Not Nina, obviously. Nina always knows what to do. That's why she's in charge.

But the rest of us: Ines, Charlotte, April, Tandy and me—Gabrielle—we didn't know up from down. Even after all the drills we'd done in school, we would have forgotten to take our fallout pills if Nina hadn't reminded us.

She'd trained for this.

We all did, I guess, but how much of your schooling do *you* remember?

And who *are* you, by the way? If we're the only ones left, who am I writing this for? Aliens?

I'll tell you one thing I've only ever confessed to Charlotte, because she knows how to keep a secret: I don't really believe there are no more people.

Don't say that around Nina. She's convinced we're the only ones left. But think about how many people are—*were*—on this planet. Billions, right? Was it 7 billion or 70 billion? I don't remember, but it was a lot.

Do I really think all those other humans died in the explosions? Not for a second. If we six survived it, others did too.

Aside from Nina, we're just average girls. Nina's superhuman, like a comic book hero. She should wear a cape. Except she's not pretty like that. She doesn't have long hair and an hourglass figure. She's stocky and muscular with golden brown skin and black hair she's kept short for as long as I've known her.

She doesn't look like Wonder Woman, but she knows how to take charge.

And we need that.

Because even if there *are* pockets of six humans here and there on the planet, we obviously haven't been able to make contact. It would be great if the space shuttle was still up there looking down on things, but that got blown up early in the conflict.

Seems like years ago. I guess it was only six or eight weeks.

It's weird how life can change in an instant. All-out war takes hold and the world goes crazy.

Now everyone's dead but us.

Maybe.

My theory is that there have to be people still around. People who lived so remotely no one would think of targeting them. Like one time I saw a show about these goat herders in Mongolia. Or maybe it wasn't goats. Maybe it was sheep. Anyway, they herded something and they were nomads. They lived in the mountains and they didn't have cell phones.

I bet they're still around.

But Nina gets mad when people contradict her, so I keep my mouth shut. That's fine. I really don't mind. The last thing I want to do is start arguing with one of the only people left on Earth.

There are so many things I regret saying. To my mom especially. And my dad, but he didn't like conflict any more than me.

That's what I talk about around the fire with Charlotte and Ines. At night we conserve energy. There's just darkness and night sky and moonlight and fire. It's actually really nice, if you tell yourself you're on vacation and you'll come home eventually and everything will be like it was.

But nothing will ever be like it was. Everything I cared about is gone.

Nina knew how to build shelter. She told us what to do and we followed her instructions. It's good to work at times like this. Physical labour gives you something to focus on, and something to tire you out so you don't toss and turn all night long. That's Nina's theory, but I actually agree with her there.

Now Nina has a new plan, and she wants to get started right away. "While we're young," she says.

There are no secrets when you live in close quarters. She found out pretty fast that me and Charlotte and April are a little different from her and Tandy and Ines. The fact of the matter is that we've got parts they don't.

And that means we can propagate the species.

That's how Nina puts it: propagate the species, like we're animals in a zoo. I don't know what I'd call her plan. To say we're getting the other girls pregnant sounds so romantic, like we'll all pair off into couples and get married or something.

To be honest, the thought of having sex with any one of my friends weirds me right out. I'd never have imagined it until Nina started all this propagation talk. But it's not like I've got a leg to stand on. If we really are the last six girls on Earth, do I really want the species to die with us?

Maybe I do.

After all, look at what we've done to this planet. We exploded everything on it, even ourselves!

Maybe we deserve to die.

Even if I don't always agree with Nina, I do trust her to make decisions for the group. And she's decided that we're doing this.

We're repopulating the earth.

Gosh. That's a lot of responsibility.

She's really scientific about it, though. She listed off all our various traits and determined that April should mate with Tandy, Charlotte with Ines, and me with her.

Let me tell you, the idea of having sex with Nina doesn't exactly excite me. I hope she doesn't find this and read it, but even if she does I hope she'll understand.

I'm not exactly into girls. I'm not exactly into anyone. I had a boyfriend but we didn't go all the way, and now I hate to think of him because it reminds me of everything we've lost.

The world is over unless we save it.

And, even if we do, it won't bring back the people who are gone.

NINA TOLD US WE'D BEGIN that night. Night was a good time. Hopefully it would be dark enough that I wouldn't have to look at her too much.

The plan was to go one at a time—one couple in front of the others. That way it would be less awkward. I'm not sure how having sex with one of your closest friends while your other friends watch could possibly NOT be awkward, but Nina said it was better this way.

She said we'd do this every night until the girls with the ovaries knew they were pregnant.

That could take ages. Makes me tired just thinking about it.

The other rule she made was that there couldn't be any canoodling behind each other's backs. Canoodling is my word, not Nina's. Actually it's my mom's word, but I don't want to think about her right now.

Anyway, the no canoodling rule was so we could keep track of which children belonged to which parents. We'd obviously have to be strict with them about who could mate with whom. Hopefully none of our kids would want to have sex with their own brother or sister, but... ewww, why did I even think that?

Here's another weird thought: if the pregnancies took, we'd all be parents before the year was up. We'd have to raise kids. The plan was to do it communally, as a group, to take the pressure off ourselves as individuals and to further reinforce that we're not three couples.

We're just six people repopulating the earth.

Oh boy. This was a lot of pressure.

I wasn't looking forward to nightfall, but it came as it always did. The day had been hot, but the night wasn't cold. We dragged the reed sleeping mats that Charlotte and Tandy made away from the light of the fire and we put them all in a circle.

Nina pulled Tandy's mat into the middle and said, "April? Tandy? You're up first."

They looked at each other cautiously, and April said, "I'm only doing this because we have to."

"Well, me too!" Tandy shot back.

They were acting like children, but when it came my turn I'm sure I would too.

At least April and Tandy were evenly matched. They both had small bodies, small breasts. Tandy was a little taller, a little slimmer. She used to be more pale but we were all shades of gold or brown now, and she was no exception. Her hair used to be darker and now it was sandy, almost blonde. She looked like an athlete but she was terrible at sports.

I'd known her forever.

This was so weird.

I'd known April forever as well. She was born in China and adopted by white parents in the Netherlands, so she speaks with an accent but not a Chinese accent. So, right from the moment you meet her, April's never what you expect her to be.

She's got a great fashion sense. I never thought she could survive in a bunker. She likes shopping too much. She was always so into her looks before. Now, with no makeup and wearing what amounted to rags, she was still very pretty, but a bit of her glow had gone.

Nina worked us to the bone, but it was necessary work. Besides, who else would do it?

"Take off your clothes," Nina said. "We're making babies, here. We need to be naked."

"No we don't," April shot back. "You can get pregnant with your clothes on. Well, if you're wearing a skirt, I guess, and you've got your panties pulled to one side."

Tandy butted in, saying, "It's okay, Nina. We'll take off our clothes."

"But we don't *need* to," April bit back. "That's all I'm saying."

"Tandy understands my intentions," Nina said. "It's about the ritual. We come together naked every night. When we're naked, we engaged in coitus for the purpose of procreation. After coitus is complete, we put our clothes back on and we go back to being who we are. Nothing we do or say while naked is a reflection on our relationships while clothed. Is that understood?"

"Yes, Nina," we all said, even though I'm not totally sure what she meant. Charlotte gave me a look which told me she felt the same way, but it was easier to go along.

I'd glimpsed everyone naked since the fallout, but that doesn't mean I'd sat there watching them undress. I felt like a total pervert staring at my friends while they took off their tops and their ragged pants.

Luckily we were far enough away from the fire that I only really saw them in shadow as they kneeled together on Tandy's reed mat. I could see that they were facing each other. I could see that they were naked, but I tried not to focus on the way their hair shimmered in the moonlight or how the fire painted their golden skin shades of tiger orange.

I tried especially hard not to stare at their breasts, which was very very difficult to do. If there are bare breasts in front of you, you're obviously going to stare at them. Even if you've seen a hundred million breasts in your lifetime, you're still going to stare.

Of course, I hadn't seen a hundred million. I hadn't seen much of anything.

So maybe I stared a little more than I wanted to at Tandy and April. Both girls had roughly the same sized breasts, but they were so different. April's were little cones with soft pink nipples. So sweet and pure the night seemed to lick them with every gentle breeze.

Tandy's were more like oranges than cones. Even in the darkness I could tell her breasts were the same pale skin I remember—a very different colour than her face or her arms or her shoulders. Pale globes with peachy nipples. Hers were soft, too. Not pointy.

I wondered if that would change as the night progressed.

"Well?" Nina asked. "What are you two waiting for, a written invitation?"

April gazed up at Nina, who was hovering over them. "I don't know what I'm supposed to do!"

"Don't tell me you've never engaged in coitus before."

"No P-in-V coitus, no."

"What other kind is there?" Tandy asked.

A blush took over April's cheeks as she said, "Just hand stuff."

"A hand job isn't coitus," Tandy said.

"Why do we keep saying coitus?" Ines jumped in. "Nobody uses that word. Call it sex like a normal person."

"No," Nina said. "This isn't sex. Sex involves love or at least attraction. What we're doing tonight and every night is simply about procreation. We're not engaging in these activities for the fun of it."

"That's for sure," April grumbled, folding her arms across her bare breasts.

Tandy rolled her eyes and said, "Thaaaanks."

"It's not you," April said without looking directly at our friend. "You know you're like... hot or whatever."

Tandy made a face. "Pfft! You're the hot one."

"Me? I'm too short to be hot."

"You can be short and hot," Tandy said. "I mean anyone can, but you definitely are."

"You're hotter."

"You are!"

April sat a little straighter. "Thanks."

Whether she believed it or not, she obviously appreciated the compliment.

"Anyway," April went on. "All I was trying to say is that I've never fucked a girl and it's gonna be weird."

"I've never fucked a girl either!" Tandy screeched.

Nina cut in at that point. "This isn't about who's been to bed with whom. It's about repopulating the planet. I don't care if it's weird. I don't care if you don't want to. You just have to do it."

"Well, Tandy's gonna have to do more than just sit there," April said. "She needs to get me hard and I'm totally not right now."

Nina pointed to Tandy. "You heard what she said. Get going."

"Going how?" Tandy asked. "What am I supposed to do?"

Seeming stumped, Nina looked to April. "What do you want her to do?"

April sighed, then sat back with both hands behind her and her legs outstretched, Tandy between them. "I guess you can give me a handy."

Tandy looked pleadingly at Nina. "Do I have to?"

"Yes."

Did she really expect the answer to be no?

"Just do it," April said. "Let's get this over with."

Tandy growled. "Fine!"

April's dick must have been super-soft and hanging between her legs, because I couldn't even see it until Tandy lifted it up, balls and all. Even then, it wasn't big.

"What should I do?" Tandy asked, cradling our friend's sack.

"Stroke it," April said.

Tandy did, with just one finger, like she was petting a dog but she was afraid of it. "It's not working."

April tossed her head back and closed her eyes. "Here, I'll pretend you're someone else."

"Oooh, who?" Charlotte asked.

"None of your business," April said with a laugh, but it wasn't long before her dick grew erect in Tandy's hand.

Charlotte said, "Whoever he was, you must have really liked him!"

April's brow creased. Her lips pursed. After a sniffle, she said, "I really did."

We were all quiet after that. The only sound, aside from the crackling fire, was the whoosh of Tandy's fist shuttling up and down April's cock.

After a while, April said, "Okay. You should get on now."

I figured Tandy would object to being on top, but she didn't argue at all. She just walked her knees up either side of April's body and held her pussy lips open. April leaned all the way down, so she was on her back. She held her shaft by the base while Tandy sunk down on it.

"Holy Jesus," Tandy said, like she was surprised how good it felt.

April covered her eyes with her arm and said, "Don't talk."

Who knows what fantasy she'd escaped into, but if it kept her hard, all the power to her.

Once Tandy had consumed April's cock, she didn't do much else. She basically just sat there straddling our friend.

Finally, April smacked her thigh and said, "Move!"

"Oww! Move how?"

"Move *sexually*!"

"Don't hit me!"

"Don't..." Instead of finishing that sentence, April just growled. "I hate you so much!"

"Oh, real nice! Tell the girl who's fucking you that you hate her."

"You're not even fucking me." April looked up at Nina. "She's not even fucking me! Make her do something."

Nina growled, then stomped behind April and grabbed her by the armpits. "Come on, get going."

I had to bite my lip not to laugh. Nina worked her like a water pump, up and down. I'd been so worried it would be uncomfortable to watch my friends putting on a live sex show, but that's not what this turned out to be. It was more like improv comedy.

"Whoa, whoa, whoa, whoa!" Tandy said as her head bobbed. Her breasts were just big enough to get a bit of bounce going, and I have to admit I felt a twinge of arousal when I noticed them.

Boobs are truly mesmerising.

April's were small enough that they remained steady as mountains while Nina bounced April on her dick. Her face was still buried under her arms, but her body was starting to show strain. I don't know if the moon got brighter or my eyes just adjusted to the night, but I could see her muscles tensing, especially around her chest and shoulders. Then her hips rose off the mat and she bucked into Tandy's cunt.

"Drop her, Nina!"

Nina backed off with both hands in the air, like Tandy was a gun the police had told her to set on the ground and walk away from.

April grabbed Tandy's hips, and Tandy jerked forward, catching herself on April's arms. Tandy kept bouncing, but now it was April driving the motion. April fucked our friend from below, so hard I could hear her dick sloshing in Tandy's vagina. It was a wet squelching sound, which made me wonder what had turned Tandy on enough to get that juicy.

"Oh God, I'm gonna come," April squeaked.

Tandy didn't say anything for a second. Then it was just: "Good."

When she started bouncing harder, I think she was driving the action just as much as April. She probably wanted to come too, but she didn't. She gritted her teeth while April cried out, and that was that.

Tandy asked, "You came, right?"

April panted beneath her, nodding. "Yeah. Oh my god. That was hard."

I'm not sure if she meant she came hard, or it was hard to come.

Tandy started to get up, but Nina said, "Stay. And try to suck her cum into your womb."

"Womb? Eww." Tandy made a face.

"Visualize yourself becoming pregnant," Nina said. "Every little bit helps."

"I don't even *want* to be pregnant," Tandy grumbled.

"None of us *wants* to be pregnant," said Ines. "But if we don't do it, no one will. The fate of the world is down to us."

Charlotte whimpered. I don't think she meant to. It was a big responsibility, though: growing little humans, raising them together. This wasn't the life I'd imagined for myself, but I guess sometimes circumstance dictates the path you'll take.

This was our path: repopulating the planet.

"Charlotte? Ines? You're up next." Grabbing April and Tandy's mat, Nina tugged it to the outside of the circle without dislodging April's spent cock from Tandy's juicy cunt.

Ines got up off her mat and dragged it to the middle. She undressed immediately, exposing herself to us all. Her skin was golden like Nina's, but even darker brown and not just from the sun. I think her dad was from like South America. I forget where, exactly, but that place probably didn't exist anymore.

Nothing really existed anymore.

Except us.

"Scared?" Ines asked Charlotte, who hadn't left the outer edges of the circle. Ines waved her over. "Come on. It'll be fun."

"It's not supposed to be fun," Nina said. "It's supposed to be productive."

"Reproductive," Tandy said with a giggle.

Nina ignored her.

Charlotte grumbled as she rose from her mat.

Ines had a young-looking body, but Charlotte didn't. Not that Charlotte looked old. She didn't at all. She just looked much fuller, fleshier. She'd lost a lot of weight since the start of the war, because of all the rationing, and even more since the fallout, but she retained her natural buxom figure even now.

Her big breasts swayed beneath her tattered shirt as she approached Ines, who was standing on her mat.

"Take your clothes off," Ines said, clapping her hands together. "Let's do this thing."

With a sigh, Charlotte lifted her shirt over her copper curls and let it fall beside her. Without a bra, her breasts hung low. Her nipples looked forward, straight at Ines. Peachy-pink nipples versus dark brown. Hard to say which were prettier. Maybe call it a tie.

Charlotte sighed again, and pushed down her pants. Ines immediately got on her knees to look at Charlotte's cock up close. Charlotte wasn't hard, but she wasn't exactly soft. Her balls were huge, which pushed out her penis while Ines approached it.

Ines parted her lips and allowed Charlotte's pink tip between them.

"Christ," Charlotte said. Her chest heaved and her breasts shook. She placed her palm on top of Ines's head. "Don't let me come in your mouth."

"Don't come in her mouth!" Nina growled.

Charlotte's spine straightened noticeably. "I won't, okay?"

"Mmm," Ines moaned as she sucked more of Charlotte's dick into her mouth.

"This really is unnecessary," Nina said.

"Unnecessary?" Charlotte asked. "How else am I gonna get hard?"

Nina growled. "Fine."

I think Charlotte was just really enjoying the blowjob, not that she'd ever admit something like that. She was so proper in so many ways. We were good friends, but if I was a prude, she was a prude times a million. She blushed whenever we talked about sex, and the topic was never initiated by her.

She always reminded me of the kind of girl who would have been a dairy maid in a past life.

Oh cheese... I'd forgotten about cheese. Maybe one day we'd come across a herd of wandering cows and Charlotte could milk them for us. Nina probably knew how to make cheese. She knew everything.

"You have to stop," Charlotte said, pushing on Ines's shoulders with her fingertips. She whispered, "Stop or I'll come."

"Already?" Ines asked. "Wow. That was fast."

I could hear Charlotte's blush in the sound of her voice when she said, "I'm sorry."

"Don't apologize," Nina said. "Quick and efficient. That's just the way to do things."

Ines folded herself down on the mat so she was facing up at Charlotte. "You want to do it this way, with you on top?"

Charlotte seemed hesitant, but said, "Okay. I guess."

She didn't move.

"I don't want to crush you," she told Ines. "I'm so fat."

Ines laughed, and said, "Don't worry about it, honey. The guys I've had haven't exactly been puny."

Charlotte gasped and covered her mouth, then laughed. "Just tell me if I'm hurting you, okay?"

"I promise."

When Charlotte got between our friend's legs, I took a good look at her cock. We were such good friends that it took some effort to convince myself to look there. I was pretty surprised. Her cock was kind of huge. I'd never seen it erect before. Even when it was soft, I'd never stared at it.

I could never picture Charlotte having sex. Even now, before my very eyes, it didn't seem real. She got down between Ines's parted legs and guided her dick toward our friend's pussy.

"You're sure?" Charlotte asked.

"She's sure," Nina growled.

"I mean you're ready?"

Ines felt her crotch. "Slick and slippery."

"What from?"

"From blowing you," Ines said. "I love sucking cock. I could do it all day."

I felt a twitch between my legs as Charlotte said, "Really?"

"Enough chit-chat," Nina cut in. "This was going so well until now."

Charlotte sighed as she pressed her pink tip between Ines's legs. I couldn't see what her pussy looked like, because of the way her legs were bent, so I watched her face as Charlotte pressed into her. At first, she wore this expression like she felt a bit of pain. That didn't last long, though. Soon enough, this blissful look took over. She sighed as Charlotte leaned in so close her breasts hung against Ines's.

"I've never done this," Charlotte said, pumping awkwardly. "Sorry. I'm bad at it, I know."

"You're doing okay," Ines said, but I knew her so well. I knew when she was lying.

When I took my turn with Nina, I hoped I wouldn't look so jerky. Charlotte leaned forward, then pulled back. She obviously didn't know what she was doing. Finally, she just collapsed on top of Ines and said, "I can't! I'm sorry!"

"Ines?" Nina said. "Take over."

"I'm sorry!" Charlotte sobbed.

Ines rolled her like a beached whale. Sounds mean, but that's exactly how it looked. They weren't even on the mat anymore when Ines climbed on top.

That girl knew how to work it. She didn't just sit there like Tandy had done. She didn't bounce like when Nina forced the motion. She kind of slid back and forth in this really slithery way that made her look sexy as anything.

I didn't want to feel attracted to Ines, but it was hard not to when she moved like that. Her small body rolled with each thrust, and I could tell (though don't ask me how) that she was rubbing her clit against Charlotte's belly.

Charlotte started whimpering when Ines grabbed her tits and squeezed. Not just squeezed, but mushed them together and took those nipples and played with them. Took Charlotte's tits between her fingers like a horse's reins and flapped them around. Those big breasts bounced, which made Ines smile.

"You'll get better," she said encouragingly. "See? You're doing it already."

At first I wasn't sure what Charlotte was doing differently. Then I noticed a subtle movement and realized she was rolling her hips, driving her dick into Ines's pussy in corresponding motions.

Ines kept on riding, getting louder and louder with every push. She was pretty driven, that girl. If she wanted to come, she'd get there. She rocked harder on Charlotte's cock, flapping those tits, calling out words that Charlotte had probably never heard before.

"That's right. Make me come," Charlotte panted.

Nina grumbled, "Well, that kind of smut-talk is not really necessary."

"Make me come! Make me come!"

As Ines got really noisy, Charlotte started making these sounds that were like sneezes, really high-pitched and weird.

"You coming?" Ines asked. "Come with me, baby. Let's go. Let's go. Let's... oh yeah..."

Charlotte made more sneezing sounds as Ines collapsed on top of her.

Nina rolled them onto their mat and pulled it back into place.

Oh god. It was our turn next. I felt like someone had reached into my gut and tied all my intestines in knots.

"Come on," Nina said. "It's getting late."

I got up reluctantly and pulled my mat to the middle. I couldn't hide my erection. It surprised even me.

"Good," Nina said. "You're ready to start."

I sighed.

When Nina stripped bare, I was glad to already be hard. Her body was so muscly and massive I just couldn't see it as attractive. Her chest reminded me of when we used to have Olympics and there were those powerful swimmers from Germany or Russia or something. They were like mini-hulks.

That was Nina. Mini-hulk Nina.

And, god, her bush. Not that any of us could talk. But hers was so full and dark it was like... did I really have to insert any portion of my anatomy into *that*?

I took off my clothes but nothing happened. Nina looked at me. There was no flicker in her eye, no evidence of attraction.

She got on all fours with her muscular ass in the air, then turned her head and said, "Go on."

I tried not to act too resistant as I kneeled behind her. Thank goodness for this abundant erection. Hopefully I'd blow my load as soon as I got inside her.

But here's the thing: I pressed my engorged tip everywhere I thought her slit might be (couldn't see that well in the dark, and with all that hair) and I just couldn't find it. Everywhere I poked it was like sticking my dick against a wall.

"Where's your vagina?" I asked.

She spread her pussy lips and said, "It's right here." She grabbed my cock roughly and stuck it where it needed to go.

It still wouldn't go in.

"Oww," I said. "You're all dry and tight. I can't work with that."

"Well, you're gonna have to!"

"But I physically can't do it." I pounded her cunt in a half-assed way to illustrate my point. It wouldn't go in. "You need to be wet!"

"Well, Jesus," Nina growled. "Ines! Get over here. If you love sucking things so much, put your face between my legs."

Nina flipped onto her back and opened her knees for Ines.

I couldn't help wondering why she hadn't asked me to lick her clit, but I wasn't going to ask. I didn't want to do it.

Ines crawled eagerly into the circle and bowed between Nina's thighs. She went right at it, burying her face in all that hair like it was her favourite dish. She licked like a cat with cream.

Nina put both hands behind her head like a sunbather, and looked up at the stars. "That's good. Keep going with that."

I sat on my heels and watched as Ines ate Nina's pussy. The more I watched, the harder I got. Maybe it was Ines's mouth that turned me on. I sort of wished she'd suck my dick. In fact, as I watched her eat Nina in messy slurps, my cock throbbed harder than ever. My dick felt so fat and thick and full that it finally hit me: I was turned on.

And I don't just mean my dick was turned on.

All of me was.

So weird, because who'd have thought watching one friend lick another one's clit would do it for me? But it was working. Oh god, I couldn't wait to stick my dick somewhere. Anywhere!

Well... not in Nina.

I can't explain what happened next. Suddenly I was kneeling behind Ines, who was on all fours between Nina's legs. Suddenly I was grabbing Ines's narrow hips and shoving my cock between her thighs and... oh god!

Not only could I find her pussy no problem, but it was hot and wet and slick and juicy and swollen and fat and everything you could ever want a pussy to be.

"What are you doing?" Charlotte hissed.

"Shut up!" I didn't want Nina noticing.

Ines started bucking back to meet my thrusts. I hadn't even realized I was thrusting! My body started acting without my brain. I was doing something Nina had strictly forbidden and I didn't even care. Ines's cunt felt too good to leave.

And when she clamped her pussy down on my dick? Forget about it! Nina would have to drag me off that girl's ass kicking and screaming. I didn't give a fuck anymore.

While Ines made Nina moan with her mouth, I planted myself balls-deep in that sweet wet slit.

I never knew it could be like this. I never knew how good a pussy could feel all wrapped around my dick. Screw Nina and her tumbleweed cunt. Ines was mine, all mine!

Of course, it probably helped that her snatch was full of Charlotte's sperm. That probably added to the warm wetness and all. In a way I felt like I was fucking Charlotte, which was kind of a weird thought. I had to remind myself I was only fucking Charlotte's cum. Charlotte's hot, sloppy cum inside Ines's perfectly swollen vagina.

Good thing Nina was having such a good time getting her pussy licked. That way she didn't notice I was screwing someone else... until I slapped the girl's ass and cried out, "God, I'm gonna come so hard!"

Nina's eyes burst open. When she realized what was going on, anger boiled in her eyes. "What do you think you're doing, Gabrielle?"

"Fucking Ines!" I screamed.

I couldn't help myself. I planted my dick way up in my friend's snatch, and I let loose, blowing my load in her hot cunt.

"You bitch!" Nina hollered, heaving Ines to one side so she could get to me.

I thought for sure she'd ring my neck. But it wasn't my neck she grabbed for.

She wrapped both hands around my swollen dick as I shot another load of cum, spilling my seed on the reed mat. Nina tried to collect every drop that came out, but I was spent. She plunged her fingers into her cunt, trying to get my sperm in her vagina.

She must have thought that wouldn't be enough, because she grabbed Ines by the hips. "Give me that sperm!"

Nina sprawled on her back with her legs splayed weirdly. She situated Ines on top of her so their pussies mashed together, then she swung that little body around like a ragdoll. Ines seemed to enjoy it, but I was starting to think maybe she enjoyed everything.

"Give me that sperm, you little bitch!" Nina called out. "I need it to propagate the species!"

To be honest, I couldn't picture Nina giving birth. Her body just didn't strike me as maternal.

Charlotte's did. It was too bad Charlotte couldn't get pregnant. She had the makings of a great pregnant-lady body.

As Nina shook Ines around on her pussy, they both hollered and shrieked. Nina's angry tone turned impassioned in a completely different tone. She cried out the same way she had when Ines was licking her clit.

They were obviously enjoying themselves.

I was exhausted.

"Wait," April said when Nina dropped Ines at her side. "If you both get pregnant, how will you know whose baby is whose?"

Nobody answered.

Tandy said, "Yeah, that's right—now if Innes has a baby it might be Charlotte's or it might be Gabrielle's."

"And she shared the sperms from her vagina," April went on. "So if Nina gets pregnant, that baby could be Gabrielle's or Charlotte's too."

Charlotte didn't have anything to add to the conversation. Ines and Nina were either too worn out of bewildered to speak.

Tandy said, "Oh my god, imagine if one of you got pregnant with twins and one of the twins was Charlotte's and the other's was Gabrielle's!"

"Is that even possible?" April asked.

"Yeah, with two eggs."

"Ohhhh."

Nina shot up to a seated position and said, in a commanding tone, "We're not going to worry about it right now. Chances are none of us gets pregnant on the first try."

We all shut up, because the implication was that this nightly ritual would go on and on and on for weeks and maybe months until every womb had a baby in it.

I glanced at Charlotte, but she was staring at the fire in the distance. If I asked her to trade me Ines for Nina, I knew she would. She's sweet like that. And, anyway, she'd be a better match for Nina. She was so submissive and Nina was so dominant. They complemented each other perfectly.

Now all I had to do was get Nina on board with the switch and Ines would be my mate every single night... until we'd repopulated the planet.

Dave's Not Here, Ma'am
Spanked by the Futa Boss

HE WAITED UNTIL EVERYONE had gone home for the evening.

The receptionist cleared out first. Then the assistants, then accounting. Sales were a tricky bunch. Sometimes they worked late into the night, if they were falling being on quotas. But it had been a strong month, so they went out for drinks. They even asked Dave along.

Any other day, he'd have said yes. He loved feeling included.

But tonight he had plans of his own.

The last to leave was his boss, Ms. Heartland. She sometimes stayed even later than the sales force. Around quarter to six, Dave knocked on her door and asked, "Didn't you have that thing tonight?"

"That thing?" She looked up at him from behind her desk, confounded, like she couldn't keep track of her own schedule once her assistant had left for the night. "Oh, that thing. No, that fell through."

Damn it! Dave was counting on her to go so he could get changed in his office. Now he'd have to do it in the restroom and sneak past her office without her seeing.

Ms. Heartland gazed at Dave with her dark-rimmed glasses halfway down the bridge of her nose. He had to admit, she looked good like that: with her mahogany hair dancing on her shoulders, her tailored suit jacked slung across one of her client chairs, her blue shirt casually unbuttoned enough that her cleavage peeked out. She was always so buttoned up during office hours. This end-of-the-day style worked for her.

Glancing at her silver-toned watch, she said, "I guess I should get going. Someone's got to feed the fish."

She always joked about being single, but not being a cat lady.

Ms. Heartland had fish instead of cats.

"See you tomorrow," Dave said, trying to suppress the giddiness bubbling up inside him. "Have a great night!"

Before heading out, she poked her head into his office and said, "Almost feels like you're trying to get rid of me."

"Not at all, not at all! Just happy it's Thursday. Good TV night, Thursday."

Ms. Heartland cocked her head and said, "Okaaay... well, bye then."

He sat totally still as he listened to her heels click-clacking along the flooring in the back corridor. The rest of the place was carpeted, but since their offices were so far from the front door, they always snuck out the back way.

Dave listened to the door opening, then closing slowly.

His heart raced.

He couldn't wait to get started.

But he did wait. There was always a chance Ms. Heartland had forgotten something. He paced the office for fifteen minutes, but he couldn't hold off any longer. He pulled out the suitcase he'd smuggled in early that morning, lifted it onto his cleared-off desk, and unzipped.

Everything smelled like perfume: his signature scent. Some of the people he partied with on Thursday nights said they could smell him a mile away, but he took that as a compliment—however it was intended. There was nothing more evocative than the silky aroma of a sensual perfume.

His hands shook as he undressed. He was just that excited.

Slinging his shirt and pants over his office chair, he peered inside his suitcase. Panties first. He'd brought three pairs to choose from, but he knew he'd get nervous about staying tucked and end up wearing all three at once. Regardless, he started with just the stretchy black pair. They were unforgivingly tight—so much so his belly popped out the top. But they felt good on, and they looked good too. His crotch even looked fairly flat once he'd tucked away what he didn't want to see.

He put the purple pair on over the black pair, and the red ones on over those. Ooh, that was a very tight squeeze, but when he ran his hand over his crotch, it felt womanly in the extreme. That would hold all night long, if it needed to.

Next, a spritz of perfume.

Oh, that was strong. Filled the office with a lusty aroma. But it would dissipate in time, hopefully before everybody got in the next morning. If it didn't, Ms. Heartland would probably think he'd had a woman in his office afterhours. Imagine that!

His bra was black, but utilitarian. It came with breasts already inside, but he taped together his manboobs to give the illusion of cleavage. Fat was good for something, if you knew how to use it.

When he was packing his bag, he couldn't decide on an outfit. He'd included a wide variety of skirts and dresses, ranging from randy to refined. He went middle-of-the-road with a sheer white top over a black lace camisole. He paired that with a tight-fitting black skirt, but not before running a pair of silk stockings up his shaved legs.

Oh, that looked good. Felt good, too. He loved the way those layers of tight panties kept everything in place, and how the skirt gripped his backside like two hands squeezing his ass.

If only he had a woman in his life: a mature woman, maybe someone older, who'd been around the block and recognized his love of ladies' clothes for what it was.

A woman who was as turned on by the same things that turned him on.

A woman with a firm hand.

That's what Dave wanted.

His toenails were painted red, but nobody would ever know that once he'd put on his high-heeled shoes. He would know how stunning his toes looked, though, and sometimes that was enough. The little things, like painted toenails or pretty panties, often got him through a long day at work.

Damn, he should have shaved before getting dressed. That was stupid. He must have been especially frazzled by his boss sticking around. Usually he didn't make these mistakes.

But he'd brought a towel along, so he took his shaving kit and makeup bag to the bathroom and locked the door behind him. The cleaning staff didn't usually come around until after eleven, but he wasn't taking any chances.

He draped his towel across his full chest, and his big breast held it in place. Perfect. Now he wouldn't end up spilling any shaving cream down his top.

Once his face was smooth as a baby's butt, he ran his lotions and potions over his skin. The friends he'd be meeting in the hotel lounge often asked how he managed such a close shave with no telltale bumps. That was Dave's little secret. He didn't have much leverage over younger dressers and those with slimmer figures. Maybe that's why he guarded his proprietary blend so closely.

Makeup was next. He used to rush through it, but he'd learned that a slow hand made all the difference.

Foundation, powder, eyeliner, shadow, a bit of blush—not too much—then lipstick with a touch of gloss. When he was done, he looked like an entirely different person. But he didn't look complete. Not until he put on his wig.

Blondes have more fun. That's why he'd gone with the long blonde wig. It even had a few lowlights mixed in so the hair didn't look like something you'd find growing out of Barbie's plastic head.

Gentle wheat-coloured waves tumbled against Dave's large breasts as he fluttered around his office, making sure he had money in his small purse. There were often men at the lounge who would buy them drinks, but Dave wasn't keen on men, so it felt like stealing. He'd rather buy his own.

His heart trembled as he asked himself if he'd forgotten anything. It was always useful to do a double-check before heading out into the night.

Shoes on his feet, stocking on his legs, three pairs of panties, tight skirt, bra, blouse, makeup, wig, purse.

That was it. Ready to go.

But the moment he gripped the handle on his office door, he thought he heard something out in the carpeted area. Could be the cleaners. There was always a chance they'd come around early. But he couldn't hear that push-cart they always had with them. He couldn't hear them talking to each other. They always travelled in pairs, for safety's sake.

Dave listened keenly. His body went on high-alert. Every muscles locked as his veins filled with ice. There was definitely somebody out there. But who?

Suddenly Dave's door opened inward. It whacked him in the chest and he lost his footing, fell backwards onto the floor—fell right on his ass.

There he sat, both hands behind him, both legs parted, knees in the air. He felt practically crustacean as his boss swanned into the room.

Her eyes widened and her jaw dropped. Dave had to admit, Ms. Heartland looked very pretty like that, with her lips parted into a luscious O and her shoulders back, nostrils flared.

"What's going on?" she asked. "What are you doing in Dave's office? Where's Dave?"

Surely she must know...

Surely she must realize this was Dave, right here on the floor. Under all these layers of panties and makeup, he was there.

But maybe she didn't. Maybe it wouldn't cross the mind of a woman like Ms. Heartland that someone in her office would don ladies' garments every Thursday night and go out on the town.

So Dave said the first thing that popped into his head, which, comically, was: "Dave's not here, Ma'am."

"Dave's not here?" she answered back. "Well, where is he?"

"Gone," Dave said, pushing his voice into the highest register it could manage. "He left. Dave has left the building."

Ms. Heartland shook her head. "Well, who are you? What are you doing in his office?"

"I'm... Sheila? And I'm... waiting for him?"

That was a stupid thing to say. And, sure enough, Ms. Heartland asked, "Well, when is he coming back?"

"Later," Dave said. "Much later. You won't want to wait that long."

"Why are you waiting that long?"

"Because..." *Think of an excuse, Dave! Fast!* "I'm not waiting. I was just about to leave."

It would help if he could get up off the floor.

But he couldn't.

He struggled, flip-flopping side to side like a turtle tossed on its shell. He figured Ms. Heartland would extend a hand to help him up, but instead she blocked his office door and said, "You're not going anywhere, Missy! Not until you explain why Dave would leave a stranger alone in his office. That's a serious security breach."

"I'm not a stranger," Dave said. "I'm his... sister?"

Ms. Heartland raised an eyebrow. "Dave doesn't have a sister."

"I meant cousin."

"You said sister when you meant cousin?"

"We're very close," Dave said. "He's always been like a sister to me."

"Don't you mean you've been like a sister to him?"

"That too."

"Well, that doesn't mean it's okay for you to hang out in his office unsupervised. There's a lot of sensitive information in here."

Dave started to feel panicky, like he really was this Sheila person who shouldn't be left alone in Dave's office. "I'm not looking at anything. I was really just leaving."

Grabbing the edge of his desk, Dave managed to pull himself to his feet. As soon as he was upright, Ms. Heartland closed the door, trapping them both in the office.

Having the door closed made Dave feel suddenly claustrophobic.

"Not so fast," Ms. Heartland said. "Someone needs to be punished for this security breach, and since Dave's not here it'll have to be you."

"Punished?" Dave cried, a little deeper down in his register than he meant to. "Punished how?"

Ms. Heartland looked around the office. Dave had zipped up his suitcase and hidden it in the space under his desk, and since he'd cleared everything onto the windowsill earlier, his desk was now totally bare.

Marching around the office, Ms. Heartland tapped at Dave's pens, pencils and the other utilitarian office necessities he stashed in a chipped mug. From it, she plucked a gunmetal grey ruler with cork lining the reverse side.

For a moment, she just looked at the black notches and numbers.

Then she tapped the cork side against her palm.

Then she slapped it against the desk.

"Bend over, Sheila."

"What?"

"You heard me," Ms. Heartland said. "Bend your ass over this desk before I get angry."

"Don't get angry," Dave said, feeling a combination of apprehension and apology. "I'll do it. I'm doing it. See?"

He bent over his desk, feeling his breasts pressing into his chest. He felt very exposed with his ass in the air, but he didn't even consider going against his boss' commandments. He could easily have confessed everything, but he had a creeping sense that this would be better.

"Have you ever been punished by a ruler?" Ms. Heartland asked.

"Punished how?" he asked, suddenly remembering the Johnny Deeper joke kids used to tell in school.

"Spanked," she said. "Smacked. Slapped."

"Oh. No. Never."

She whapped his ass with the cork side, but under a skirt and three pairs of panties, he couldn't really feel it.

"How was that?" Ms. Heartland asked. "Have you learned your lesson?"

"I suppose so."

She tsked her teeth. "That's as good as a no. Let's try this again."

Flipping the ruler around, she smacked his ass with the metal side.

"Still nothing?"

He decided to be somewhat honest. "I think I'm wearing too many layers."

"Too many layers?" Ms. Heartland asked. "How many layers?"

"One skirt," he said. "Three pairs of panties."

"Three pairs of panties!?!"

"I need all three," he explained.

Ms. Heartland grunted. "I see." Setting the ruler down on the desk, she said, "I think you might have to pull up that skirt, Missy."

"Okay..."

"And I think I might have to roll up my sleeves."

Dave turned just in time to catch his boss slipping off her suit jacket and tossing it over his office chair, right where he'd tossed his work clothes before packing them away in his luggage. She then unbuttoned the cuffs of the blue shirt and rolled each one up to her elbows.

She really took her time doing it, too, and every second spent watching her made Dave's crotch a little warmer. Sure his penis was tucked away, but he could still feel aroused. Instead of getting hard, he got wet. Natural lubrication drizzled from his cockhead, soaking through one, then two, then all three layers of panties while he pulled his skirt all the way up to his hips.

"Nice ass," Ms. Heartland said.

"They're panties," Dave replied, his heart pounding in his throat.

"Nice panties, then." She shot him a smile that could almost be interpreted as loving. But just as quickly, her expression hardened. She grabbed the ruler and whapped his ass with it in a perfect backhand.

Strangely, the first thought that entered Dave's mind was, "Wow, she must be a killer on the courts."

But tennis quickly came and went, replaced swiftly by the sharpness of that blow to his butt.

"Oww," he said, surprised by his reaction. "That hurt."

"Your skirt must have been masking the pain." She bent her arm farther back and whapped him again with the metal side. "How's that for punishment?"

He'd never been hit with a metal thing. He could feel the cold unforgiving nature of the ruler, feel its thinness in the way it vibrated against his butt like the flat side of a handsaw. He couldn't think of anything else that felt this way. And, the truth was, he liked it.

"Pull down these red panties. What's underneath?"

"Purple ones," Dave said.

"Well? What are you waiting for? Take them down."

Dave's apprehension tripled in less than a second.

If she asked him to take down the red ones, would she ask him to take down the purple ones too? And the black ones after?

Would he really do that? Allow himself to be so fully exposed?

He had a sneaking suspicion he would.

Slowly, Dave hooked his thumbs around the waistband, being careful only to catch the top layer. He pulled those panties down his thighs, opening his legs a little wider to feel the elastic stretch against his skin.

"Very nice," Ms. Heartland said. "Oh, I really like the purple ones. They hug your ass so snugly."

But liking them didn't mean she'd show Dave any mercy.

Without warning, she whacked his ass—and not just once, this time. One, two, three blows in rapid succession. This time she didn't backhand it. She stood on the other side of his ass and brought that ruler down so hard is sang as it cut through the silent office.

When the ruler met Dave's panties, the sound was muffled and metallic. The feeling was closer to his skin, getting closer all the time. It was starting to hurt, but he couldn't ask her to stop. He didn't want her to stop.

Ms. Heartland didn't tell him to pull down the purple ones. She slapped the ruler on his desk and yanked at those panties herself. She wasn't dainty about it, either. She really pulled at them. Hard. So hard he felt it in his crotch and his waist and his thighs.

But he didn't complain. He didn't say a word.

"Black panties now," she said. "Is this the last layer?"

"Yes, Ma'am."

"Very good," she purred.

But she mustn't have been as pleased as she sounded, because she picked up that ruler pretty fast and brought it *smack* down on Dave's ass even faster.

"Oww!" Dave screeched, flying halfway across the desk. "Oh God! That kills!"

"Does it?" she asked, then slapped him again.

The sound and sensation combined pleasure with pain, making Dave's pelvis glow with the warmth of arousal. Now that he was down to only one pair of panties, his penis wasn't cooperating the way he wanted. A good little dick would stay tucked away deep inside him. Not anymore! It crept forward, sneaking out, drooling pre-cum all down his slick panties.

Ms. Heartland punished his panties with the ruler, making his cock throb and grow.

But that obviously wasn't good enough.

"I want the black ones off too," she said.

Dave gulped. "I really don't think that's a good idea."

"I don't care what you think. This is a punishment, not a play party." Backing away, Ms. Heartland set the ruler beside Dave on the desk and said. "I suppose it would only be fair if I took off a few layers, too. What do you say to that?"

Dave replied without thinking how this might impact his work relationship with his boss. "I say... yes?" He didn't care about work stuff right now. He just wanted to see Ms. Heartland without her clothes on.

"Very well," she said, unbuttoning her shirt.

Ms. Heartland was wearing black lingerie, too. Hers was nicer, though, with lace around the cups. She had real boobs, of course: full, fleshy, bouncy boobs that jiggled inside her bra as she slipped her slim skirt to her feet. When she stepped out of it, Dave got his first look at the gorgeous garter holding her stockings in place. He wished he had one of those! Though, he had to admit he enjoyed the way his lace-rimmed stay-ups gouged into his flesh.

"There," she said, standing behind him, but somewhat to the side. "I would say we're just about equal."

Really? Because Dave couldn't even see her underwear beyond the low-cut lace garter belt. Still, he couldn't complain. His boss looked like a genuine vixen in that black lingerie.

"Your turn," Ms. Heartland said. "Pull down your panties, young lady."

"Yes, Ma'am!"

Dave did as he was told, dragging his panties slowly down his thighs. When he released them, the tight elastic snapped against his skin. It was good preparation for the ruler, which he saw Ms. Heartland pick up in his peripheral vision.

"Are you ready for this?" she asked.

"Yes, Ma'am."

Dave's muscles stiffened as his penis slowly untucked. He could feel it slipping gently from his body and settling modestly in a pool of pre-cum on his desk.

"Very well, then," Ms. Heartland said as she waved the ruler in the air.

She brought it down so quickly the metal slashed the air. It sounded like a whip, but the sensation against his ass was something altogether different.

He felt the sharp edges more than the metal middle.

And then she did it again, grunting with effort as she struck him. This time, he felt the middle every bit as much as the edges. The sensation wasn't the same as when he'd been wearing panties.

It was colder, for starters.

Sharper, too.

It hurt, but no longer in a way that brought him pleasure.

"Stop," he begged his boss. "I don't want this anymore. I don't like it."

"Well, that's just—"

WHACK!

"—too—"

WHACK!

"—bad."

WHACK!

She smacked his ass with that terrible instrument of torture twice more before tossing it on the desk. Then she said, "Fine. You don't like it, I'll just have to punish you in some other way."

Dave's cock twitched beneath him when he turned enough to see Ms. Heartland pushing her pretty panties down her thighs. Actually, "pretty" might not be the word for them. They were black, but fairly heavy duty compared with the lace bra and garter.

Oh, wait—those hadn't been the panties at all, because here came another pair. These ones were black lace, same as the bra set.

That was strange. Dave didn't realize women at the office wore their panties in layers too.

But wait... what was this? Just below Ms. Heartland's garter, he saw a meaty slab of flesh. It couldn't be... but it sure looked like... wait a minute, did his boss have her very own cock?

She held it in her hand for a moment while Dave stared unapologetically. "Is that what I think it is?"

"Depends," Ms. Heartland said. "What do you think it is?"

"It looks like a cock, to me."

She shot him a saccharine smile. "Very good, Sheila."

Sheila? Who was Sheila? Oh right—he was. He'd almost forgotten what started this whole thing.

Then Dave's legs started to tremble, and he said, "Don't tell me that's what you're going to punish me with."

"As you wish," she replied as her cock grew in her hand.

She started rubbing it, and it grew even larger. The girth was quite impressive—not that Dave had a lot of experience with dicks. That is to say, he had no experience with them. Other than his own. He'd always sort of wondered what this would be like, but not enough to act.

"Tell me what you're going to do," Dave begged.

Ms. Heartland cocked her head and said, "I think I'd rather show you."

Reaching into her jacket pocket, she snagged a pillow of lube, which she opened with her teeth.

"Open your ass for me, baby." Ms. Heartland's expression grew dark and dangerous. "Hurry up. My cock is ready to go."

"Oh God!"

Dave's knees felt weak as he parted his ass cheeks for his boss.

This had to be a dream.

Ms. Heartland had a cock and she was about to fuck him with it?

How could this possibly be real life?

When she drizzled that packet of lube down his ass crack, Dave shivered. It was damn cold, and it felt weird when she pushed a finger inside him.

"Hmm," she said, inserting a second finger too. "Good stretch. Should do fine."

"I've never done this before," Dave said. "Go easy, okay?"

"You're a virgin?" Ms. Heartland asked.

"Yes," Dave replied, like he needed to convince her of the fact. "Yes, I'm a virgin, so please go slow with me."

Ms. Heartland cooed lovingly as she finger-fucked Dave's ass. "Aww, I will. I'll take good care of you, baby."

With that, Ms. Heartland pulled both fingers from his hole and set her thick, throbbing cockhead in place. Dave could feel his boss' pulse through the sensitive ring of his lubricated anus. Her big tip was sitting right there, waiting to be granted entry. So he splayed himself across his desk and, staring at the carpet, allowed his muscles to relax.

"Ohhh," Ms. Heartland said, sliding her throbbing dickhead into Dave's virgin ass. "Oh, that's very good. Very good indeed!"

She slipped herself in a little further, really digging into his ass, encountering resistance despite Dave's valiant attempts to keep breathing and loosen up. Gripping his wrists, the boss pushed harder, harder, harder, finally breaking through that initial resistance. Dave felt kind of a POP inside him, and he would have worried she'd broken him somehow if he hadn't heard tales of anal sex from the very friends he was supposed to be meeting right now.

"Damn it!" Dave said.

"What's wrong?" Ms. Heartland grunted as she drove her dick deeper inside him.

Panting, Dave replied, "I'm supposed to meet some people. They'll be wondering where I am."

"It's no worry," Ms. Heartland replied. "When you tell them about the massive punishment I'm laying down on your ass, they'll be so jealous they'll forgive you in an instant."

"Oh!"

Ms. Heartland rammed Dave's ass, driving her dick balls-deep inside him. Wow, when her big balls whacked his hairy sack, that felt almost as good as when she dicked him. She went at it again, pulling almost out, so close Dave could feel her bulbous cockhead resting just inside his ass ring. She held there for a moment, making him nervous. He'd heard about this too: when it feels like you're going to take a big shit all over the person fucking you. But you're not. But you feel like you will, like the second that dick leaves your body, it's going to pull your innards with it.

Dave just kept telling himself it would all be okay. His mind was playing tricks on him. All he had to do was lie still on the desk and he'd be perfectly fine.

When Ms. Heartland rammed him again and her balls met his balls, he wondered for a moment why she hadn't mentioned noticing them. Seemed like something she would have shamed naughty Sheila for. Good girls weren't supposed to have big hairy balls. But Ms. Heartland had balls, and she was a strikingly seductive woman. So maybe ballhood was no big deal, in his boss' books.

"God," Ms. Heartland moaned, driving her dick deep inside Dave. "God, you've got a nice ass."

"Thank you," he said. Nobody had ever complimented it before. Made him feel like one hot mama.

"Oh, Sheila, I'm going to come so hard!"

Fucking him roughly, the boss growled and groaned. She tightened her grip on Dave's wrists and drove her dick in him rapidly, building up speed.

"Oh God, I'm so close!" Ms. Heartland cried. "You're making me come so fast!"

The compliment brought a blushing heat to Dave's cheeks. "Thank you, Ma'am."

"So close," she moaned. "So fast!"

She rammed him one last time and their big balls pressed together. Hers sat heaving on his as her thick shaft pulsed with the onslaught of ejaculate. Cum ran through her dick in such large supply Dave could feel it moving from her body and into his. He felt its warmth filling him, deep down in his ass. He'd never experienced anything like it.

"Thank you," he panted, repeating those words again and again as she pulled her dick from his ass.

"So you enjoyed your punishment, did you, naughty Sheila?"

"Yes," Dave assured her. "Yes, I loved it."

"Well, roll over," Ms. Heartland said. "Let's see just how much you loved it."

Dave wasn't sure if he should, but his boss picked up the ruler and whapped his ass again. He rolled toward the centre of his desk, so he was sitting on it, but leaning back, supporting himself with both hands behind him.

His dick stuck straight up.

Since his skirt was pulled up over his waist, there was no looking anywhere else. He felt rumpled and sweaty, but his cock was ready to rock.

"My goodness," Ms. Heartland said. "What are we going to do about this?"

"We?" Dave asked.

"Well, I can't send you into the night with a stiffy the size of the Eiffel Tower. We need to bring this baby down, and fast. Didn't you say you've got people to meet?"

"Yes, Ma'am."

Ms. Heartland made a motion like she was rolling up her sleeves, even though she wasn't wearing a shirt. She then reached for Dave's erection and wrapped both hands around it. When she closed her grip around his lusty shaft, he very nearly exploded. It wouldn't take much to put him over the top, and that was very unusual for his lumpy old body. He wasn't exactly an old man, but he wasn't exactly a young one, either.

"Goodness, you've got a mighty sword," Ms. Heartland said.

Dave laughed at the turn of phrase, but he stopped laughing when his boss pumped it slowly, up and down. Oh, she'd sure done this before. She knew exactly how to give a handy, even twisting her hands slightly, building pressure in his body, touching his cockhead only to tease him. He knew the second she really went at it, his cream would be all over her.

"Do you want to come?" Ms. Heartland asked.

"Sure," Dave said. "Who wouldn't?"

"Well, you are still being punished," she said. "Perhaps you should wait until I say so."

As soon as she said those words, Dave wanted to come immediately. "Can I come now?" he asked.

"No." She tapped at his cockhead, slathering his pre-cum all over his full, fleshy tip.

"Oh, please!" Dave begged.

Tell him he couldn't have something and that's all he wanted.

"No," Ms. Heartland said.

"Please?" He could barely keep it together.

"No."

His thighs trembled as she ran her firm hands up and down his erection, sculpting it like clay, forming his body into a work of art.

"Oh God," Dave said. "I need to come. I have to. I'm going to."

"No," the boss instructed as she wrapped one hand around his cockhead.

That did him in.

No amount of castigation could keep him from blowing his load in his boss' hands.

He came so hard it blasted through her fingers like a geyser.

He watched it soak her skin, rebound off her hand and back down onto his cockhead. She squeezed his tip and that just made him come harder. He couldn't remember the last time he gave up so much cream. It seemed to be everywhere, and it all seemed to happen in slow motion.

Weeks seemed to go by in waves. He came and came and his boss looked at him sternly, then lovingly. She smiled as she cradled his cock. She wrapped him tightly between her hands and touched him until he was too ticklish to speak.

When she let him go, she said, "You know you came without permission."

"Yes," Dave said. "I'm sorry."

"Well, you'll need to be punished for that too."

"Okay," Dave said as she placed a tissue box beside him. "I understand. But I'm supposed to meet my friends."

Ms. Heartland grabbed her clothes and headed toward his office door wearing nothing but stockings, high-heeled shoes, a garter belt, a bra, and a smile. Her spent dick hung lazily between her legs, and she didn't seem to care. She was such a beautiful woman. Why would she?

When she arrived at his door, she put one hand on the knob and paused before turning it. "I insist upon punishing you, but not now. Next week—next Thursday. Be here after hours, after everyone else has gone. I'm sure your cousin Dave will let you in. I'll be waiting for you in my office. He can show you were that is."

"Okay," Dave said, keeping up the charade. "Yes, I'm sure he will."

She nodded resolutely and opened the door. "See you next week. Don't forget."

As she headed out and closed the door behind her, Dave sighed, "How could I ever?"

ABOUT THE AUTHOR

GIA MARIA MARQUEZ knows her stuff. She's been writing for as long as she can remember—not about sissies and cross-dressing and domestic discipline, though. That's close to home, so she's kept it to herself until now. Writing spicy stories is easy, but sharing a piece of herself with the world? That's the tough part.

Other books by GIA MARIA MARQUEZ include:

Femdom Futanari
And Sissy Makes Three
Rear Eye for the Straight Guy
The Sissy Convention is Next Week!
Watching My Wife Feminize Her Ex
and much more!

Milton Keynes UK
Ingram Content Group UK Ltd.
UKHW020714310723
426074UK00018B/1199

9 798223 432333